Freeing his Tiger

Weres & Witches of Silver Lake
Book 6

Vella Day

Tattooed and pierced, Anna Fairchild sets out to find her birth mother in Silver Lake, Tennessee, but finds something sexier and more enticing. To her disappointment, the rugged and hot white tiger shifter has no interest in a walk on the wild side—no matter how hard she tries.

Straight-laced, Officer Dalton Garner plays by the rules and right now, he's determined to keep his head in the game. After all, a murderer is on the loose, and he's hellbent on taking him down. But Anna's alluring scent, killer body, and carefree spirit make it very difficult to focus. And Anna refuses to relent as she chips away at his tough-guy exterior. Torn between following orders and following his heart, Dalton struggles with his desires. But when the killer attempts to take away all chances they have to be together, he's forced to choose. Will he save his mate or save his career?

Beneath the calm and shimmering surface lie intrigue, power, magic, and danger.
Welcome to Silver Lake—where appearances can be deceiving, and what you see isn't truly what lies below.

Chapter One

To learn about Vella Day's other new releases, contests, and find new authors, subscribe to her newsletter and get three free books!
http://smarturl.it/o4cz93?IQid=MLite

An Unexpected Diversion (book 1 of Hidden Hills Shifters)
Bare Instincts (book 2 of Hidden Hills Shifters)
Montana Desire (book 1 of Rock Hard, Montana)

OFFICER DALTON GARNER leaned back in his office chair, worried about Anna Fairchild, the woman who smelled of warm honey kissed by the summer sun. She'd said her therapy was going well, but even after three months of meeting with James, she still seemed skittish—not that he was keeping tabs on her or anything.

Dalton couldn't blame her for always looking over her shoulder. Hell, if someone had driven him off the road and then dragged him somewhere, tied him up, and beaten him, he'd have had a hard time recovering too. Of course, that could never happen since Dalton was too fast to be caught. Being a shifter and a Wendayan had its advantages.

Mine, mate, his tiger growled.

Stop it, he told the persistent animal. So what if he had been the one to carry Anna out after her abduction? It didn't mean she was his—yet. *Anna's not ready,* he told his tiger.

That was an understatement. Anna had only learned shifters

existed that fateful night because his sister had altered her form right in front of her. It didn't matter the act was needed to kill the man who'd kidnapped Anna. He figured the shock alone of learning his kind existed would be enough to scare her to be around him.

Damn. Dalton wished there was something he could do to help her get over the trauma, but any move on his part might frighten her more.

When are you going to tell Anna she's your mate? his tiger asked.

Dalton didn't answer this time.

"Garner!" Phil Smythe, his boss at the sheriff's department, shouted Dalton's name as he rounded the corner from the hallway containing the department offices. The big man barreled toward him, his face contorted. Smythe was as military as they came with his short hair, ramrod posture, and booming voice. Dalton's partner, Kalan Murdoch, was right behind him, appearing equally serious despite his long brown hair flying behind him.

Dalton sat up straighter. "Yes sir?"

Smythe tossed a piece of paper on his desk. "Crystal Wedgewood was murdered in her home tonight. I want you and Kalan to take the lead. Paramedics responded to the call by the husband, but she was already dead when they arrived. The coroner is there now, and I've dispatched the crime scene unit. If you hurry, you'll beat them there."

Typical Smythe. His discourse was always to the point and with a minimum number of words. Good thing they'd switched shifts with Thompson and Compton. Otherwise, he and Kalan wouldn't have been assigned the case.

Dalton stood and then had to rush after his partner who was charging toward the exit, acting as if he'd been told his mate was in trouble. Kalan had lived in Silver Lake his whole life and must have known the victim.

Kalan strode to his vehicle that was parked in front of the building, jumped in, and slammed his door shut before Dalton reached the squad car. He managed to slip into the front seat just as Kalan took off.

"I take it you knew the vic?" Dalton asked.

"Yes. She owns the Silver Lake Bookstore," he answered. From the way, Kalan's knuckles were clenched on the wheel, he knew her quite well.

"What kind of person would kill a lover of books?"

"Someone with a grudge, I guess. It's not like she was in the wrong place at the wrong time. She was murdered in her own house for goddess's sake." He slapped the wheel.

Violation in the sanctity of one's own home was the worst. "Could be she didn't stock some sexy romance novel the killer wanted," Dalton said trying to lighten the tense mood, but the moment the words escaped, he regretted his inappropriate response. Kalan cared for this woman, and Dalton had trivialized his concern. The fact his partner didn't even glance his way proved it.

"Whatever the reason," Kalan announced, "I'm going to find out who killed her."

Dalton wisely kept quiet. They reached Elkwood Lane six minutes later and didn't need to check the numbers on the houses because the flashing ambulance lights led them straight to the door. At the end of the drive, Kalan stopped and jammed the gearshift into park, leaving his lights flashing. "How about you talk to the husband while I check the back for a possible entry point?" Kalan asked.

"Can do." Speaking with a grieving spouse was the worst part of his job, but it might be more difficult for Kalan, especially if he was a friend of the husband.

The neighborhood looked upscale with most homes sitting on at least an acre lot. All were manicured and had long driveways and mature trees. The Wedgewood's home was a two-story brick mansion with tall pillars at the entryway and was possibly the nicest place on the block.

As soon as Dalton entered the foyer, the paramedics were on their way out with their gear. Dalton stopped Trevor Harden, one of the paramedics he played pool with. "What can you tell me?" Dalton asked. He didn't expect to learn much from them, but paramedics were trained to check their surroundings.

"The wife was dead when we arrived, and the husband is pretty shaken up. Dr. Williams is in there now. He'll be able to tell you more. Whoever did this was a damned fine shot. The bullet hit her squarely in the chest."

"Or else he stood close."

"Always possible. The Doc will have to give you that information."

"Thanks."

Dalton stepped into the living room and was surprised by the opulence. Because Mrs. Wedgewood owned a bookstore, he'd pictured flowered curtains, brown recliners surrounding a wooden coffee table, and antiques crammed onto shelves—kind of like his old-fashioned rental. This place couldn't be further from his image nor could it be any colder. That might be because Dalton wasn't a fan of modern. About the only things that weren't black or white were the beige curtains and a throw rug that had a few splotches of red woven through it.

The coroner and his assistant were working on the body while a man of about forty-five was on the sofa with his head back and his eyes shut. Before speaking with the husband, Dalton glanced around, hoping to find a weapon conveniently sitting on a table, but luck wasn't pointing his way today.

He returned his focus to Mr. Wedgewood. Most middle-aged women would call him handsome in a square-jaw kind of way. His tailored suit looked expensive as did his shoes and silk tie.

Dalton moved closer. "Mr. Wedgewood?"

The man looked up then swiped a hand over his eyes and down his jaw. "Yes?"

"I'm Dalton Garner with the sheriff's department. I'd like to ask you a few questions."

"Of course. I'll tell you what I can. I want my wife's killer found."

Even though he sounded sincere, it didn't mean the man wasn't guilty. Dalton always asked questions based on the assumption that this person could be the killer. Tonight would be no exception. "We'll do our best. If you don't mind, I'd like to record our conversation." Dalton pulled out his phone.

"Sure, but I don't know much."

Husbands were a wealth of information whether they believed it or not. "Can you walk me through what happened?"

Carlton Wedgewood pulled out a monogrammed handkerchief from his pocket and blew his nose. "Crystal's shop closes at six on Mondays. She owns the Silver Lake Bookstore." Dalton nodded. "I usually arrive home before her, but tonight I had to stay late. I was working on a client's portfolio and didn't leave until six thirty. When I walked in, I found Crystal…like that." He swallowed hard.

"Do you own a gun?"

A tic appeared around his left eye. "Yes, but it was stolen about a month ago."

He'd heard that story a hundred times. "Did you report it?"

"Yes."

Dalton made a mental note to check that out. "You have blood on your shirt. How did that happen?"

Mr. Wedgewood looked down at the red smears then glanced off to the side. He sniffled. "When I came home and saw her, I thought Crystal might still be alive, so I cradled her in my arms, hoping my body heat would help revive her. When she didn't moan or respond in any way, I called 911."

That explained the blood—assuming his story was true. Kalan came in through the front door, but didn't indicate what, if anything he'd found. Instead of joining him, Kalan made a beeline toward the coroner and his assistant.

"Does your wife have any enemies?" Dalton asked.

"No. Everyone loved her."

Someone didn't. "Do you think one of her employees could have been angry over something, like not getting a raise or a promotion?"

"I don't know. Crystal ran her business, and I ran mine."

How sad. Not that he believed he'd end up with Anna, despite her being his mate, but if he did, he'd want to know everything about her job like how many customers came in that day and who was nice and who wasn't. At least he knew Anna's boss well since Elana was Kalan's mate.

"I realize this is overwhelming, but I'll need you to come down to the precinct."

"What? Why? I didn't kill my wife." His grief was replaced with disbelief tinged with anger.

Dalton held up his hands. "I'm not accusing you of anything. We need to process your clothes."

"Why? I told you my wife's blood is on my shirt." He acted as if he couldn't believe someone would think he'd done something wrong.

"I understand, but it's procedure." They'd need to test for gunshot residue too, but he did not intend to mention that to Mr. Wedgewood.

Just then two policemen arrived along with the crime scene unit. Dalton nodded to Will Mathers, one of his coworkers. "Can you help Mr. Wedgewood pack for a few days?"

Wedgewood jumped up, his jaw tight and his hands clenched. "What, so now I can't even stay in my own home?"

The man was losing it. "Mr. Wedgewood. It will take a day or two to process the scene, which means you can't be here. Is there anyone you can stay with; maybe a friend, a coworker, or a family member perhaps?"

His breathing calmed as he tried to figure out his options. "Yeah, sure."

As soon as Will Mathers escorted the husband down the hallway, Kalan joined Dalton. "What did you learn?" Dalton asked.

"Forced entry in the back. I'll have CSU dust for prints. Doc Williams confirmed she died about an hour ago. The bullet hit her in the chest, but he won't know how far away the shooter was standing until he gets her to the lab. You?"

"The husband has blood on his shirt. He said he found his wife on the floor and picked her up in his arms. We'll take him down to the station and have his clothes and hands processed for gunshot residue."

"Does he look good for it?"

Dalton shrugged. "He said he was at work until right before he called 911."

Kalan nodded. "We can follow up on that later. Come on. Let's let the CSU do their job. We don't need to be contaminating any more evidence."

EVEN THOUGH ANNA told her therapist she didn't need to have weekly sessions anymore, James insisted she return one final time. As far as she was concerned, no amount of talking or counseling could erase what happened to her. One thing he said rang true. Her future was up to her. Either she could walk around in fear or embrace the challenges of life and move forward. Anna's whole life had been one battle after another and moving forward had always been her motto. First, her parents had given her up at birth, and then her first foster home failed to take care of her properly, putting her back into the system until she was adopted at the age of six. Unfortunately, her new parents were only supportive when it suited them. All in all, she'd been dealt a raw hand. Until a few years ago, she'd allowed self-pity to guide her decisions. If nothing else, James had shown her there was a lot of good in the world, and it was there for the taking—if she had the courage to grab it.

Her thoughts shot to Dalton who personified good. He'd been there for her when she needed him, which was more than she could say for anyone else in her life—except maybe for Elana and Jillian. When she questioned James about Dalton, he just shrugged, claiming he didn't feel comfortable telling her about another person. After all, James was a therapist whose role was to respect a patient's privacy.

It didn't matter. She wasn't in therapy to discuss her lack of a love life anyway. She was there because Frank Whitlaw had kidnapped her. With much work, James had finally convinced her that involvement with the man had been a fluke. Not only had James helped her put the trauma in perspective, he'd been a font of information, especially when it came to what she'd seen the night of her capture. Anna hadn't wanted to believe that her friend had shifted from a human into a white tiger, or that her boss's brother, Brian, had transformed into a bear right in front of her eyes, but apparently they had. For weeks, Anna had been positive she'd lost her mind, but James had explained she was perfectly sane. Then again, she was aware of the powers of witches so why should she be surprised someone could easily change form?

Apparently, people who could shift from an animal into a human were appropriately called shifters. He even went on to say that Silver Lake was full of these shifter-like creatures. Now that was scary. Every time someone came into the flower shop where she worked, she tried to decide if they might be one. Of course, she was unable to detect if they were, but it was interesting to guess nonetheless.

After a week of deep reflection on the topic, Anna dredged up the courage to ask James for more info on shifters, as well as Wendayans, since she'd only learned she had been one when Dalton's sister told her. James seemed happy to oblige and explained such concepts as a shifter's mate and what happens after a shifter bites the one he is destined to be with. The whole idea of a fated mate still freaked her out though she did like the concept that when a shifter found his fated mate, he would protect her at all cost and would be totally devoted to her. Now that she could get used to.

Sadly, the pairing was not up to the shifter or the other person. The gods decided it. Talk about another paradigm shift! Because of being in the system, she hadn't been brought up with a religious background. Still, the idea of gods and goddesses was hard to get used to. According to James, she had no control over that part of her destiny. She might be mated with a shifter or she might not.

Regardless of whether she had any control over her fate or not, she still dreamed of Dalton. Then the underdeveloped rational side of her brain told her the gods would never pit someone who was so straight-laced and uptight with someone like her. He'd balk for sure. Anna loved art and all things relating to nature, and she bet Dalton feasted on spreadsheets and logic.

It was silly to even dream about something like that since she wasn't buying into the concept of a destined mate. However, no harm ever came from a little make believe.

Just in case she was wrong, at the next session she asked James how someone could tell if two people were destined to be together. All he would say was that the answer would be in the shifter's eyes.

Great. The whole window of his soul thing didn't help her at all.

Bottom line, she needed to push the whole idea aside, and let nature take its course. She had to admit the whole biting stuff scared her, despite the end result being worth it. If a shifter bit his human mate, then the human became a shifter too. Having an ability like that would seriously allow her to protect herself.

James did stress that the shifters and Wendayans worked together in Silver Lake, and that the shifters protected their fellow witches. In the end, it didn't matter if her mate turned out to be a shifter or not. Someone would be there to protect her, and Anna received great comfort from that fact.

For weeks after that talk, her head didn't stop spinning from all the information James had so calmly tossed out at her. But weird shit like that wasn't all they'd discussed. They had talked about her life growing up and her need to find her birth parents. She'd always believed that knowing why they'd given her up might help heal her belief that she'd somehow been unlovable. James told Anna that she personally had nothing to do with her parents' decision. Circumstances might have dictated that they give her up. While probably true, she'd come this far in her search and would like to learn their identities.

They'd briefly talked about her powers and why she only could detect the traumatic past of a person if they had unresolved issues surrounding it.

So here she was at his house for the last time. Anna had finally put to rest what had happened to her, yet a bit of melancholy had seeped in. She liked talking to the old man. Not only was James wise and so sure of himself, he possessed an aura of pure knowledge. What she wouldn't give to unlock what made him tick.

Anna smiled thinking back to the first time she'd arrived at the ancient looking stone house. It had given her the creeps for sure with its dark interior, but after a few weeks, she began to feel safe inside. It might have been because James didn't judge her or because he was the only person she'd never been able to get any kind of reading from when she had touched him. No, that wasn't true. She hadn't been able to get a reading from Dalton either. Each of them seemed to be able to block her talents whenever she touched them. While she'd never asked James, she wouldn't be surprised if he, too, was some kind of Wendayan like Dalton.

Anna knocked on his door and James answered quickly. "Anna, how nice to see you again. Please come in."

The smell of freshly baked cookies caused her stomach to grumble. As soon as she entered the main room, she spotted a plate filled with chocolate chip cookies on the table.

"My wife baked them," he said answering her unasked question.

"She did?" Anna had assumed the woman had passed. Never once had she been around when Anna visited, though it was possible she worked the night shift at a hospital or perhaps was a waitress at an all-night diner.

"Yes, last night, but Naliana had to leave today. Otherwise, the two of you could have met." She didn't need to touch his arm to feel his pain—not that she could see into his past either.

"I'm sorry."

He smiled, but the joy didn't reach his eyes. "Thank you. She'll return in a month."

"A month? That must be tough to be separated for so long."

"Indeed. Shall we begin?"

Chapter Two

ONCE THEIR HOUR session concluded, Anna thanked James for all his help. While she'd never forget the man who'd held her captive, she understood a bit more why he'd taken her, and why he hadn't gone after Jillian directly. James was certain that if the man had known Jillian was a tiger shifter instead of say a werewolf, he never would have attempted to silence her in the first place.

Before Anna left, she needed a favor from James. "Can I ask you something?"

"Anything."

She doubted that, but he might answer this one. "As I've mentioned, I've always wanted to find my birth parents. Two years ago, I learned my mother's name was Mary Carlyle and that she might be living in Silver Lake." She'd found no trace of her father, which saddened her.

"Ah, so that was the real reason you came to live here," James said.

"That and I never liked the really cold weather out west."

He smiled. "I understand. What is it you wish to know?"

"You've lived here a long time. Do you know anyone by that name?" *Or can you help me find her?* She'd never voice her request. James was a therapist and not a detective though she found it strange he had no certificates anywhere on his walls. When she'd asked Dalton what James's last name was, he said he didn't know. At first, she was leery of the man, but he'd proven to be amazing.

"Hmm. Carlyle you say? No I haven't, but she should be easy to find."

"Here's the thing. I've asked around, and no one has heard of her." James was her last hope. "I'm guessing she's married and has a different last name, or else she only passed through here."

"I'll see what I can find and let you know if anything comes up," James said.

Anna did a mental fist pump and then surprised James with a hug. "Thank you for everything."

When Anna walked out, she thought she'd be relieved to put the past behind, but she was still unsettled, not so much about the assault, but about Dalton and shifters in general. A ton of questions kept popping up at the oddest times.

One thing she could say about James was that he'd provided her with a sense of security. She would miss that now that her sessions were over. He'd refused payment for his services, which was doubly odd, but it meant she couldn't keep going and rehashing the same old stuff with him. It was time to move on—time to take back control of her life.

Even though it was a little after six, she wasn't looking forward to returning to her tiny apartment and being by herself. When her boss's brother moved out of the apartment above the store where she worked, Elana had suggested Anna rent the place, if only to cut down on driving to and from work.

Anna had agreed, but they both knew the commute wasn't the issue. It was driving that bothered her, as Anna had an unhealthy fear of being run off the road again. It was why James suggested she take shooting lessons. He believed it would help her feel more secure. She'd agreed.

So for the last month, Anna had gone to the shooting range twice a week, not only to practice, but also in hopes of running into Dalton. After all, he was a cop, and cops need to practice their skills too. When she closed her eyes, she imagined him standing behind her, with his arms wrapped along hers, helping her with her aim.

Anna was the first to admit that she wasn't enamored with Dalton just because he'd saved her or because he was drop dead gorgeous. Sure, he was tall, maybe six-one, with broad shoulders and slim hips, but it was his intriguing smile that sent sparks shimmying up her body just from looking at him. His medium brown hair had a slight wave that was thick on top. He combed it back, highlighting his straight nose and piercing brown eyes. The fact he often had a five o'clock shadow, even early in the day, gave him that sexy bad boy look. While she enjoyed being near him, his demeanor was often too serious, but with a little loosening up, he'd be fun to be around.

While the shifter mystique still intrigued her, she wanted to learn more about him specifically—what made him tick and why he was so driven. Even before she knew about shifters, the two of them had bonded—or so she wanted to believe. When she was in the hospital after the assault, Dalton had visited a few times just to talk. He actually blamed himself for not arriving sooner, and no matter how many times she told him she was eternally grateful that he'd found her at all, he still believed he and McKinnon and Associates could have done more.

When he'd first stopped in at the hospital, her face had been too swollen to talk, so Dalton carried on a rather one-sided conversation. He chatted about where he'd grown up, his love of law enforcement, and why he'd moved to Silver Lake. While he never came out and said it, she sensed Dalton had grown up lonely—just like her. The only difference was that when she was sad, she would escape to the woods where she'd look for animals, colorful mushrooms, and butterflies, or merely seek out the mountain views. The majestic slabs of granite always seemed to renew her soul. Dalton's answer to life seemed to be burying himself in work.

After she returned home from the hospital, he called a few times to make sure she was doing okay, and he even stopped by the flower shop to see her. She truly thought he'd ask her out, only he never did. It was almost as if he was afraid she'd break or something. Anna might have been emotionally distraught in the beginning, but three months with James had done wonders for her mental health.

Now that she was stronger, Anna yearned to change Dalton's mind about her fragile state, but then thought better of it. As a shifter, he'd end up breaking her heart the moment his fated mate walked into his life. Besides, Jillian had told her Dalton was married to his job. A straight-laced cop like him wouldn't want a woman he believed might crumble at any moment. It didn't matter he held her gaze longer than necessary when he came by or that he seemed to heal her from the inside out one cell at a time. She just couldn't chance becoming too attached. If he walked out of her life, she'd be devastated.

In the end, she decided it would be better if she just steered clear of him, which was easier said than done. His eyes contained such sadness and longing that they spoke to her on a deeper level. How could anyone ignore that? Answer? She couldn't.

Without paying attention to where she was driving, she found herself in front of the shooting range. It was a fitting place to end up. It was her place to let off steam.

Anna had purchased a new weapon, one that was heavier than the first one. The gun she had owned had been used to shoot Jillian, and she wanted nothing to do with that fateful event. She'd thought the cops would have confiscated the weapon, but she'd later learned that much of the crime against her hadn't even been reported. Now she understood why. Shifters had killed Whitlaw, and humans didn't know they existed, which forced the shifter cops to create a different version of what had gone down.

Once inside the range, Anna bought a box of bullets. With her ear protection in hand, she found an empty stall. As she loaded her gun, the hairs on her neck rose, and her heart dropped to her stomach, forcing her to twist around. Instead of looking into the eyes of a killer, Dalton was there. His inscrutable gaze was focused on her face, and his eyes had turned a lighter color. Other than being serious, she couldn't pinpoint his mood.

While she wanted to pretend as if meeting him didn't affect her, she couldn't keep the smile off her face. "Hey."

"I'm glad to see you're practicing. How's it coming?" Dalton asked, nodding to her weapon. He moved closer, causing her pulse to soar.

He smelled expensive, as if he'd gone to France and had the manufacturer make a scent just for him—sexy and strong like mountain air. "I'm slowly improving. At least I hit the target now."

"That so? Why don't you show me? I might be able to give you some pointers."

Her throat turned dry fearing she might disappoint him. She glanced away. "That's okay."

Stop it. I need to act strong and prove to him I'm not afraid of my own shadow.

He placed a hand on her shoulder, and when the heat spread down her body and hardened her nipples, she thankfully didn't jerk away. A second later, something blue flitted off her hand. That was weird. The static electricity around here must be intense.

His brows rose. "Do you think I'll judge you?"

Yes. "No."

"You want to improve, right?"

He acted like a drill sergeant. If he'd loosen up, she might have been able to relax. "Yes. If I'm ever approached by a creep again, I want to know I can shoot my gun—and hit the mark."

He smiled. Wow. Not only did his eyes light up, it lit up her insides too. Is that what James meant by the eyes would let her know what Dalton was thinking?

She knew what *she* was thinking, and it had nothing to do with shooting a gun—well not the kind of gun that had bullets. Dalton Garner was way too good looking with his tanned skin, even white teeth, and precisely cut hair. Definitely swoon worthy. Most likely, every eligible woman in town had her eyes on him, which meant she didn't stand a chance.

Great. Anna should be happy Dalton would end up with some-one else since she really didn't need a man to complicate her life, but damn, a little fling sure would help her forget all the bad things that had happened to her.

She and Jillian had lunch a few weeks back, and Anna had asked her if her brother dated a lot. To her surprise, Jillian said she didn't know, but that she guessed he didn't. He'd always been focused on work. At thirty-two, he wanted to move up in rank. While commendable, a person needed to take time to smell the proverbial roses.

"Let me see your grip," Dalton said with a clear, professional tone.

His words brought her back to why she was there. Anna saw no reason not to learn from him. He was, after all, trained. She picked up the gun and adjusted her hands. When she raised her weapon, Dalton stepped behind her, slid his hands around her shoulders just like in her dream, and then cupped her hands. Instantly, her brain ceased to function at his touch. "This isn't right?" she asked, not able to come up with anything else to say.

"It's close. Move your right hand up as high as it can go."

That required about a half-inch adjustment. "Like this?"

"Yes. Your left hand is there to keep the gun steady."

She made the adjustment. "That does feel more secure."

"Good. Now be sure to lock your wrists over center." He moved her hands into position, and she had to admit the grip was more solid. He then nudged the back of her left foot forward with his toe. "Always stand square to the target."

"One of the men here told me to use something called a Weaver stance."

"That hinders your ability to move right and left with ease. If you need your gun in a hurry, you won't be able to get into position quickly enough that way. Trust me; you'll want to face the target."

"Okay."

Dalton stepped out of view. With her grip now correct, Anna raised her weapon to eye level and took aim. She held her breath, squeezed the handle tight, and then pulled the trigger. The recoil caused the gun to move, but not as much as usual.

"You hit the target. Good job," Dalton said.

She set her gun down, twisted around, and lifted her ear protection off one ear. "Thanks. Care to show me what you can do? I learn better when I see someone else do it correctly."

"Sure thing."

Anna stepped back to give him room. He loaded his weapon then readjusted his ear protection. With the experience of someone who'd practiced a lot, he lifted his weapon in one smooth motion and let six bullets rip in rapid succession. Whoa. His broad shoulders and wide stance exuded power, and she wondered if his tiger helped guide his hand.

He pressed a button on the side of the lane to bring the target closer. One bullet hit on the edge and six others were dead in the middle. "I'm impressed," she said.

Dalton slipped his gun back into his holster. "Thanks. I've spent endless hours practicing."

Precise. Determined. Ambitious. Just as Jillian had described. *Ask him.* "Does your *other* talent help you with your aim?"

Every muscle froze. "My other talent?"

She looked around, not sure if she should say anything in public, not that anyone could even hear their conversation. She hadn't wanted to be the one to discuss his ability to shift just yet, thinking he'd bring it up. "Let's just say you appear to be as tightly controlled as say a large cat."

His beautiful cocoa-colored eyes turned a darker shade. "How do you—"

"James and I have had some interesting discussions."

Now it was his turn to glance around. "Have you eaten?"

She hadn't expected that question. "No, I came straight from therapy."

"Do you like pizza?"

"Love it." Oh my God. Was he actually going to ask her out on a date?

"Care to join me for dinner?"

"Sure." Her body shook with excitement. As much as she wanted to study his eyes, she didn't dare. Pretending he was hers, if only for an hour, would be good enough.

Chapter Three

DALTON SAT ACROSS from Anna at a table in the back of Nate's Pizzeria, and the cozy setting caused conflicting emotions to bombard him. Anna was kind, accepting, and intensively hot. His inner tiger wanted to drag her into bed, but Dalton refused to consider it. While he wanted someone to share his life, his job was as dangerous as it came, and he refused to put Anna in anyone's crosshairs again.

That's an excuse, his tiger nudged. *You're just scared.*

Fuck you. What he wouldn't give to shut up his animal. Always pushing. Always horny. The tiger was way too needy, and that was not who Dalton Garner, the man, was.

Did he like the security of having a mate? Maybe, but Anna would never accept his way of life, nor would he ask her to.

You want to be alone all your life? Without your mate, you'll die a slow death.

Dalton refused to listen and, instead, refocused on why he'd asked her to dinner. He needed clarification on her comment about him being like a cat. She'd seen Jillian change into her tiger form, but had Anna believed what she'd seen?

She makes you feel good inside—alive for the first time in your life, his animal said.

Dalton pushed aside that ridiculous comment. Every time he solved a case, adrenaline coursed through him. It made him thrive. He didn't need a woman for that.

"Dalton, are you okay?" Anna asked.

Damn. Had he spaced out? "Yes. Just wondering when the food will arrive. I'm starving." Okay, that was lame.

He checked the area to judge how safe it was to talk. Of the ten tables, only three were occupied, and none close by. Good. It appeared as if most people had come for pickup service instead of dining in.

However, between the order taking, the customers in line chatting, and the music, it was difficult to hear, despite his shifter abilities. Dalton didn't want to consider his need to strain was due to the fact his heart was pumping hard from wanting her so much. No doubt about it, being around his mate was messing with his head—along with a few other body parts.

His mate. That's right. Anna Fairchild was his mate, but he wasn't going to do anything about it for a long time. She might be Wendayan, but even that concept was new to her. She didn't need another shock of learning he was a shifter. If she understood what had happened that fateful night, she would have made a comment during one of his visits to the hospital.

Talk to her, his tiger urged.

"So how does it feel to be finished with therapy?" he asked, pissed at himself for sounding rather distant.

"Now that I'm done, believe it or not, I'm actually going to miss it. James was really nice."

He was happy to hear the immortal had been able to help. "I've never met him."

"Really? Then why did you recommend him?"

"Kalan thought it would be a good idea."

"Oh. Well, I learned a lot."

She brushed back wisps of hair from her delicate forehead. The rest of her long brown hair was pulled back into a braid. The top had blonde streaks running through it that looked like the summer sun had bleached it. The soft curls contrasted with the shiny gold eyebrow ring. Given her sweet demeanor, he figured the adornment was more for show.

Her dark chocolate eyes spoke of pain, but her full, curvy lips screamed imp. The contradiction intrigued him. Because Anna only came up to his chest, it made him want to protect her even more.

Protect her, yes, his tiger reminded him. *Always.*

Dalton blew out a breath. It was true he'd met Anna under the worst of circumstances, but it suited him better if he believed she was too shy to be mated. It was a handy excuse.

She's not ready, he told his tiger.

It's you who isn't ready. Damn animal needed to stop butting into his thoughts.

The twenty-year old behind the counter finally delivered their pizza. "Here's a Coke for the lady and a coffee for the gentleman." He placed a large pepperoni pizza in front of them to share.

As soon as the kid left, Dalton picked up a slice. "You said something back at the shooting range."

A knowing look crossed her face. "Are you talking about my reference to your catlike reflexes aiding you in shooting?"

Damn. Could she read his mind? "Yes."

"James explained everything to me."

His gut churned, and he quickly swallowed. "Care to define what you mean by everything?"

She glanced around. "Should we be discussing this here?"

He leaned close, needing to know. "Did he tell you how it was possible that you saw a tiger in the building that night?" he whispered.

Anna grabbed a slice and bit off a large chunk. It was as if she was trying to think of what to say. Once she finished chewing, she inhaled. "Yes."

So she did believe that shifters existed. Did that scare her? He waited for Anna to continue, but she must have wanted him to drag it out of her. "And what did you think?" His leg bounced up and down.

"It took me a while to get used to the idea. You have to admit that your talent is…um…unique."

"No more than yours."

She sipped her Coke. "I hardly think what I do is all that special. I can merely tell what's happened in a person's life that adversely affected them."

Jillian had explained how Anna had been able to see the night her friend Dalia had been murdered, right down to the detail of the striped wallpaper in the spare bedroom where her friend had been staying. Dalton stretched out his arm willing to let her touch him. "Want to tell me something about myself?" She shook her head. Okay, that confused him. "Why not?"

"You always block your thoughts from me."

That's because you're mates, his animal said, butting into the conversation once more.

Had James told her they were mates? If he had, Dalton wasn't sure if he wanted to throttle the man or hug him. "I don't do it on purpose."

"Are you sure?"

Was she challenging him? Most women never dared, though coming from Anna, he found it rather refreshing. "Yes, I'm sure."

Anna leaned back in her padded seat, looking smug. "If you loosened up a little, you might be able to get in touch with your feelings."

That made him laugh. "My feelings?"

"Yes. You've made it quite clear that your life has been focused on one path and only one path—that of being a detective. Never in the telling did you talk about traveling to a foreign country, hiking the Appalachian Trail, or jumping out of an airplane. You're so rigid in your thinking that you don't seem to enjoy life. I think it's why I can't learn anything about you."

"That's rich. What about you? Are you that open then?" He wanted to learn more about this free spirit.

"I am. I dream a lot."

"Dream of what?" She had him curious.

"I dream of seeing the world's most exotic gardens, of paddling around in the Grotta Azzurra, in Capri, Italy, of rolling in a field of dandelions and blowing their seeds everywhere. Fun stuff like that."

"You don't think I have fun?"

She stared at him. "Honestly? No."

He tried to come up with the last spontaneous thing he'd done that she might consider fun, but all he could think of was when he'd played flag football at the annual sheriff's department picnic. He doubted shooting pool a couple of times a month counted. "I don't know what gibberish James filled your head with, but you have the wrong idea about me."

"Oh, really? Perhaps you should try to change my mind."

That would require him to spend more time with Anna, and his concentration was bad enough. He had a murderer to catch. "I'll give it some thought."

She leaned forward on her elbows, looking way too pleased with herself. "Speaking of James, there's something that has been bothering me about the man."

Dalton's senses shot to high alert. James might be married to a goddess, but Kalan swore he was highly honorable. "What's that?"

"Why doesn't he have any diplomas on his walls?"

Dalton sank back against his seat. Keeping her in the dark about goddesses and immortals would only piss her off later when she learned about them, especially if Elana or Jillian mentioned it. Most of the Wendayans in Silver Lake knew about James even though they had never met him or his goddess wife. "Because he's not an actual doctor."

Every muscle in her body seemed to tense. "What do you mean? You told me he was a therapist."

Kalan promised that James would give her solid advice. "Let me ask you this. Did he help you come to grips with what happened?"

"Yes. And more. He explained things to me, things I had no idea existed."

"That's all that matters."

She shook her head. "No, it's not. You might not have said he was a doctor, but you implied it. Why not send me to a licensed professional?"

Anna had every right to be angry, but he had his reasons. "Because if you'd mentioned what you saw that night—Jillian shifting—to a human therapist, you might have been committed to a psychiatric hospital, and I couldn't let that happen."

"*You* couldn't let that happen? You don't own me."

The walls were starting to crumble all around him. "No, but I was trying to protect you."

Anna bit down on her lip and then blew out a breath. Dalton looked off to the side as his thoughts turned to mating.

"You're right. I'm sorry. Thank you for having my back," she said. "What I don't get is why didn't you tell me about your sister's *talent* when you visited me in the hospital? You must have realized that when I saw her change I would have been a bit confused."

For months, he feared this conversation would occur. Now that it had, Dalton wasn't sure how to handle it. "Would you have believed me, if I had told you that people could turn into animals and then back again?" He kept his voice low. "Admit it; you would have said it was too farfetched."

"Maybe, but you could have at least tried to convince me. Hell, all you would have had to do was change...you know...into something big and white."

Dalton appreciated she was trying to be circumspect. "The thought crossed my mind, but I'm not sure I could have handled seeing you in shock. I did what I thought was best."

"By saying nothing?" She jammed another bite of pizza into her mouth and washed it down with her soft drink. When she swallowed, she leveled him with a glare. "What other secrets have you been hiding?"

Too many. He sipped his coffee, but this time the rich brew didn't calm him in the least. "James is not who you think he is. He knows things we ordinary humans don't." Dalton looked around to make sure no one could have overheard.

"I'll grant you he's smart, but what do you mean by ordinary humans? I wouldn't even put you or myself for that matter, in the *ordinary* category."

He liked her spunk, but it was time to come clean. If she learned of their identity from someone else, she'd never forgive him. "James is an immortal, and his wife is a goddess," he whispered.

Anna laughed. That wasn't the response he expected. "I'm not that gullible."

"But it's true. Do you see why I didn't tell you about my kind?"

Glancing away, she stared at the street outside. With a big inhale, she faced him. "Did I mention his wife made cookies for me last night?"

"No, but I believe she could have. It was after all a white moon. I've heard she's fond of baking."

"White moon? As opposed to what?"

More questions she deserved answers to, but a busy restaurant was not the place to be discussing something so sensitive. "How about we finish up then go back to my place? Fewer ears are there."

"Really? Your place?" Her eyes glowed, acting as if he'd asked her to bed. That could be trouble.

Yes, bed. Mate, mate, his tiger chanted.

Shut up. It's too soon. I want her to like me first.

She likes you just fine.

Dalton chose to ignore him once more. "You have questions, and I have some answers. We can go to your place if you'd feel more comfortable."

"No. Your place is good."

He finished off the last slice of pizza. "Ready?"

ANNA WAS SUPER excited to go to Dalton's house. This wasn't a date, but that was okay for now. Seeing how he lived would help fill in those missing puzzle pieces when she dreamed about him. His house would be obsessively neat—that she was sure. If he had any artwork on the walls, there wouldn't be much because he wouldn't have had the time or desire to decorate. Efficiency was his game. Take his kitchen for example. It would be sparse but would contain everything he needed to make a simple meal. His closets would be organized according to use—his uniforms on one end and his casual clothes on the other.

That was one reason why she didn't want him to see how she lived. She was clean, but definitely not neat. Her old apartment had been highly eclectic with plaids mixed with polka dots, but the new place above the store was a work in progress. For weeks, she hadn't been up for decorating, but during her drive to the range, she decided she was ready to tackle the world.

"Do you want to pick up your car at the shooting range and follow me home?" he asked.

"Sure. I don't want to leave my vehicle there longer than necessary."

Once they arrived at the range, he parked close to her Volkswagen and waited for her to start the engine before he took off. She followed closely behind, and for the first time in a long while, felt totally safe, having no doubt that Dalton wouldn't let anything happen to her.

He lived on the north end of town in a neighborhood where most homes were surrounded by chain-linked fences. He pulled in front of a brick home, and she parked behind him.

Before she could even blink, he was at her door and had it pulled open. He held out his hand, and when she placed her palm in his, blue sparks shot off. "Holy crap."

"You sound surprised," he said.

"Hell yes, I am surprised. What was that?" She meant both the blue sparks and his ability to move faster than the eye could blink.

"James didn't tell you?"

"Tell me what?" she asked.

"Come on inside. I can see it's going to be a long night."

Her heart pounded, but Anna couldn't tell whether it was because she was about to see where he lived or that she'd be alone with
her fantasy man. If she asked him to shift for her, would he? She'd
always had a love of animals, and petting such a large cat would be a
high. Somehow, she sensed he'd say no, claiming shifting was done
only when needed.

Dalton held open the front door. "Just so you know, the place
came furnished. It's not my style."

She stepped in and looked around. The kitchen was against the
far wall. Given the tired looking brown sofa and worn brown chairs,
she hadn't expected the home to be open concept. "It's nice." Neat
but rather sterile.

"Can I get you something to drink? A wine or some beer?"

If Anna drank, no telling what she'd do. She never could hold
her liquor. "Water's fine."

"Water it is."

As he strode over to the kitchen, she sat on the sofa and looked
around. The white walls could use some artwork—something with
color. "You said you've lived here for over a year?"

"Yes. Kind of sad isn't it?"

She chuckled. "Depressing might be a better word. You know
some colorful pillows could do wonders for the place. Bright red
slipcovers and a multicolored throw rug would go a long way to liven
up the place."

"I'll keep that in mind." He handed her a glass and sat across
from her. Darn. She'd been hoping for something more intimate.

"I have a lot of questions, starting with what happened outside.
One minute you were at your car and the next by my door. I didn't
see you move."

"Jillian didn't tell you of her ability to move fast?"

"She did, but I never witnessed it. It's like you disappeared and
reappeared someplace else."

Dalton crossed his feet at his ankles and leaned back in his seat,
looking relaxed for a change. "I only do it when I know I'm in

friendly territory."

"How do you know some neighbor doesn't have her binoculars trained on your house?"

He laughed. "Why would she?"

Because you're hot? "She's bored?"

He sucked in his cheeks as if he was about to laugh. Anna had to admit seeing the glint in his eyes and the cheer on his face turned her on even more.

"I'll make sure to be more careful," he said.

"Your ability to move fast was unique, but did you notice those blue sparks floating around me? That's the second time I've seen them."

She swore his face reddened. "I take it you're unaware that when a Wendayan is sexually excited that he or she glows blue?"

"Really?" Okay that was embarrassing. His eyes said he wasn't lying. Still, she found it hard to believe. "Do shifters turn green or something when they're excited?"

Now he laughed. "Hardly. Our nails and teeth sharpen. Hair sprouts on our bodies. Thankfully, mine is light in color so it's harder to notice. I've been told my eyes turn something akin to gold. As for your blue sparks? I'm Wendayan too, but I'm no expert. Here's what I know, though Jillian can describe it better." He explained about the blue sparks growing larger and larger until they turned into a bubble of blue.

"That's embarrassing, but if you're a Wendayan too, why don't you have those blue sparks?"

He shrugged. "If I'm capable of having them, I've never seen them."

Crap. That could mean he wasn't excited when he was around her. Well damn. "Moving on, tell me the significance of the white moon, and please don't say Silver Lake has vampires."

Chapter Four

ANNA DIDN'T THINK she could be shocked any more, but Dalton had managed to twist her worldview once more. Immortals and goddesses started the ball rolling. He then moved on to listing the different kind of shifters and what happened during and after the shift. In her opinion, it would be terrible to return to human form after shifting back from being an animal only to be naked. "Was Brian…um…naked after he left the warehouse?"

She'd been saved by Dalton before Brian in his bear form had finished fighting the evil Whitlaw.

"Yes, but all shifters keep an extra set or two of clothes in their cars. Since Brian hadn't known he'd shift, Kalan probably offered him one of his spare sets."

"Smart." Anna didn't think she was ready to learn any more oddities about shifters at the moment. "Back to your previous topic. Tell me more about James. Do you know how old he is?"

Dalton shrugged. "I have no idea. Hundreds of years I'm guessing, and because his wife is a goddess, he knows more than any other human. From what I've heard, she knows everything, including who will be mated to whom."

"Are you talking about fated mates?" A bubble of excitement burst inside her. Maybe Anna could ask James to set up an appointment with his wife to learn the identity of Dalton's mate. As soon as she thought of it, her brilliant idea came to a crashing halt. A goddess wouldn't tell her shit, especially something about a shifter. Besides, it would be better if she didn't know who Dalton would end up with for the rest of his life.

His eyes turned a few shades lighter. "You know about mates?"

"As I said, James was a font of information."

"What did he say about them?"

Dalton probably wanted to know what she'd learned so he could fill in the gaps. "I'll tell you what he told me."

She described how in the state of high passion, the shifter would bite his mate, and then if his mate were human or a Wendayan, she'd become a shifter too. "It sounds pretty far-fetched, but what do I know?"

"It's not."

Wow. "James once commented that when a shifter met his mate, he recognized her right away, but he never said how the shifter knew."

"His or her body goes wild with need. Instinctively, he knows."

Which meant blue sparks would be shooting off of Dalton if they were mates. Well, damn.

Common sense told her the man wasn't a virgin, which meant he'd had sex with women who weren't his mate. She wouldn't mind being one more in his collection. Of course, she'd have to work hard to steel her heart from further hurt, but to make love with him even once would be a dream come true.

The easiest way to start the seduction would be to ask him to shift. Then when he shifted back, he'd be naked! Eazy peazy. The hard part would be figuring out how to lead up to the request. "James said the shifter community always protects the Wendayans. I'm curious how my kind learned about shifters in the first place?"

He leaned back. "I don't know. It might be a Tennessee thing. In California, no one even discussed shifters. Hell, for most of my life, I thought our family was unique. It wasn't like you asked your neighbor if he could shift."

Poor Dalton. "Really? James told me that shifters could sense other shifters."

He finished his glass of water. "True, but as a kid, I didn't know what that odd sensation meant when I was near one. Our dad died when we were young, so we had no direct instruction. I supposed I could have asked my mother since she was married to a shifter, but I never did. I can tell when I meet one now, though."

"That's good. So basically, when you moved to Silver Lake, it was the first time you could free your tiger, so to speak."

He shook his head. "To be honest, I've never shifted in front of anyone here."

That surprised her. "Why not?"

"Kalan would talk about the Changelings and how the other wolves and bears disliked them. I feared they might not take kindly to a tiger either. Rationally, I understood why they were prejudiced against the mutant wolves, but I didn't see the need to take the chance and expose what I was."

No wonder Dalton lived a controlled life. He'd been forced to keep his true identity wrapped up tightly. "Mutant wolves? Who are they?"

He spent the next half hour describing who they were and why they were evil. At the end, she was sorry she'd asked.

"The Changelings should come with a warning label," she said.

He laughed. "Don't we wish? Most shifters can't tell one shifter from another or whether it's a Changeling or not, which helps make them more powerful. There is one woman though, who can tell the difference. Her name is Ainsley Chancellor. She's mated to Jackson."

Jackson. Yes. The man who'd figured out where she was being held captive. "She's lucky." Anna slapped her thighs, wanting to refocus on her goal of seducing him. "So will you shift for me?"

Dalton froze, and then so did she. Slowly, his chest expanded, and she let out a breath.

"Why?" he asked.

Because I want to see you naked, hopefully making it easier for me to seduce you. She shrugged. "I think it would be fun to pet you."

The moment she said it, his lips thinned, and his jaw tightened.

Crap.

"Not going to happen. Shifting is for emergencies only, not for playing around."

That was just a controlled excuse. "Spoilsport." Since he wasn't going to play along, she decided to move away from the whole shifter talk, but she wouldn't give up on getting him to shift for her later. She'd just have to seduce him using a different approach. He might, however, let down his guard if she asked about his work. "Someone came into the shop and mentioned that Crystal Wedgewood had been murdered. Is that true?" An ache swelled in her belly at the remembrance.

"Yes. Did you know her?"

"Yes. I was in her store all the time. She was a nice lady."

Dalton sat up straighter. "How did she treat her employees?"

Anna thought the question rather odd until she realized it was something a cop would ask. "I never heard her yell at them, if that's what you mean, but who knows what went on behind closed doors. The manager, Meredith Wilson, could tell you, I bet."

"I plan to speak with her tomorrow."

Anna finished her water. "I'll stick to arranging flowers. Your job is too stressful, not to mention dangerous."

A black cloud crossed over his face. What had she said to warrant that reaction?

"It is. While I've never shifted to catch a criminal, the time will come when I'll have to."

Like Jillian had to in order to save Anna. Now that they'd discussed shifters and the role of goddesses, there was no reason for her to stay. Dalton's mind seemed way too engaged in work to be thinking about having sex anyway.

Who was she kidding? No shifter would be highly motivated to pursue a woman unless she was his mate. Clearly, she wasn't meant for him, or Dalton would have made his move already—especially now that he knew she was aware of shifters. She hoped she hadn't voiced her opinion about the whole concept of being bitten. If he knew it freaked her out, he'd stay clear.

Anna stood. "I should be going. Thanks for dinner and our little chat."

Dalton jumped up, but she couldn't tell if he was relieved she was leaving or not. Anna slung her purse diagonally over her shoulder and pushed the bag toward her back. She then walked slowly to the door before spinning around to face him. Just as she'd hoped, he'd followed her.

"I want to thank you for everything you've done for me," she said. While she'd told him that many times, she'd never shown him. Dalton would either like what she was about to do, or ease her out of his arms and tell her he wasn't interested. No pain no gain, right?

Drawing on her inner strength, Anna reached up, cupped his face, and drew Dalton's lips to hers. The two seconds before their mouths actually touched seemed to take an eternity. Her pulse soared, and doubt tried to nudge its way in, but she pushed it away.

Their lips met, and boy did her blue sparks fly. Not only did her body sing from the softness of his lips, his fresh mountain air scent made her skin tingle. His hands latched onto her hips, and when he pulled her closer, she melted against him. For those few seconds, her dreams came true. When his lips slightly parted, her breath caught. Was that an invitation?

Just as she was about to delve into his mouth, he stepped back. At first, she thought the blue sparks were only coming off her, but when she glanced at his hands, he was glowing too. Yes!

"We can't," Dalton said, his voice strained.

Was he kidding? "Why not?" she managed to say, despite her mouth turning dry. "You can't tell me you didn't feel anything." He slipped his hands behind his back probably because either more sparks were shooting off his arms or else his nails had grown. Dare she hope it was because he was trying to keep his hands off her?

It didn't matter the reason. His eyes gave him away. They had been cocoa-colored, but were now a mixture of yellows, greens, and oranges.

"It's not that," he said. "You've been through too much."

He was going to pull that line? "Let me decide when I'm ready. I've been discussing my issues with James for three months. That's right—three whole months." She tapped him on the chest. "Am I scared it might happen again? Hell yes, but I'm not going to let it ruin my life. News flash, I like you."

"I like you too."

She planted a hand on her hip. "Well, you sure have a funny way of showing it. I don't understand why you stopped." When he didn't answer, she stepped closer. "You know what your problem is?"

A hint of enjoyment filled his eyes. "Tell me."

"Besides being a control freak, not to mention a neat freak, you lack spontaneity. In case you don't understand what that means, kissing for no apparent reason is the epitome of being spontaneous."

He leaned down, and not only did her pulse soar, her body vibrated with an intense need. She wanted to touch him again, but she didn't want to make the same mistake twice.

"I can be spontaneous." The challenge in his eyes held her captive.

He grabbed her to his chest and kissed her like she'd never been kissed before. Her eyes rolled back, and her breath lodged in her throat. When he teased open her lips, her damned knees weakened. Thank goodness, Dalton was holding her up, or she might have dropped to the floor.

The moment their tongues touched, he probed, swirled, and dipped into her, and it was as if electricity had charged through her body. When she answered his next thrust, her tongue met one of his sharp teeth, and cut her. Pain sliced through her.

They jerked apart. Dalton held onto her shoulders. "Oh, fuck. I'm sorry. I didn't think my teeth would sharpen like that."

Between the elongated incisors, the change in eye color, and the white hair sprouting on his face and arms, she'd say he was turned on. "It's okay. What's a little blood between friends?"

"Anna," he huffed. "As you can see, I'm attracted to you, but you don't understand what my life is like."

Here it comes—the brush off. She'd heard it a hundred times. "Is it the nose ring or the tattoos?"

His brows pinched. "What?"

"You know what I mean. A lot of guys are put off by my appearance."

He shook his head, actually looking confused. "Are you kidding? No, you're perfect. Have I dated anyone like you before? No, but that just means you're unique."

She held up her hands, needing a lot more time to think about what all that meant. He had liked the kiss, there was no denying it, but she wouldn't be getting him into bed tonight. "Okay. Thanks." *I think.*

She twisted away, pulled open the front door, and stepped outside. Dalton suddenly appeared before her.

"Wait, please," he said holding up his hands.

"You don't have to apologize. I get it." The July air was rather muggy, and she wanted to go home and take a shower. She'd truly thought the two of them had chemistry, but somehow Dalton didn't want to take her up on her offer.

"My job is dangerous."

"Yeah, well, you are a cop." She worked at a flower shop and had been kidnapped, but she kept quiet.

"I don't want to put you in danger."

He was pissing her off again. "I appreciate your protective nature, but I'm a big girl and can make my own decisions."

His chin lowered, clearly not buying it. "What are you saying? You want to see if this can work?"

Hope soared through her. Anna lifted her chin. "Yes."

He lowered his arms and stabbed a hand through his hair, clearly needing some time to think. "Okay then. How about we take things slow and see how it goes?"

Her heart jumped to her throat. She'd take what she could get—for now. "Slow is good."

"Okay. I'll call you this week, and we can set up a time to go out again."

She hoped this wasn't a pity date. "Can I ask you something?"

"Anything." His eyelids lowered, and he leaned toward her, almost as if he wanted this moment to last forever.

"Do you know who your mate is? I mean at what age does the goddess reveal it to you?"

Dalton didn't even blink or breathe. Then as if some fairy god-mother waved a magic wand, he let out a breath and looked off to the side. "She doesn't reveal it per se. Look, it's complicated."

"I understand that you're a cop who's trained in negotiations, but I'm not some terrorist. Just tell me."

"It's not that simple."

He'd just said that. Dalton was stalling. She planted a hand on her hip. "Did I say I wanted simple?"

"No." Dalton blew out a breath.

"Tell me."

"Okay. You asked for it. *You* are my mate."

Chapter Five

ANNA'S HEART DROPPED to her stomach. If dusk hadn't fallen, she might have been able to read the expression in his eyes. "Is that a joke?"

"Why would I joke? Even you said I'm not capable of having fun."

True. "Then why don't you seem happy about us being mated?"

Dalton grabbed her hand. "We need to talk."

Hell, if she was his mate, they needed to be doing a lot more than talking, but she let him lead her back inside. Anna didn't know whether to laugh from joy that she could spend more time with him or prepare herself for the big letdown. "What's there to discuss?"

For most of her life, she'd been told she was too brash, too forward, and too impatient. That had been true, but in the last few years she'd grown—or at least she liked to think she had. As soon as she started working in the flower shop under Elana's guidance, Anna's anxieties had fallen away. It was only when that terrible man nearly killed her that she'd regressed. With the help of James and her friends, she had improved.

"We need to talk about *us*," Dalton said.

He walked over to the kitchen, pulled out a beer from the fridge. "Change your mind about having something to drink?" he asked, waving the bottle.

Maybe she did need the fortification. "Sure, a beer's good."

He grabbed a second one, walked around the center island, and guided her to the sofa. This time he sat next to her then handed her the drink. Dalton leaned back and held his drink with both hands. "When I said it was complicated, I meant it."

"Okay, then explain it to me. I'll work hard to understand." That came out a bit too snarky, but she didn't like being treated like a little kid. He was only seven years older than she was.

"Having a mate and being mated are two different things."

She nodded. "James explained it to me. I'm not asking to jump into bed with you and have you bite me. Even I know relationships take time to develop, but a little kissing and touching can go a long way in learning about each other."

He chuckled. "You are something else."

"You are right; I am, which is why you need to listen to me and not let your logical mind dictate everything. This is about emotion, not facts."

He tipped back his beer and looked away. "I'm used to being in charge."

"No shit, Sherlock, but if I'm your mate, you need to be more flexible."

Dalton set down his bottle. "That may be, but I can't help it. I want you too much."

A laugh escaped. "You sure have a funny way of showing it." If it were true that he really wanted her, it should make him want to create a win-win situation. "Just so you know, I want you, too."

Dalton blew out a breath. "The truth is, I *more* than want you," he responded without addressing her comment.

Men. "Care to elaborate?"

"I'll try. Ever since I rushed into that building where you were being held, I knew you were my fated mate. Why do you think I saved you, rather than helping my sister kill that bastard who beat you?"

She focused on the first half of what he said. He knew way back then and didn't tell her? She had always wondered why he'd saved her, instead of rushing to his wounded sister. At the time, he might not have known Jillian had been shot. Arguing about why he never mentioned it before wouldn't change things or help make their relationship stronger. "I figured you thought she could handle herself."

"I did, but here's the thing you need to understand about shifters who've met their mates. I'm going crazy thinking about you all the time, and that could interfere with me doing my job. I'm even having a hard time sleeping, and when I'm near you?" He shook his head. "It's ten times worse."

Her pulse raced, replaying his words in her head over and over. He really thought about her all the time? No one had ever said anything like that to her before. For the last three months, Dalton had acted like he didn't even like her. "Then why didn't you ask me out?"

"Because you needed time to heal."

"In the past, maybe, but not now." She studied him. "Have you ever heard of asking a person what she wants? I would have told you that I'm ready."

He grinned, and her libido shot into high gear. "You sure?"

His dreamy eyes nearly did her in. "Yes."

Dalton slipped her beer from her fingers and set her bottle next to his. A second later, she was on his lap, and the kiss that followed spoke of a future, of passion, of love. Anna was delirious, still not believing she was his mate or that he wanted her more than life itself.

Right now, she wanted to do everything in her power to make sure he didn't change his mind. Even though he'd said he liked to take control, she needed to show him that being the recipient of some loving could be an even greater turn on.

Letting her desire rule, she tugged on his shirt to dislodge it from his pants, but she only managed to free the sides.

Without breaking the seal of his kiss, he helped her loosen his shirt the rest of the way. He moaned and then slipped off her sandals, implying they'd be naked soon. That thought alone had her sex throbbing.

Needing some air, she broke the kiss and undid the buttons on his shirt as fast as her fingers could fly. As soon as she revealed his chest, her heart nearly stopped.

"You're beautiful," she said, running a palm over his lightly sprinkled coffee-colored chest hair.

"Men aren't beautiful," he grunted.

"Fine, you're hot. Is that better?" Why was she even having this conversation? Her witch was screaming for her to touch him everywhere and then lick him until he screamed her name.

In one quick move, she slipped her top over her head and when his eyes widened, she crossed her arms over her chest to cover her small breasts.

"Don't," he commanded. "I've told you that you are perfect. You have to believe me."

His words were like hot chocolate on a cold night. He peeled her arms from her body, and a moment later, she was flat on her back. Excitement sizzled through her at what was to come. A quick pinch on the back of her bra, and it became history. Dalton then unzipped her jeans and dragged them off along with her panties.

His mouth opened as he stared at her nakedness then he licked his lips. "I don't know if I can keep my tiger at bay. It's been so long."

So long since he'd had sex or since he'd let his tiger loose? It didn't matter which one. "Try."

Dalton rose onto his haunches and lifted her legs over his shoulders. This position of vulnerability might have bothered her in the past, but right now, it excited her. Anna appreciated his inventive spontaneity.

Leaning over, he inhaled deeply then swept his tongue over her opening. Holy hell. Not only did sparks fly off of both of them, she glowed blue and prayed she wouldn't self-destruct. To maintain some control, she clutched the sofa cushion.

When Dalton sucked on her nub, the pleasure was so intense it almost bordered on pain. She let go of the cushion and grabbed his shoulders. The moment he flicked her tiny pearl again, she dug her fingernails into his skin. Who knew that part of her body was her *On* switch?

"Please, I need you," she begged. She hated that she was easy, but Anna had fantasized about him for months.

He answered by slipping two fingers into her and wiggling them around until he found a spot that skyrocketed her upward. With each lick and finger movement, her moans grew into what sounded like a feral cry. Finally, the dam broke, and she came hard.

As soon as the waves of lust subsided, Dalton sat back and smiled. "Did you like that?"

"You couldn't tell?"

He chuckled, and she was pleased he took her comment the way she'd meant it. He slipped out from under her, stood, and shucked his shoes and pants in record time. Anna raised her arms for him to return to the sofa and continue their lovemaking, but instead of doing what she expected, he pulled her to her feet.

"I can't wait any longer," he said.

She wasn't asking him to. He walked her backward to the center island, and when she bumped into it, he captured her lips again. While their breaths increased, indicating he was on edge, he took his time, exploring her lips one little nibble at a time. Then their tongues mingled and plunged, and the divine sensation thrilled her beyond words.

He pressed his cock against her stomach, and she was unable to keep from slipping a hand between them and wrapping it around his long shaft. Heat poured through her palm at the touch.

"You don't want to do that," he said between gritted teeth.

"Are you telling me what to do again?" She raised a brow.

"No. I'm merely warning you."

Just as she was about to shoot off another smart response, hot cum splattered her knuckles, and she released him. "Oh."

"Told you. Now turn around," he said as he twisted her toward the counter and bent her over.

Anna clasped onto the edge. When he spread her legs, the anticipation caused not only her blue glow to pulse and radiate, it was as if
an electric current made every nerve ending crackle with delight.

He leaned over her back, brushed her hair to the side, and kissed
her neck. She stiffened, awaiting the bite. What she got instead was a
soft nibble that was so erotic she nearly came again. As much as she
loved this position, it didn't allow her to rub her hands on his body
or kiss him, but all thoughts of dismay flew out of her head when he
cupped her breasts and pressed on her nipples. Her body went wild
with need, sending strong pulses straight down to her core. To say
she was glowing would be an understatement.

"I need you," he said in the deepest, sexiest voice possible.

"Yes." That one word was about all she could speak.

The second his cock pressed against her wet entrance, he drove
in, stretching her so wide, she thought she'd split in two. A second
later, total bliss enveloped her. Dalton planted his forehead on the
back of her head and made a sound that was close to a purr. He then
lowered his hands to her hips and held on tight as he withdrew then
pounded into her once more. Her fingers curled on the counter, and
she lifted her head to gulp in some much-needed air. Never had she
felt anything so wonderful or intense in her life.

With each thrust, she soared higher and higher, and the only
sound reaching her ears was the strong beating of her heart. Each
plunge was amazing, fantastic, and life altering.

Wanting to participate more fully, she pressed her hips back and
reached one hand around to his hips. The texture of his skin seemed
different—rougher, as if his tiger was trying to get out. She wasn't
sure she could handle that happening, but she certainly wasn't going
to stop!

"You feel so fucking good," he whispered, almost as if his comment wasn't meant for her to hear. His words instantly dismissed her
concerns.

"You feel pretty great too."

When he twisted one of her nipples, her climax swamped her,

pushing her over that huge cliff of erotic bliss. She squeezed her eyes shut and yelled his name as his hot seed filled her, searing her insides.

Dalton grunted, wrapped his arms around her, and then dropped his head on her back. His ragged breathing matched hers, and they remained motionless for another few minutes. When they caught their breath, he slipped out, trotted around the island, and retrieved a towel from the drawer. After wetting it, he handed it to her to clean up.

"That was... well, I have no words for it," she said. *My dream come true?*

His eyes widened, and then they darkened, scaring her in their intensity. "Fuck. I was so excited, I didn't use a condom. I'm sorry."

They'd been spontaneous, and she loved it. Anna mentally calculated the timing from her last period. "I'm not. It's safe."

"That is good news." He took the towel from her and dried himself off. Instead of tossing it on the counter, he dropped it in the sink. At least he hadn't taken the time to place it in the washing machine.

When he walked back to her, she took in his body. Magnificent didn't come close to describing him. He was a tiger. Pure and simple. Sleek and muscular with eyes that held a person captive.

"Maybe we should get dressed," he said.

Why? Surely he couldn't want her to leave. Not now. Not after what they'd experienced together. Or was he nervous for some reason? Needing to convince him that what just transpired had been unbelievably amazing, she reached out and grabbed his arm. "Come here you. I'm not finished."

Before he could question her, she plastered her chest against his and kissed him again. As if they hadn't just made love, he devoured her lips, teasing, probing, and tasting her. He slipped his hands under her butt and lifted her onto the counter so that they were of equal height—eye to eye, lips to lips.

Anna wrapped her arms around his neck and returned his passion, stroke for stroke.

This time, Dalton stepped back. "Do you see why it's dangerous for us to be around each other?"

"No. I think it's natural for two people who are attracted to each other to want to kiss and touch."

He smiled. "I agree, which is why I can't continue."

Her heart stopped, though his smile took off the sting. "What do you mean you can't continue?"

"I'm saying that we have to take it slow."

She grinned. "Like we just did?"

"That was all your fault. You tempted me too much."

Her jaw dropped. "I did no such thing. If I recall, you dragged me onto your lap."

He winked. "See? I can be spontaneous."

Anna tried to punch his arm, but he was so fast, he twisted out of the way. "Fine. I'll be good and stay out of your way," she said, having no intention of doing any such thing.

"You're lying, and I can prove it."

She lifted her chin. "How so?"

He stepped back and lowered his still erect cock. "I dare you not to suck on it."

She glanced down at his larger-than-life steel rod that looked as if he'd never climaxed. *Decisions, decisions.* She wanted to taste him really badly. Hell, any mortal woman would drop to her knees and suck on him, but she wasn't ordinary.

She shrugged, and without a word, walked past him, picked up her panties and slipped them on.

Dalton laughed, and she fell a little bit more in love with him.

Chapter Six

D ALTON FOLLOWED KALAN into the Silver Lake Bookstore that was thankfully open for business. "I thought the manager, Meredith Wilson, would have closed the doors until after Crystal Wedgewood's funeral," Dalton said.

Kalan shook his head. "Guess not. Maybe she wasn't broken up over the owner's death."

"Always possible," Dalton said, "but if she did harm the owner, she should have at least pretended to be upset over it. Hell, maybe that meant she wasn't guilty." Of late, his logical mind had fallen off the rail, and he blamed Anna for it.

Mate, mate, his tiger panted.

Not now. He did not need to think about her. Last night had caused him to lose too much sleep, which really sucked. Kalan and he needed to catch a murderer.

Dalton pulled open the door and stepped inside. No surprise, it smelled stale, like years of collected dust, bringing back memories of his childhood. Dalton had spent hours in the California public library, reading sci-fi stories, wondering if perhaps his family had been some alien race who had landed on earth years ago. The old worn books, read by so many, had become precious to him. While his imagination had shut down when he'd grown older, it had been vivid as a child. He sighed. Those were the days when he had few cares in life.

Like when you're with Anna, his tiger reminded him.

True.

Never in his life did he think he'd find a mate as amazing as Anna. Once he realized he had to take over as the man in the family, he became a firm believer in routine, accuracy, and careful planning. Anna on the other hand, seemed to have a wild side, taking chances that he never would have dared.

How many human women, upon hearing her mate could change into a tiger, would start cheering? One. Anna. She should have run, but for some reason she hadn't. He hoped it wasn't because he'd carried her out of the building where she'd been held captive. He was no hero—a whole team of men had been responsible for finding her.

And then there was the sex. Never before had he met anyone who was more open, spontaneous, or who responded to his touch like her.

"You okay?" Kalan asked.

Dalton jerked out of his musings. *Do you see why you can't let me think about her?* he asked, chastising his tiger. "I'm good. Just thinking about how much I loved books as a kid."

Kalan smiled. "That doesn't surprise me. You seem the studious type."

Dalton wisely didn't answer. Kalan was always busting his chops about being too serious.

No more than four customers were in the store browsing, which would make questioning the suspects easier. A short woman, between forty and fifty, with medium brown wavy hair was taking inventory of the books on the shelves, occasionally turning some outward while straightening others. Her spiked heels, black pencil skirt, and cream-colored blouse put her in the running to be the manager.

A second woman, who was rather pretty with short-cropped black hair, stood behind the counter, working the cash register. Dalton put her at about forty, but he never was good at guessing a woman's age. Hell, he'd thought Anna wasn't more than twenty. Turned out she was twenty-five.

Kalan tapped his shoulder. "Why don't you take the woman in

the black skirt, and I'll speak with the cashier?"

"Works for me." Because neither of the two male employees was visible, he hoped they were working today.

As Dalton headed toward his assigned woman, a man emerged from the back of the store with a tablet in his hand, making a beeline toward her. Sporting a slight paunch and a bad haircut, Dalton judged him to be about the same age as Meredith.

"Hi, Merry," he called. "I just got off the phone with Voracious Publishing. About three hundred of John Stenton's books are still on backorder."

Merry must be short for Meredith. Her shoulders sagged. "When will they be in?"

"Two weeks."

She stood up straighter. "Call Renaldo Framingham and ask if he can help expedite things."

"Will do." The man spun around and returned to the back of the store. The male worker had to be either Tom DeLuca or Ed Santaria.

"Ms. Wilson?" Dalton asked.

She turned toward him, and when she ran her gaze up and down his body, he didn't know whether to blush or be put off by the perusal.

"How may I help you, officer? I trust this is about Crystal?"

"Yes. Is there a place we can speak in private?"

"Sure. We can talk in my office."

He followed her around the many stacks of books. While the store was large by Silver Lake standards, the place was terribly crowded. Space was at a premium in the small town.

Inside the manager's office, a cluttered wooden desk sat in the corner. The rest of the space was taken up with boxes of books stacked halfway to the ceiling. Without any windows, the room was rather claustrophobic. Most likely, it had been designed as a storage closet, and they'd run out of room.

"Sorry about the mess," she said, dragging a folding chair from against the wall and opening it for Dalton.

He sat while Meredith took a seat behind her messy desk. "Do you have any idea who killed Crystal?" she asked.

That was going to be his question. "Not yet, Meredith. Do *you* have any suspicions?"

"Call me Merry, please. Only my mother called me Meredith, and that was when I'd done something bad." She flashed him a smile, and his thoughts jumped to Anna. "To answer your question, Officer, no I don't know, though Ed Santaria has never liked Crystal."

He pulled out his phone. "Mind if I record this?"

She waved a hand. "I have nothing to hide."

He tapped the record button on his phone. "Go ahead."

"Ed used to own this bookstore before I came to work here. I've heard that due to his poor management, he ran into financial trouble and had to sell the place. The only buyer was Crystal."

"Seems to me she did him a favor."

"I guess so, assuming it was a fair price, but for as long as I've been here, she's treated him like dirt. Crystal made him do all the dirty work, almost as if she was punishing him for running the place into the ground."

"Why did he stay then?" No one deserved to be treated with a lack of respect.

She shrugged. "I don't know. You'd have to ask him."

Dalton would do that. "How did the other employees feel about her?"

She glanced off to the side. "For the most part, good, I guess, but about three months ago, Crystal was approached by a big box store who wanted to buy the bookstore."

From the way her lips thinned and her chest caved, she wasn't happy about it. "Do you know the name of that bookstore?"

"Books Galore. They're fairly large in North Carolina."

Kalan had spoken about how Silver Lake was slowly being taken over by bigger chain stores and many of the folks were upset. "What would that mean to everyone here?"

"Most likely we'd lose our jobs." Her chin trembled. "It is possible they'd keep some of us as I doubt they'd bring a fully staffed team."

That might give someone a motive to kill Crystal. "Was Crystal considering selling?"

"Yes. She said she was tired of working all the time and wanted to retire. The timing was perfect since her husband had succeeded in building a large clientele." Merry looked off to the side as if she could see the irony of it all. Crystal would never have to work again.

"What does he do for a living?" It was something Dalton planned to ask her husband.

"He's some kind of wealth manager. He deals in large investments, or so Crystal liked to brag."

Crystal might have married Carlton for his money rather than for love. Dalton was glad he wasn't wealthy for that very reason. "Who had the most to lose if everyone was laid off?"

Her lips pursed. "I'd have to say me. Jobs aren't easy to find in Silver Lake, especially at my age. My husband had a stroke last month, and he hasn't been able to work since then. His medical bills are mounting, and I'm our sole supporter."

"That has to be tough." She almost looked as if she was about to cry. Uncomfortable with a lot of emotion, he moved on. "What can you tell me about Linda Darnell?"

Her chin tucked under. "I don't know what you mean. She's hard working."

"Was she upset about the possible sale?"

Merry blew out a breath then reached for a tissue on her desk and swiped her eyes. "We all were upset, but I think she was hoping she and Tom DeLuca would move to North Carolina together if the new company didn't need her services. He'd always talked about his cabin in the Blue Ridge Mountains. Of the four of us, I think those two would have had the easiest transition if we lost our jobs."

A knock sounded on her door, and Dalton tensed. A shifter

signature was out there. The door eased open, and a man who was closer to sixty than fifty with thinning salt and pepper hair poked his head in. From the ruddy complexion and sallow eyes, it looked like he drank a lot. "Sorry. I didn't know you were busy, but I need to discuss something with you."

"Can you give me a minute, Ed?"

"Sure." He closed the door.

"That was Ed Santaria," she said. "If you think one of us killed Crystal, I can assure you it wasn't me, and I don't see Tom or Linda for having done it, either."

That left Ed. "I appreciate your candor." Dalton stood. "It's my job to ask where you were the night of Crystal's murder."

"I was home."

"Alone?"

"No, my husband was there, but if you ask him, he won't be able to tell you, as he was asleep when I arrived."

Convenient. Dalton stood. "Thanks for being so open. I'll let you two get back to business." He fished out his business card and handed it to her. "If you think of anything, you can contact me here."

Merry stood and shook his hand. Her palm was dry. "I will."

When Dalton stepped out of the office, Ed was there, and his face reddened as if he'd been eavesdropping. "When you finish with your boss, I'd like to ask you a few questions," Dalton said.

The man stiffened. "Why me? I didn't have anything to do with Crystal's death."

That was what everyone said. "You might be able to provide the clue that helps us find the killer."

He puffed out his chest. "Oh, then sure."

Note to self: Ed seemed to possess a low self-esteem and wanted people to think of him as having power. "I'll be out front."

Dalton could use Ainsley Chancellor's expertise right now, as she was the only one who could tell a good shifter from a bad one. If Ed headed the suspect list, perhaps Kalan could ask his brother if his mate might be available.

Dalton went in search of his partner who was finishing up with Tom DeLuca—the man who'd delivered the news about the backorder. Kalan must have finished with his interview with Linda Darnell already.

Kalan stepped away from Tom and met Dalton near the back of the store. "What did you learn?" Dalton asked.

"Not much. Linda said that Ed Santaria was unhappy with Crystal because she was in the process of selling the store. Apparently, he was the original owner but ran into money problems. After Crystal bought him out, she kept him on even though she treated him like dirt."

"That's the exact thing Merry told me," Dalton said.

"Merry?"

"Meredith, the manager. I find that both Merry's and Linda's finger pointing at Ed are eerily similar."

"You think they decided to pin this on him when in reality one or both of them did it?"

Dalton shrugged. "We've seen stranger things."

"That we have."

"Merry also told me that Linda has the hots for Tom DeLuca," Dalton said. "She felt that if the store sold, those two might leave together and live in North Carolina."

"That's not what Tom said. He admitted that he cared deeply for Crystal and that Linda was jealous of their relationship. It didn't seem to matter than Crystal was married or that the two of them weren't dating."

"Did he say that Linda might have killed Crystal to pave the way for her to step in as the new love interest?"

Kalan shrugged. "No. Nothing is making sense. What's even stranger is how eager everyone was to rat out the others."

"Reminds me of the movie, *Murder On The Orient Express*." Kalan looked blank. "It was where everyone stabbed the victim so the authorities couldn't tell who had done the actual killing."

The door to Meredith's office opened, and Ed Santaria emerged. "I was waiting to question him. He's a shifter. Do you know him?"

Kalan looked up and studied the man. "Never seen him before."

Dalton hoped he wasn't a Changeling. If Kalan didn't know him, it just might mean he lived outside of town.

"I'll speak with Linda again about Tom and Crystal," Kalan said. "See if she confesses to lying."

"Sounds good." Only two customers were in the store, and they were on the other side, so Dalton didn't see the need for privacy. He made his way to Ed Santaria. "I want to ask you about Crystal Wedgewood."

"Sure, but I don't know what I can tell you."

He sounded like Carlton, the husband. "Do you know if she had any enemies?"

Ed glanced back at the office where he just emerged. "Other than Merry?"

"Merry? Why do say that?"

"She was freaking out about the fact that Crystal was planning to sell the place."

That matched what Merry had said, but he would have thought such a conversation would have remained private. "Did you overhear some argument?"

"Hell yeah. It was after hours about a month ago, and Merry had a bunch of stuff go wrong that day. Being in a foul mood, Merry told Crystal that it wasn't fair to sell the place without asking what everyone else wanted."

Employees usually didn't have a say in how corporate America worked, but Dalton jotted down the conversation anyway. He would have recorded what Santaria said, but for some reason, he thought the man would balk.

"What about you? I heard you used to own this store. That must have upset you to know some big box store would take over."

His hands clenched. "Not really. I'm ready to retire anyway. Back then, I fell on hard times and had no choice but to sell. I was thankful Crystal came along. It was her store, and I figured she could do what she wanted."

Dalton didn't believe a word of it. "So you had no hard feelings that a female bought you out?"

Ed's face reddened. "I didn't kill her if that's what you think. Merry had the most to lose."

"Where were you the night Crystal was murdered?"

"What time was she killed?"

Dalton was surprised Merry hadn't asked him that question. "It's hard to say. The coroner said death was between five thirty and six thirty."

"I was here—at the store."

"Good. What can you tell me about Tom DeLuca?"

"Tom? Nothing other than he was in love with Crystal."

"And not Linda?" That was what Tom claimed, but it was good to get a second opinion.

Ed waved a hand. "No way. Sure, he and Linda dated before they moved here. In fact, Linda followed Tom to Silver Lake a few months after he arrived. The problem was that Tom immediately became enamored of Crystal. When Linda arrived, things turned ugly."

"Tom does know she was married, right?" Dalton asked. In his opinion, infidelity ranked high on his list of heinous acts.

"He didn't care. That schlub of a husband was cheating on Crystal anyway."

That wasn't the impression he had of her husband, but then again, Carlton Wedgewood never gave off the vibe that he was in a marriage made in heaven.

Dalton almost smiled. Naliana lived in heaven, and she had chosen Anna for his fated mate, so he supposed Anna and he had a match made from there.

Ed shifted from side to side, obviously wanting this interview to finish.

Dalton refocused. "Did you ever meet Mr. Wedgewood's girlfriend?"

"No."

Because Carlton Wedgewood claimed he and his wife didn't mix their businesses, it wasn't a surprise. What frustrated Dalton was that none of the stories were lining up other than everyone claiming Ed Santaria was a bitter business failure. Dalton handed Ed his card. "If you think of anything, contact me here."

Kalan had finished his discussion with Linda, and Dalton wondered what his take would be on the interaction between the employees.

Kalan nodded at Dalton and motioned they should leave. Now the fun would begin—trying to figure out who was their top suspect.

Chapter Seven

W HILE ANNA'S BOSS, Elana, was in the front of the store helping a customer, Anna finished putting the final touches on one of the arrangements. Too bad she was having a hard time keeping her mind on her job. Everything reminded her of Dalton—like the texture of the rose petals that were as soft as his lips, and their scent, which was as divine as his mountain freshness.

The bell above the front door chimed, implying either that customer had left or another one had arrived. A second later, Elana walked into the back room. "How are you coming with the arrangement?"

"It's slow going." *Because I keep thinking about making love with Dalton again.* She cut the stem on one of the roses and tried to place it in a precise spot, but she missed repeatedly.

Elana smiled. "Kalan just texted me. I hear you had a date last night."

Heat raced up Anna's face. "I did. I'd finished up the last of my therapy sessions with James, and I wanted to blow off some steam."

"How did you swing a date with Dalton?"

"You know how I've been bemoaning the fact that I've had my eye on him for months now, and while we'd interacted on occasion, he's never asked me out. I finally decided to take things into my own hands, but before I could, Dalton stepped up to the plate."

"Tell me what happened." Elana's eyes glistened.

"When I went to the range to do some shooting, I ran into

Dalton." She faced Elana. "We went to dinner probably because I hinted that I knew he was a shifter."

Elana chuckled. "That would drive Dalton crazy wondering what you knew."

"True. I confessed that I was aware of his kind, and I asked him about James. He told me that James isn't really a therapist. Did you know that?"

Her boss and friend looked to the side. "I figured he wasn't, but he was helpful, right?"

"Very."

"Well, that's all that matters." Elana leaned her elbows on the counter. "So tell me about this date."

Anna needed to decide just how much to tell Elana about the amazing sex. After all, both of their mates were partners, and Anna didn't want the gossip to get back to Dalton. From the way her friend's head was tilted to the side and her eyes were shining, her friend wouldn't be put off.

Anna blew out a breath. "Once at dinner, I told him I knew he was a shifter. Dalton told me he had yet to mention it because he thought I'd be shocked to learn about his kind." She lowered her gaze. "And no one else bothered to tell me about them either."

Elana held up her hands. "I was having a baby at the time, if you recall. You should chastise Jillian. You saw her and my brother shift. They should have asked if you were okay with it."

Anna waved a hand. "In the end, it didn't matter. James filled me in."

"Back to your date. From the way your eyes sparkle when you say Dalton's name, more happened than just dinner."

Anna was bursting to tell her. "Yes. It was amazing."

"Do tell."

Fortunately, no customers had come in, despite it being a beautiful sunny day. "I kept prodding him for information about shifters and mates and stuff. I finally wore him down, and guess what?"

"What?"

Anna inhaled. "He told me I was his mate." Just saying those words had her pulse soaring.

Elana hugged her. "I'm so happy for you." She instantly sobered. "I never thought Dalton would ever find anyone. He's so devoted to the job."

"I know. My new goal will be to loosen him up. I want to teach him to enjoy life and to take a chance on things."

"If anyone can do it, it's you, but it won't be all fun and games. Dalton is a cop. There will be days when you're scared something bad will happen. I know our men heal fast, but it's not like they're invincible."

Anna hoped Dalton's speed would help him avoid any bad situations. "Every relationship has its risks."

Elana smiled. "That it does. So now what happens?"

"What do you mean?"

"When are you going out again?"

She shrugged. "I guess when he's free."

Elana's brows rose. "Good luck with that. He and Kalan are in the middle of a murder investigation."

"He has to have fun sometime, though I know whenever I become single-minded I can lose perspective."

"Tell me about it, but as soon as Kalan comes home and sees Aiden, he forgets about his job. I'm glad Dalton has you."

"We're not mated yet or anything." To make that happen, however, Anna had already decided to help things along. For starters, if she could find some dirt on who wanted Crystal Wedgewood dead, it would go a long way in helping the two of them bond.

She'd always been a big lover of mystery novels and had often asked Meredith Wilson for suggestions since they seemed to have the same taste in reading. Of anyone, Meredith would have known Crystal the best. Not that Anna planned to rush into the store and ask questions, but maybe she could find another way to extract the information.

Duh. If she casually touched each of the employees, surely, one of them would reveal if he or she had killed Crystal. They wouldn't be able to hide the horror of what they had done. Unfortunately, it wouldn't help bring the killer to justice. Juries liked real evidence, not something based on magic.

Well damn.

WHEN DALTON AND Kalan arrived back at the station to compare notes, Dalton carried his laptop over to Kalan's desk.

"You going to make one of your famous spreadsheets?" Kalan asked with his typical grin.

"Just because you can't bother to be organized, doesn't mean I can't be."

Kalan held up his hand. "I'm not complaining. I've learned your way has merit."

"Give me a sec to set it up. Seems to me we have six suspects."

"Six?" Kalan asked.

"That would be the four employees in the store, the husband, and his mistress."

Kalan's brows rose. "Do we know who she is?"

"No, but it shouldn't be hard to figure it out. With Carlton's wife dead, his mistress will be around more, pretending to console him."

"My brother's been saying he's been bored lately. Maybe Jackson will want to do some surveillance."

"The department will never sanction the expense."

He shrugged. "He might do it for free."

"I'd rather use him to keep an eye on Ed Santaria. Maybe he can have Ainsley go with him and tell us if Ed's a Changeling."

"That would be interesting to find out." Kalan snapped his fingers. "Speaking of Changelings, it's possible the store is sitting on a lode of sardonyx. Perhaps someone in the big box store knows that, which is why they want to buy it."

Dalton hadn't even considered that. "Or the Changelings know the sardonyx is under that store and will do whatever it takes to make sure it isn't sold. They might have been planning to buy the place or even burn it down like they did the Donaldson place."

"Jackson has the map that will show if the bookstore is sitting on one of those spots."

"In a way, I hope it isn't."

"Why's that?"

"That will expand our suspect pool to include all Changelings."

"Fuck." Kalan stabbed a hand through his hair then leaned closer. "If they are involved, we'll definitely have to ask McKinnon and Associates to help."

Dalton understood that anything related to the Changelings needed to be kept on the down low. It sucked if the real perpetrator of a crime was a Changeling. If a fight to the death occurred, he and Kalan weren't above altering some evidence to make sure the courts understood that the Changeling had been guilty. If he managed to escape, his own kind would take care of him, since failure was unacceptable to them.

Dalton returned to filling out his spreadsheet. "To keep it simple, let's assume for the moment that the Changelings aren't involved. Here's how I see it. Meredith Wilson admitted she was scared that Crystal would sell the bookstore. With Merry's husband still recovering from his stroke, losing her job would affect more than just herself."

Kalan nodded. "That sounds like a good motive, but with Crystal dead, most likely the husband would sell the store."

"Good point."

"You said Ed Santaria was bitter. Did he say if he loved the bookstore still? Or is he waiting for his chance to dig up the sardonyx?"

"Anything is possible, but we can't know if he's aware it's there. It's only been recently that the Changelings have started their search."

Kalan looked off to the side, grunted something before refocusing. "Let's assume Santaria doesn't know about the sardonyx. You said he told you that because Crystal now owned the place, she could do whatever she wanted."

"Yes, but I didn't believe a word of it though," Dalton said.

"What are you thinking?" Kalan asked. "That he feared the small-town feel of the place would be lost if it was bought out?"

Dalton nodded. "He might have had it written into the sales contract that he was to stay on for a year or two in order to help with the transition. During that time, Crystal didn't like him meddling and treated him poorly. Ed could have been fed up with her treatment and killed her."

Kalan picked up a pencil from his desk then twirled it over his knuckles. "It's reasonable. What are you thoughts on Tom DeLuca?"

"You said he's in love with Crystal. It's possible he asked her to leave her rich husband, and she laughed at him. That would be motive enough to kill her."

Kalan smiled. "I like your imagination."

"I'm trying to be more spontaneous." Anna would be proud. "I know we'll have to pull the phone records to see how often Tom spoke with Crystal, but I like to have a working theory."

"You're right. Next there's Linda," Kalan said. "I can't figure her out. For the sake of argument, let's suppose that she wants Tom, but Tom wants Crystal. She feels with Crystal out of the way, Tom will turn to her for solace."

Kalan was on a roll. "We can't prove any of it."

"I know, but it's fun to speculate. Then there's the one who always seems to be the killer—the husband. According to Ed Santaria, Carlton's having an affair. Perhaps Crystal found out and threatened to divorce him and take all of his money, so he shoots her."

"As long as we're making things up, let's take it one step further. The girlfriend wants the rich husband for herself but Carlton Wedgewood said he won't leave his wife, so the girlfriend kills Crystal." Dalton filled in the information in the spreadsheet. "Hell, maybe they all did it."

"Don't even go there," Kalan said.

BY THE TIME Dalton rolled into bed, it was close to midnight. Thankfully, Kalan and he had tomorrow off. Then on Friday, they would return to their normal shift hours. Dalton intended to check out the husband again to see where he was staying. The crime scene unit had finished at the Wedgewood house, which meant Carlton Wedgewood could return home. The big question was whether he'd return alone.

Stop thinking about work!

It was a bad side effect of being a cop. Dalton tried counting backward from one hundred, but that didn't work. Neither did thinking about Anna help, but at least that was more pleasant than going over the suspect list.

Their lovemaking still rattled him as the intensity was off the charts. While he was pleased he'd refrained from biting her, he'd been tempted. Anna's sweet scent still resided inside him.

As much as he wanted to ask her out tomorrow, he feared she'd side track him again. It didn't matter that they'd met three months ago or that he'd visited her in the hospital a few times and then again at her shop. For the last two months, he'd had to be content to walk by the store window or ask Kalan to ask Elana about her.

Coward, his tiger said.

He was a coward. What if Anna didn't like being around him for long periods of time? Sure, she said she liked him, but that was after one dinner. She was a free spirit who'd had a temporary setback after the kidnapping, and he was stodgy and set in his ways.

You can change, his feisty animal said.

His father's death had caused him to assume responsibilities that were meant for someone older. A little recreation might help clear his head. Hell, he might be able to put the case into perspective if he could relax.

Ask Anna to help, his tiger urged.

I won't put her in danger. His job was the main reason why he should stay away from her. Only, right now, he didn't seem to be able to. He closed his eyes, rolled onto his back, and hoped that by tomorrow he'd have more clarity about how he was going to balance his work life with this intense yearning to be with Anna.

Chapter Eight

ANNA USED TO love her days off, but that was BD—which stood for Before Dalton. After he rescued her, she'd spent far too much time thinking about ways to get him to notice her. Work helped her focus on something other than him. Now that she'd connected with Dalton on an intimate level, her thoughts about him invaded her nights too.

Elana told her that Kalan and Dalton had the day off today, despite them being in the middle of an investigation. Even cops needed some R&R, she'd said. Elana warned that Dalton often went into work even on his days off because some aspect of the case bugged him, and he had to take care of it.

Anna usually didn't take Thursdays off, but she asked Elana if she could switch days in the hope Dalton would call her. Knowing him, Dalton would say he wanted limited contact, because while he enjoyed her company, she distracted him. Well tough. He needed to deal.

Summer was in full bloom, and she wanted to take advantage of the beautiful day. Soon, the leaves would fall, and the snow would arrive. What better way to enjoy the day but with a picnic? With Dalton, of course. Excited, she mentally went through what she needed to buy. Once she made a list, she located her phone to call him. Before she could find his number, her cell rang. When she spotted his name, shivers of delight blasted her. If they'd already mated, she might not think it so strange, but being on the same wavelength was almost spooky.

"Hello, Dalton," she said, her voice holding too much joy.

"Hey, I have the day off and was wondering if you wanted to have lunch and maybe shoot some pool."

He could have asked if she wanted to eat worms with him, and she would have said yes. "Sure. Do you even play pool?" That would mean he actually had fun. Forget it. He probably played with total focus. Joking around wouldn't be his thing. One more thing she'd have to work on.

"I do."

"I don't, so I don't think you would have much fun."

He chuckled. "Aren't you always accusing me of not looking for fun?"

"Playing with a novice might throw off your game, and I picture you as this intensely focused player."

"Our date isn't about me winning some tournament. It's about being with you. Besides, you're wrong. I suck at pool. I play just for fun."

His definition of a good time might not match hers. "I'd like to see that."

A long pause followed. It was almost as if Dalton was trying to figure out how to comment on her concern.

"I can laugh, you know," he finally said. "How about I pick you up at noon?"

"Perfect. I'll meet you in front of the store."

"See you then."

Once he disconnected, Anna spun around. "I have a date with Dalton!"

Oh crap. She needed to find something sexy to wear. She had to be able to move easily if she would be playing pool, but she also wanted to entice him—keep him off kilter and not focused on the game. Shorts fit the bill, as did her hot pink off-the-shoulder top.

Once she dressed, she rebraided her hair, but then decided she'd look more mature if she let it hang loose. Today was all about luring

Dalton Garner into bed. She was pleased he wanted to get to know her before they mated, but if he bit her now, she wouldn't complain. Surprisingly, their push-pull type of relationship excited her in part because Anna always loved challenges.

She must have taken a little too much time with her makeup, because when she stepped outside, Dalton was there in his sporty new white SUV. Before she reached the car, he slid out and had her door open for her.

"Thank you," she said then took a moment to drink him in. "I like the cowboy look."

"Cowboy look?"

"The boots, jeans, and white T-shirt." Make that a tight white T-shirt that hugged his muscles. *Grr.*

"Standard fare around here."

"I still like it. Gets my motor running." When that got a grin in return, she smiled back at him, and then slipped into the air-conditioned car. Dalton returned to his side, jumped in, and took off.

"How does McKinnon's Pub and Pool sound?" he asked.

She chuckled. "Given it's the only pool hall around, I say yes."

He glanced over at her. "I like you. You speak your mind."

That she did. "I like you too."

"Well, you smell good and look even better." His voice sounded thick, as if he had to work hard not to drive them back to his place and let his tiger claim her.

"Thank you." She wouldn't complain, though Anna was in the mood to hear him laugh more often, and the bedroom wasn't the place for that—although it could be if Dalton played his cards right.

"Just so you know, it's hard to focus right now. My tiger is going crazy."

Good to know. Being a bit devilish, she slipped a hand over his leg. "That so?"

He gently pried her fingers from his thigh and placed them back on her side. "You do realize tigers can't drive cars." He winked.

She supposed that would be bad. "Okay, I'll be good."

Dalton smiled. "I'll trust you."

"You shouldn't."

Apparently, the man knew how to flirt, and that pleased her to no end. He pulled in front of the bar where about ten vehicles were parked, many of which were motorcycles. "Don't get any ideas, young lady. Motorcycles are dangerous."

"You can read minds too?" she asked.

"No, but I can see those wheels in your head spinning. Plus, you glanced over at them and drew in your bottom lip."

She had to remember he was a cop and was good at reading signals. "Fine, I was thinking how fun it would be to ride one with you. Have you ever owned one?"

"I grew up in California where the roads were really congested. So no."

Too bad. He came over to her side and helped her out. With his hand on her back, he led her inside. Just being next to Dalton had her hormones zinging. His touch alone had her jumping ahead to what they could be doing after their fun adventure.

On the way to a booth, she checked out who was there. Finn McKinnon was behind the bar, but Molly McKinnon, his cousin, was either in the back or not working today. Laughter spilled out from the poolroom. "Someone's having fun," she said.

"As will we." Dalton chose a booth with a view of the street. "Ladies first."

Anna slipped in and Dalton sat across from her. "So how is the case coming?"

He lowered his chin. "I can't talk about it."

She opened her mouth. "I'm not just anyone. I'm a good sounding board. I promise I won't say a word, not even to Elana."

"I appreciate that. All I'll say is that we have many suspects."

"I didn't know Crystal all that well, but how could so many people want her dead?"

He lifted one shoulder. "The usual motives: money, greed, power."

"I didn't think the store was doing that well."

"We haven't delved into the case enough to tell."

Anna leaned back in her seat. "If you ever need to narrow down the suspect pool, I can always touch them. I might get lucky and see one of them kill Crystal from one of his memories."

Dalton stilled, acting as if he might consider that. "Solid police work is needed to build a case, not magic."

"Just saying, if you want to speed things along, I'm your woman."

He grinned, and his handsome face almost made her forget about the crime. "I'll keep that in mind."

A server came by and handed them menus. "What can I get you to drink?" she asked.

"Iced tea please." Anna wanted to keep her wits about her.

"Same here."

The server disappeared. Dalton reached out and placed a hand on her arm then let go without saying anything. Even if she hadn't been a witch, she would have been able to tell he'd been about to say something. "What is it?"

"It's complicated."

She huffed. "When you die, I'm going to have them engrave that on your tombstone."

Dalton dropped back his head and laughed, the sound rich and delicious, and joy burst through her. "You're right. It's complicated, but it's because it involves you. Trust me when I say I want this to work between us, but I don't want you to get your hopes up. I'm difficult to be around."

She held up her hand. "Your job comes first, I get it, and I'm not so easy either. Just ask your sister."

"She's never mentioned any such thing. Here's the deal: You are my mate," he whispered. "As such, you are the most important person in my life, which is why I want to take things slow. I want you to understand what you'd be getting into."

She looked upward. "Hmm. Refresh my memory. Did I call you today and ask *you* out or was it the other way around?" Anna wouldn't comment that she was seconds from calling him. "So who was rushing things?"

He glanced to the side. "I just meant that I fear I'll disappoint you if I have to leave in the middle of a date for a case. Shit comes up all the time, and I don't want you to take it personally. Then there are the times when I'm on surveillance duty and have to be out for hours. I know you. You'll worry. And heaven only knows when a case is gnawing at me, I can't stop thinking about it. Then again, that was before I met you."

"That's sweet of you to say, and you're right. I would worry. However, Elana seems to have adjusted to Kalan's job."

"She has, but it's hard on everyone."

"Fine. Can we change the subject? It's depressing."

"Sure." A sparkle returned to his eyes. "Why don't you tell me about flower arranging?"

That made her laugh. "That would definitely bore you. How about you tell me what you like to do for fun? I told you last time."

"Fair enough. I like to read, though I wouldn't call that fun."

"I love to read too. Do you read fiction?"

He shook his head. "I read police manuals, foreign policy papers, and treatises on economics."

Anna grinned. "You're full of shit."

His grin dimpled his cheeks. "You're right. I was just testing you. I like to read science fiction novels, though I do enjoy a biography now and again."

She could deal with that. "What else? And please don't say you like to play chess."

Before he could answer, the waiter stopped by and delivered their drinks then asked what they'd like to order. Anna really didn't care what she had, so she went with something easy and quick. "I'll have a hamburger, medium rare, with lettuce and tomato."

"Same here," Dalton said.

"You don't have to order what I'm having," she said after their waiter had disappeared.

His brows rose. "Not spontaneous enough for you?"

"That's not it. I want to learn about you. Do you really like tea and medium rare hamburgers?"

"I do."

Time would tell. "So who do you like for the Crystal Wedgewood murder?" If she asked him enough times, he might give in.

"You know I can't tell you, so how about if you explain your talent to me."

Did that mean he wanted to use her ability to help him solve the case? Excitement sped through her. "It's hard to explain. Jillian called me a Wendayan, but I had no idea those kind of witches existed because I didn't know my parents."

"What do you mean you didn't know your parents?" His brows furrowed.

"Jillian didn't tell you?" He shook his head. "My parents gave me up as a baby." She explained about the foster care that came after that and then how a family finally adopted her.

He studied her for a long minute. "How did you develop such a positive attitude in life?"

"My attitude isn't always positive. Trust me. I have my bad days, but I finally decided that the more positive I am, the better my days will be. In fact, my luck began to change a few years ago. Did I mention I've been searching for my birth mother my whole life?"

"No."

"Well I have been. About three years ago, I learned her name and that she'd moved to Silver Lake."

He leaned back in his seat. "Ah, which is how you ended up here?"

"Yes. I asked around but unfortunately got nowhere. I then decided if it was meant to be, I'd find her, though I would like to know why she gave me up."

"Does it really matter? Most likely it had to do with finances."

"I agree, but that's not the only reason I want to find her. I've never known a mother's love. Don't get me wrong, the people who adopted me were nice and all, but I never felt as if I were a member of the family."

He sipped his drink and looked off, as if he were remembering his family. "Jillian and I were close until she became so focused on her job that we kind of lost touch." He held up a hand. "I'll admit I was just as bad. I hadn't realized why I felt so off kilter until she came to visit—or rather to seek refuge from Frank Whitlaw. When we reconnected, it was as if I had my family back."

She liked his sentiment. "And your mother?"

"She still lives in California. Now that Jillian is here, she might consider moving to Silver Lake, but she's torn. Mom really likes her life on the west coast."

"Do you see her often?"

Dalton shook his head. "No, I haven't had the time, but we speak at least once a week—that is until recently. We're all fairly close, especially since she was basically a single mom. I know I should fly back to California to visit, but I wanted to get established here first."

Wisely, Anna decided to keep quiet. She would have made more of an effort.

Dalton held up a finger. "Speaking of not knowing your heritage, the same thing happened to Elana's brother. His mom had an affair with a shifter and neither Brian nor the mom knew."

"Elana told me, but only after James informed me about shifters. I can't imagine not being aware of something that important."

"Weren't you in the same boat? Jillian said you didn't know you were Wendayan."

"I knew I had a talent, just not that I belonged to a group of witches called Wendayans."

"So how did you learn you had some abilities if you had no one to guide you?"

She drank some of her tea. "I was maybe four or five when I

happened to grab a caseworker's arm. Suddenly, frames from a movie rolled through my mind's eye. I could see this woman's life as clearly as if it was happening right then."

"What did you see?"

"The caseworker remembering when she must have been about twelve. I saw a man on top of her. She was yelling and crying. Of course, at that time, I was too young and didn't understand it was rape, but I knew something bad had happened."

"Did you ask her about it?"

"Yes, but she told me she and her dad were just playing around. As a kid, I accepted it. As I grew older, I began to understand the visions better and how to interpret them. Most of the time, I didn't let on what I'd seen. After all, they had already lived through the event, and I figured they didn't need a reminder."

"I can't imagine keeping all of that bottled up inside. I think I'd stop touching people."

She smiled. "I did that for a long time. Who wants to invade someone else's privacy anyway?"

"I agree. Are the images always bad?"

"Yes, but when Jillian and I discussed it, we both thought it was because my upbringing was so difficult. To be honest, of late, I feel as if I'm losing my touch."

"That might be a good thing."

She didn't want to mention it occurred after Dalton had come into her life. "I guess."

Their meal arrived, and she was suddenly super hungry. "It smells amazing, and my stomach is growling like an animal," she said.

"Roar."

She laughed. A silly Dalton was such a high. They both devoured their meals like rabid animals that hadn't eaten in days. Hamburger juice dripped down his chin, and Anna had the urge to lick it clean.

"You're staring," he said.

She touched her chin and Dalton picked up his napkin and dabbed it clean. "Sorry."

"So what kind of movies do you like?" she asked.

His chin tucked under, acting as if he had either never been to a movie or else no one had ever asked him before. Seconds later, he relaxed back against the seat. He must not have realized the purpose of the question. "Action adventure. You?"

"Horror."

He chuckled. "Seriously? I pegged you for the romantic comedy type."

She stuck out her tongue. "I like romance, but I want to experience it for myself, not watch it on the big screen. That stuff in the movies is so fake, especially when I know the actor is married."

"Good point. Why horror?"

She'd never really questioned her reasoning. "I guess I like the adrenaline rush. When I'm sitting through a scary movie, life is totally pushed aside."

Dalton finished off his tea then waved for the check. "I might have to try that."

"You should. It's when you aren't actively thinking about the case that your subconscious is at work."

He winked again. "Then I guess a horror movie is in my future."

Yes!

Chapter Nine

WHEN DALTON WAS with Anna, his worldview changed. He was actually able to put work aside and concentrate on the woman he hoped to spend his life with. She was quirky, sassy, forward, and totally delightful. However, he refused to let her alter him in any other way. He liked his ambitious nature, his focus, and his desire to help others.

After he paid for their lunch, they headed to the back room where three of the four pool tables were free.

Anna checked it out. "Is this where the magic happens? I mean the fun?"

He waved a finger at her. "Time will tell. You ready to be schooled in some pool?"

"Totally." She looked up at the Tiffany style light over the table. "I like the stained glass look. It's pretty."

"McKinnon's is a classy place."

"I wouldn't expect you to take me to any other kind of bar."

Hadn't she said it was the only pool hall in town? What a flirt. He cleared his throat. "First, we need to find you a stick." Dalton walked over to the rack on the wall. He wanted to make sure Anna had a stick that was right for her small size. After he picked one out, he handed it to her. "How does this feel?"

The second she ran her hand up and down the wooden shaft, his tiger went wild, imagining her doing that to his cock. From the sparkle in her eyes, the little minx knew exactly what she was doing.

"I like this one just fine."

He did not respond that he had something like it just as hard, only much thicker, and way more comfortable. He silently grunted at his inappropriate thoughts. He'd promised her a date, and a date he would give her. Dalton didn't want her to think he was obsessed with sex—or rather his tiger needed the constant gratification.

He racked up the balls.

Mate, mate, his tiger chanted.

Please let me concentrate. Life isn't all about sex.

His tiger grumbled.

"How about you break so I can see how it's done?" she asked.

That made him smile. "Watching and doing are two different things." If Anna broke, he doubted more than a few balls would move.

She placed her cue stick against the table across from him. Placing her hands on the rim of the table, she leaned over, exposing the tops of her breasts. His nails extended and his teeth sharpened.

Down boy. Please. While most in the bar were shifters, not everyone was, which meant he had to be extra cautious. Dalton prided himself on his ability to keep cool under the tensest of situations, but he'd never been tempted like this. Hell, he'd be lucky to even hit the stack of balls.

Returning his focus to the table and not on the luscious woman a few feet away, Dalton drove the stick into the cue ball. It hit off center, not spreading them as he'd hoped. At least a stripe ball managed to land in the pocket—thankfully. While he wasn't great at pool, he normally sunk more than one ball on the break.

"I guess I'm stripes and you're solids," he managed to say with enough calm to fool most people that he had everything under control.

Anna stepped over to the pocket and looked in. "How appropriate! You're stripes."

He smiled. "Well, I am partial to them."

"You go again, right?"

"Yes." Dalton wanted to impress Anna, so he took his time, walking around the table, looking for the best shot. He wasn't worried about leaving the ball in a difficult position for her, like he would have with a more experienced competitor.

On his second trip around the table, he swore Anna purposefully was in his way just so he'd have to touch her. As much as he liked being close, his tiger would only stay hidden for so long.

"How long do games usually last?" she asked. While she sounded innocent, it was a dig.

"Not long." Dalton lined up his shot and sunk another striped ball. Wanting to give her a chance, he clipped the corner on the next ball. "Your turn."

Anna walked around the table precisely two times, clearly mimicking him. "I think I'll try for the number two ball. Do I have to tell you which pocket?"

He thought she'd never played. "No."

She bent over, wiggled her cute little butt a few times while taking aim. Dalton didn't know whether to scope out her body or tell her to place the tip of the cue stick lower. As much as he wanted to wrap his arms around her and help, he was afraid something catastrophic might happen, especially since they were in public.

The stick slipped off the cue ball and it only rolled a few inches. "Ah, crap." She stood and faced him. "Does it count if the white ball doesn't hit any balls?"

Yes. "No. Try it again."

She grinned, and he immediately recognized he'd been taken advantage of. This afternoon, the game wasn't about winning—it was about having fun. This time, the white ball connected with the number two ball, but she didn't sink it. "Darn."

"Next time," he said, wanting her to enjoy the game and not become discouraged.

Now it was his turn. When he lined up his cue stick, Anna moved next to him. "Don't mind me," she said. "I want to see how you're holding the stick and where on the white ball you're aiming."

He couldn't tell if she was serious or not. "Where I hit the white ball depends on how much spin I want."

"Oh."

From her furrowed brows, she didn't have any idea what that meant. Already, her scent had completely infiltrated every cell, and his tiger was pushing to be balls deep in her sweet body. He doubted he could sink any ball on the table right now. Not only would that make him look bad if he missed, the game would never end, and Dalton had plans for later. He sunk the next one then missed the following one. "Your turn."

Anna might profess to play just for fun, but she was a fierce competitor too. With a smooth stroke, she sunk the ball and then raised her arms in victory.

"Awesome." Without thinking, he grabbed her and swung her around. The glee on her face was worth the pain of trying to keep his animal in check.

For the next twenty minutes, they battled it out. He'd sink two, and she'd sink one. Once all the stripes were off the table, he purposefully sunk the cue ball along with the eight ball.

"Damn. You win," he said.

"I did?"

As soon as he explained about the eight ball, Anna lifted the stick over her head in a victory stance. "I say we go again."

Dalton laughed, never expecting that reaction. "I have a better idea. How about we pick up some popcorn, go back to my house, and watch a horror movie?"

Her eyes widened as if he'd given her a present. "Really? I'd love that. Do you have Netflix?"

"No, but we can order something On Demand."

"That works."

He'd never dated a woman who was so easy to please. He hoped that if they didn't finish the movie, she wouldn't be upset.

ANNA HAD TO reevaluate her impression of Dalton. He wasn't as serious as she'd first believed. It was when he was in his cop mode that he seemed overly focused. She'd had a blast shooting pool, and as much as she tried to distract him, Dalton had kept his cool, despite a few random sparks that had escaped.

He did flirt, however, especially when he would lean close and try to help her. She had thought he'd drape himself over her back, but apparently that would have been too much for his tiger.

At the grocery store, they grabbed the promised popcorn as well as another six-pack of beer. She couldn't wait to show him how amazing horror movies could be. When he pulled into his drive, random sparks shot off her arms in anticipation of snuggling next to him.

Dalton cut the engine and glanced over at her, nodding to the sparks that were streaming off her. "None of that. We're watching the movie. The whole movie."

She'd see about that. "Yes, sir."

Inside, he turned the television to the On Demand channel. "You find something good, and I'll fix the food."

Content to do as he asked, Anna dropped down on the sofa and searched through the horror movie section. A few Wes Craven movies showed up, but she decided a classic would be better, so she picked John Carpenter's *Halloween*. It would be a great introduction movie to the genre.

As she searched through the menu, loud popping noises came from the kitchen, followed by a divine smell that wafted toward her. She couldn't remember the last time she'd watched a horror movie with someone while eating popcorn. Seconds later, Dalton arrived with a bowl in hand then returned with two beers.

"Ready to educate me?" he asked.

"Yes. I picked the movie *Halloween*. It's a classic."

"I hope it's real scary." He grabbed a handful of popcorn and shoved some into his mouth. "I need to warn you that I've seen my share of dead bodies, so don't expect me to jump when someone pops up out of nowhere."

She hadn't thought he'd be that jaded, but it made sense. "That's okay. For me, at least, these kinds of movies take my mind off of what's troubling me."

He picked up her hand. "You're troubled? I don't like hearing that."

She smiled. "Not so much anymore. Mostly, it was in the past when I couldn't understand why I had these visions. I thought I was a freak."

"Me too! Maybe that's why Naliana paired us up. We could be from planet Blue Stripe."

She punched him. "I love it. Planet Blue Stripe. Or it could be Planet Blue Spark."

He laughed. "We'd be the Blue Stripe Spark aliens. Watch out world!"

She laughed, and Dalton leaned over. When his eyes turned a delicious shade of amber, her body went wild with need, and the kiss that followed set her body on fire. Their tongues touched, and all of her pent up sexual energy brimmed over.

Twisting toward him, Anna grabbed ahold of his large biceps, and when he flexed his muscles, a rush of endorphins shot through her. Everything about the man thrilled her. He was confident and sincere, all the while capable of enjoying himself—at least while they were together.

He lifted his hand, threaded it through her hair, and then tugged, making her heart beat too fast. Blue sparks shot everywhere. By now she was used to her reaction to Dalton, but when his arms started glowing blue, she almost broke the kiss and shouted for joy. The only way she'd been able to tell his level of enthusiasm had been by the hardness of his cock. The sparks told her more.

Dalton broke the kiss and dragged her shirt over her head. "I can't get enough of you," he said in what sounded more like a groan.

"There's a lot more to explore for both of us." Because he'd started the seduction, Anna saw no reason not to continue it. As soon as she undid the top button on his jeans, a woman on the television screamed. Anna pretended that person was warning her about what might happen tonight, and that her life might change forever, but she wasn't worried. She was totally ready for it.

"I need more room," he said. In a flash, he stood then lifted her in his arms. "You're coming with me."

Anna wrapped her arms around his neck, never wanting to leave his embrace. She loved his strength, his determination, and his need for her. Once in the hallway, the photos on the wall flashed by, but she was too busy watching him to pay much attention.

At the end of the hall, he turned left into his room. It was dark and for some reason Dalton didn't seem to need any lights. She'd play along. He turned down the spread then placed her on the made bed.

"I need you naked." He flicked on the dimly lit lamp next to the bed, creating a soothing ambience. The room appeared small, but that might have been because he had a king-sized bed taking up half the space. Besides the nightstand, there was a dresser on the far wall. She liked everything about the room except for the ugly brown floral wallpaper. Some aspects of rentals sucked.

Before she could flick off her shoes, he tugged them off. "Wait," she said. "I want to take off your clothes first."

"You know what might happen. I'm already on edge." He gritted his teeth, probably to show off his longer and sharper eyeteeth.

Oh, my. "I'll go slowly."

Dalton groaned. "That will make it worse."

Anna would store that tidbit for later. Dalton was standing in front of her so she stood and slipped her hands under his T-shirt. She ran her palms up his chest, not able to get enough of his ripped body. "I could drag my hands all over you for hours."

"I'd have to stop you because I'd never last."

That was probably true. Anna stood and slipped the soft white T-shirt over his head. When she leaned over and licked one flat nipple, he growled. Just as she moved to the other side, Dalton grabbed her shoulders and eased her onto the bed. In one quick tug, he removed her shorts and panties. Reaching around her back with one hand, he unclasped her bra on the first try. A second later, it was history. And to think she'd spent all that time just to pick out the perfect one.

"How come I'm always naked first?" she asked.

"Because I'm bigger, stronger, and faster than you. Also, I just want you more."

She held out her hands, and they glowed blue. "How can you say that?"

He grinned. "Gotcha."

Anna attempted to punch him, but he caught her fist and brought it to his lips. The moment he kissed her knuckles, she melted into the bed. "So undress already."

Dalton saluted then toed off his boots and divested himself of his jeans in a flash. "There."

As Anna stared openly at his body, a trail of heat slid over her. When he picked up his jeans to fold them, she couldn't hold her tongue. "Drop the pants officer and get on the bed, or I will have to use force."

The jeans found the floor and landed in a heap. Dalton stalked toward her. "I was stalling to control my desire, not because I had the urge to be neat."

"Uh-huh. You don't need to control your desire around me." He smiled, and when he climbed on top of her, she tapped him on the shoulder then pointed downward. "Did you forget something, Officer Garner?"

Dalton gave her a lustful stare. "I figured you might like to unholster my weapon, but be forewarned. It is fully loaded."

Anna giggled and grabbed the waistband of his underwear. "Oh my, why Officer Garner, what a big gun you have!"

Dalton laughed as he leaned down and kissed her playfully; a kiss that quickly turned heated and passionate. He looked at her with heavy eyes filled with desire, and Anna couldn't wait for what came next.

Chapter Ten

ANNA SLOWLY SLIPPED his briefs over his hips, but with Dalton on top, she wasn't able to remove them completely. What she was able to do was reach between them and grab his exposed shaft. He growled as soon as she touched him then dipped his head to kiss her again. The man could rival Houdini because he kept the seal on the kiss while he discarded his briefs. Just being naked with him had her glowing fiercely.

Anna didn't want to dwell on whether he'd bite her or not. She just wanted to enjoy their second encounter. Dalton slipped down between her legs and stopped when his lips hovered above her breasts. The first swirl of his tongue around her sensitive nipple had her arching her back and clamping down hard on his shoulders. He seemed to know exactly where to lick, how hard, and how often. No doubt about it, Dalton was a master seducer.

Wetness pooled between her legs, but she refrained from begging him to take her. He deserved to enjoy the seduction, even if it drove her wild.

Just when she thought she couldn't take it any longer, he slipped lower and dipped two fingers into her wet hole then wiggled them around. Her inner walls contracted with need, forcing her to claw his skin. Maybe she was a shifter in disguise and didn't know it, because her need was growing by the second.

Dalton leaned over and when he nudged her clit with his tongue, waves of delicious delight swamped her, accelerating her heart rate.

"Let me suck on you," she begged.

"You know what happened the last time."

A squirt of cum had risen up, but it hadn't affected his performance in the least. "I'm willing to chance it. Please, Dalton."

As if he dismissed her request, he continued to draw her tiny pearl between his lips, and her lower body rose off the bed. Her need was so strong that bolts of electricity shot across her body, and she came hard. Even though she'd just climaxed, he continued to flick her nub. Anna pushed at Dalton's head. "Stop, it's too sensitive right now," she said, panting. It was time to tease Dalton. "Get on your back, please."

He looked up and grinned. "Are you going to ride me?"

She hadn't considered that position, but it might be fun. First, however, she was going to take great pleasure in sucking on him. "Sure."

With Dalton on his back, Anna straddled him. He latched onto her arms, presumably to help guide her, but after she grabbed his shaft, she pushed her hips back, bent down, and then drew him deep into her mouth.

"Fuck, girl." Dalton's nails grew, and so many sparks flew off him that his arms pulsed a color closer to navy than royal blue. Her glow was lighter.

Because she couldn't swallow all of him, she wrapped her palm around his length and pumped her fist up and down his big cock. His growl deepened, and his hold on her intensified. When two squirts of cum escaped, she pulled off.

"Warned you," he said, his voice low and oh so sexy.

"You did." With her gaze on him she rose to her knees and inched forward until she was in position to be impaled.

With a firm grip on him, she pressed the head of his cock against her opening and eased down. Whoa. He seemed to have grown even bigger, forcing her to lift up and try again.

Dalton's eyes were closed and his breathing ragged. *Please don't shift on me now,* she silently begged.

Anna needed to figure out just how much he could handle before he blew. Dalton took the decision out of her hands the moment he clasped her hips and held her still. With her firmly in place, he drove into her, and heat swamped her. When she leaned forward to kiss him, the change in angle made his size easier to handle but felt so much deeper. On the next thrust, Anna nearly came again. Here she thought shifters were the out of control ones.

Dalton lifted his head and captured her lips, and the intensity of his passion had her body's blue glow nearly encompassing him. Even Dalton's aura was large enough to almost reach hers. Hoping this was the moment when he would make her his, she broke the kiss and dragged her lips to his neck. She inched her way to his earlobe, and when she gave it a tug, his responsive groan edged her closer to that perfect climax.

He sucked on her neck, and his sharp teeth scraped along the skin.

"Oh, Anna." Dalton tunneled into her so deep, he pushed her off that climactic cliff, and she yelled her release. A second later, his hot seed filled her.

Exhausted, Anna collapsed on top of him. Dalton held her tightly, kissing the top of her head. "You make me happy, Anna Fairchild."

He made her feel like she belonged for the first time in her life. "Ditto."

"Ready to watch that movie?" Dalton patted her butt.

"In a minute. I need some recuperative time." He kept his arms around her, and when her breathing returned to normal, she lifted her head. "Okay. I think I can move now."

He tapped her butt again and slipped out of her. As he walked to the bathroom, presumably to get a towel, she called after him. "You are so going to be scared."

He laughed. "We'll see."

DALTON YAWNED AS he climbed the steps to the sheriff department the following morning. Anna and he had stayed up late watching the movie *Halloween*, which he had to admit, had been somewhat frightening. The best part was having her clutch his arm and suck in an audible breath when Jamie Lee Curtis believed she had killed the evil Michael Meyers, and then turned her back on him. When Meyers sat up, Anna whimpered and shouted at Jamie Lee to turn around, and then buried her face into his shoulder. Dalton loved that Anna turned to him as if she needed his protection.

She said it didn't matter how many times she'd seen the movie, that scene always got to her. Given what he did for a living, he preferred something lighter.

If he were to spend more time with the sexy siren, he'd have to figure out a better sleep pattern though. Usually at night, he'd go over the day's cases and often would fall asleep on the sofa. With his mate close by, sleep was the last thing on his mind.

When Dalton walked into the station, Kalan was at his desk, looking refreshed. Lucky guy. Aiden, their baby, must be sleeping through the night. Dalton stepped up to him. "Solve the case yet?"

His partner tossed down his pen. "Fuck no. The more I think about it, the more convinced I am they all did it."

Dalton pulled over a chair from the empty desk next to Kalan's. "What did Jackson say about the possibility of the *stone* being under the bookstore?" While the humans wouldn't have any idea why sardonyx was important, Kalan, and he feared they might slip and mention the Changelings by name.

"It was marked on John Ernst's map."

Dalton drummed Kalan's desk with his fingers, not sure if that was good news or not. It added another suspect or suspects to the already growing pool. "How do you want to handle this?"

"I don't know. We do need to investigate Carlton Wedgewood to see how close he was with his secretary. I'd like to know if there are any surveillance cameras that will show Carlton in his office during the time his wife was murdered."

"I can ask George to pull the traffic feeds near his office and look for his vehicle. You want me to take Wedgewood?" Dalton asked.

"Sure."

"What are you going to do?" Dalton asked, wanting to make sure no stone was left unturned.

"I want to speak to the person from the big box store who wanted to purchase the Silver Lake Bookstore. If nothing else, I need to inform him that his client is deceased."

"Are you thinking someone from there might have harmed her? That if the owner was dead, the store might be sold at a cheaper price?"

"I'm not sure what to expect, but I want to cover all my bases. I don't trust any of the workers, or the husband for that matter."

That was one lesson he'd learned from Kalan—everyone was a suspect. Dalton pushed back his chair. "Touch base with me if you learn anything," Dalton said.

"You too."

Dalton's first chore was to find the make and model of the husband's car. Once he learned that, he asked George to check the few traffic cameras in town to see if Carlton had driven by them when he said he had. After an hour of looking, they weren't able to prove or disprove Carlton's claim. The one black Mercedes that drove by had mud smeared on the plate enough to obscure most of the numbers. Damn.

That meant a trip to Wedgewood Financial's headquarters on River's Edge, located three blocks from the sheriff's office. Come to think of it, given where Crystal's husband worked, it was possible he wouldn't have crossed any traffic cams driving from work to home. That made things harder.

The exterior of Carlton's office looked rather run down, which wasn't what Dalton expected for a high-end financial firm. Then again, perhaps Carlton's clients didn't want the whole town to know they had money.

As soon as Dalton stepped inside, however, he realized the brilliance of the man's strategy—unassuming exterior and lavish interior. Music that sounded like it was recorded in a Costa Rican jungle was piped in. It went well with the hand painted walls that contained monkeys, toucans, and large colorful lizards. It was possible this building had been a travel agency at one time.

The part that didn't fit was the expensive marble flooring. No travel agency would have installed something like that. Dalton liked the ten-foot tall waterfall feature on the far wall that added a relaxing element to the environment. Anna for sure would get a kick out of it.

Whatever theme Carlton Wedgewood was going for, Dalton couldn't guess. Was it work or vacation?

A tinny squeal coming from the hallway reverberated toward him, followed by the clickety-clack of heels coming his way. A stunning redhead wearing clothes that looked like they were purchased from Rodeo Drive approached him. "May I help you?"

"I'm here to see Carlton Wedgewood."

"Do you have an appointment?" He couldn't tell if she was displeased to have been disturbed or merely wanted to know his reason for being there.

The fact he wore a brown sheriff's department uniform should have told her why he was there. "No, but I'm here on official business."

"Of course. Follow me, Mister...?"

"Officer Garner. Can I ask you a question, Miss?"

"Julie Dominick. I'm Mr. Wedgewood's secretary."

It would be bad manners to ask if she was having an affair with her boss, so he kept that question to himself—for now. Even if she were involved with him, it wouldn't mean she'd killed Crystal. "On the night of Mrs. Wedgewood's murder, were you with Mr. Wedgewood?"

Her cool composure crumbled for a moment, but she quickly regained it. "Yes, Carlton and I were working late that night."

"So you were with him the whole time?"

"Yes." A pulse beat hard at the base of her neck, almost as if she were hiding something.

Both of them could have been in on the murder and decided to use each other as alibis. He'd seen it before in Los Angeles.

She inhaled and then twisted around. Dalton followed her down the hall to the end office. Julie knocked then held it open for him. He was surprised she didn't have him wait in the lobby while she spoke with her boss, but that might have been because she'd just been in his office, and Carlton was free.

"Mr. Wedgewood, an Officer Garner to see you."

"Show him in." Carlton stood and walked around his desk with his hand out. Dalton shook it. "Have a seat. Do you have news of my wife's killer?"

"I'm afraid not."

Either the husband was innocent or he was a good actor. Given he had a mistress—or at least someone thought he did—Dalton was surprised at his level of concern for his dead wife.

"What can I do for you?" Wedgewood asked.

"Besides your secretary vouching for you, can you verify that you stayed at the office late the night of your wife's murder?"

Carlton Wedgewood's brows pinched. "Verify? I don't punch a clock if that's what you're asking."

"Did you order any take out, speak with anyone on the phone, or send any emails during the time of your wife's murder?"

Sweat beaded on his forehead as he glanced around. "I don't think so."

This wasn't looking good for the man. "What about the janitor? Did he see you?"

"Hank doesn't come in until eight." Mr. Wedgewood looked off to the side again, acting as if he was reliving that night. "I don't see why my secretary's word isn't good enough. Do your other suspects have to have two witnesses?"

"I'm not at liberty to say." Or rather he couldn't say, as he hadn't asked them.

"You shouldn't be wasting your time with me. I didn't kill my wife. I loved her." Wedgewood's face reddened.

"What about Julie? Do you love her too?"

A tic formed around his eye, and his chest expanded. "We had a brief affair a few months back. I told Crystal about it, and then we moved on."

"Why would you tell your wife?"

Wedgewood ran his hand through his hair then straightened his tie. "She found out and confronted me. I'm not proud of it."

Dalton had heard enough. "Thank you for your honesty. I'll see myself out."

Even after he left the building, Dalton wasn't sure what to believe. Hoping Kalan had learned something, Dalton headed back to the station. When he arrived, his partner was on the phone and waved him over.

Seated, Dalton tried to follow the conversation. Kalan leaned back in his seat and looked at the ceiling. "Could someone else have spoken with Mrs. Wedgewood?" he asked the person on the other end. "Well, thank you for your time." Kalan hung up.

"What's going on?"

"You won't believe this. No one—and I mean no one—has ever heard of Crystal Wedgewood at Books Galore."

"Perhaps Merry got the name wrong." As soon as he said it, he realized the likelihood of that was slim. "Or not. So where does that leave us?"

"It's possible our friends up the mountain decided they wanted the building. What better way to gain access to the store than to pretend to be big time buyers? They probably figured that Crystal wouldn't want to sell the store to just anyone. She might agree to the sale if she thought the new owners would transform her store into something special, and the best way to convince her would be to pretend to be the big retailer Books Galore." Kalan picked up his pen and twirled it on his knuckles. He'd told Dalton that his pen fixation helped him think.

"It's a good theory, but how are we going to prove it?"

"I'm not sure."

"Do you think your brother and his firm could do a little investigating on the possible sale? There might be chatter in the mountain community about the purchase. I'm sure it wouldn't have come cheap, and many of *them* would have to agree."

"I can ask Jackson," Kalan said. "All real estate in Silver Lake costs a lot, especially downtown."

"If our *friends* couldn't buy this bookstore, what's to stop them from moving on down the road? Hell, they might end up buying half the town in order to procure enough of their precious stone. Can you imagine what they'd be like if they did get a hold of that much red stuff?" Talking in code was frustrating, but they were used to it.

"Fuck. This could turn into a nightmare." Kalan tossed the pen on the desk. "I'll talk to Jackson and Rye."

"Why Rye?" Most likely Kalan who was the Beta to their Clan wanted to keep his Alpha appraised of anything that involved the Changelings.

"If that stone is the cause of this mess, he'll need time to develop a plan."

"I see."

"So what did you find out?" Kalan asked.

"Not much, other than Carlton Wedgewood admitted to having an affair with his secretary."

His partner's eyes opened. "Could they be the killers?"

"I have no proof they weren't where they said they were, nor do I have any proof they had anything to gain by killing Crystal. I'll try to find out if Carlton and Crystal had a prenup or a large insurance policy. It's possible Carlton needed the money."

Kalan pressed his lips together. "If he was broke, he'd want the sale to go through to bring in the cash."

"He did say they kept their businesses separate, but with her dead, Carlton would get the money. On the other hand, she might have wanted the money so she could break away from Carlton. Crystal knew about the affair."

"Why kill her before the deal was done?"

"You're right. That was what bothered me the most. I guess it's time to turn our attention elsewhere."

Kalan glanced to the side and rocked in his chair. "Do you think Crystal was planning to leave town with her sweetheart? What's good for the goose is good for the gander, so to speak."

"Ed Santaria said that Tom DeLuca was sweet on her. Maybe they were having an affair, but unless Tom comes out and tells us that, we'll never know."

As interesting as it was to talk about the possibilities, all of these theories were just that—theories. They needed something solid and soon or this case would go cold.

Then the image of Anna appeared. "I know this is unorthodox, but Anna said she could touch a person and possibly tell if that person killed Crystal. If one of our suspects did kill her, Anna might be able to point us in the right direction."

"I'm all for her narrowing down our pool of suspects if Anna can be circumspect. If the killer catches on, whatever we learn after that will be thrown out of court," Kalan said.

"Well damn. Seems like we're no further than when we started."

Chapter Eleven

JUST THINKING ABOUT her wonderful date with Dalton last night—from the wild sex to the popcorn and movie—put Anna in a great mood all day. Dalton may have acted as if the movie hadn't scared him, but when the scene came from Michael's point of view, and he was following someone with a knife in his hand, Dalton had clutched the seat cushion. Oh, yeah. He'd been scared.

In the future, however, she might have to suggest something lighter, like science fiction or a comedy. After all, Dalton was a cop who worked with dead bodies. He probably needed something happier in his life.

When five o'clock rolled around and Dalton hadn't texted her about his plans for the evening, Anna decided to head to the bookstore to buy him a science fiction book. He'd mentioned he wanted to set a slower pace to their dating, claiming he often needed time at night to review the facts of a case. Given he was in the middle of a murder investigation, she was okay with not seeing him—but only for a night or two.

Smiling, she pictured their future together with them sitting around and reading in front of a roaring fire. That would only happen of course after they had wild sex. Hell, they couldn't be in the same room and not kiss and touch. The draw between them was that intense.

She sighed. Anna had never felt as adored as when she was with Dalton. He was special, and it wasn't because they were mates. The whole idea of being cherished by someone, and then being able to lavish affection back on him unconditionally resonated with her.

Stop thinking about it. She was already turned on and didn't need to be more excited.

Needing some fresh air, Anna decided to walk to the bookstore, which was on Robin's Ridge about a half mile north of the flower shop. The summer evening was warm and delightful, and the streets were filled with folks shopping after work.

She told herself she was just going to check out books, but that if she happened to touch one of the employees—by mistake, of course—so be it. What she learned wouldn't be admissible in court, but it might help Dalton direct his search.

When she reached the store, she paused before going in. *Just buy the book and leave.* Yes, that was what she should do.

Inside, several customers were milling about the book-packed store. Anna's biggest complaint about the place was that the aisles were spaced too close together. The benefit was that it allowed for more choices.

As she walked past the front, a slightly overweight man was working the cash register. Off to the side was Linda Darnell who Anna had spoken with on several occasions about books on flower arranging. Anna would have spoken to her about finding a science fiction book, but Linda was talking with an elderly woman.

The manager, Meredith Wilson, came out from the back carrying a stack of books to one of the shelves near the romance section. Anna would ask her.

She painted on a happy face and strolled over to her. "Hi," Anna said.

Meredith spun around. "Oh, Anna, hello. Let me put these books down. How have you been? I haven't seen you in a while."

Anna reached out and touched her arm. "Let me help."

"I've got this."

Anna held on a little bit longer than was necessary, but in that time she felt waves of pain emanating from the woman. A vision flashed in Anna's mind of a person who looked like a younger version of Meredith, lying in a hospital bed. An older couple was standing off to the side. From their age and the worry creasing their faces, they might be her parents. A rather dark skinned woman in scrubs handed what appeared to be a baby to the woman in the bed. The woman broke into sobs, as if the baby might have been still born. After kissing and rocking the newborn, she handed the child back to the nurse and looked away.

Anna shivered at the heartbreaking scene. Now she wished she'd never touched Meredith. Anna had hoped she'd have seen Meredith toting a gun or perhaps having a shouting match with Crystal Wedgewood.

"Anna, are you okay?" Meredith asked.

"Yes, I'm fine." She really needed to figure out a way to hide her reaction to these visions.

Meredith had already set the books on the shelf. "What can I help you with?"

"I'm looking for a science fiction book for a friend of mine."

"Do you know what kind? Space opera, military, alien invasion, or something else?"

Anna sagged. Here she thought she understood Dalton and could figure out his likes and dislikes, but apparently, she had a lot to learn about him. "I'm thinking military." After all, he was a cop.

"Come with me." At the science fiction section, Meredith stopped and ran a manicured nail along a row of books before pulling one from the shelf. "How about *Alien Nomad*? It's about a Starfleet commander's exploration of space. It's one of our bestsellers."

It wasn't her cup of tea, but perhaps Dalton would like it. If he didn't, he could always return it. "Sounds great."

As soon as Meredith held the book out to her, Anna's vision blurred, and her heart started pumping too hard.

"Are you sure you're okay?"

Anna placed a hand over her heart and grabbed onto the shelf.

"I'm not sure. I just need to rest."

Meredith looked up and waved to someone. "Tom, could you get Anna some water?"

"Sure," he called back.

"Anna?" She looked up, and found Rye hovering near, his expression grim.

"What are you doing here?" She hoped nothing had happened to Dalton.

"Izzy sent me here to pick up a book for her. You don't look well." He wrapped an arm around her waist, and for a moment she was able to pretend it was Dalton. "Let's get you some fresh air."

Anna nodded and placed the book back on the shelf, but not in the correct place. Glad to have someone to steady her, Rye led her toward the exit. As soon as she was halfway to the door, all of her symptoms disappeared, and she halted. "That's odd."

Rye let go and faced her, his brows pointing downward. "What is it?"

"I'm suddenly feeling fine."

Tom, the employee, came over and handed her the water. "Thanks," she said, and then tipped back the paper cup and drained it. She handed the empty back to him.

Meredith drew near. "You seem better."

"I'm so embarrassed. I have no idea what came over me. I know I'm not a big sci-fi fan, but that reaction was ridiculous." Anna laughed, but the sound came out hollow.

The manager smiled. "As long as you're okay, that's all that matters."

"I am, thanks."

Meredith glanced at Rye, nodded, and then returned to stacking her books.

Anna snapped her fingers. "I almost forgot. I don't want to leave without picking up what I came here to buy. I appreciate you helping me."

As she returned to the sci-fi aisle and reached the book Meredith had recommended, another wave of lightheadedness assaulted her. What the hell? A brief thought that she might be pregnant crossed her mind, but it wasn't possible she'd experience symptoms so quickly.

"Anna, let me take you home," Rye said, suddenly reappearing at her side.

This time she didn't complain. With the book in hand she let him lead her toward the front again. For the second time in only a minute, her symptoms disappeared halfway to the door. "Rye, I'm sorry, but I'm suddenly fine again. I must be allergic to something on the shelves."

He glanced around. "So you only felt ill in one spot?"

He made it sound like she was faking it. "Believe it or not, that was what happened."

"Hmm. Would you do me a favor?"

He was the Alpha. She might not be a shifter—yet—and Dalton wasn't a member of Rye's Clan, but everyone looked up to Rye. "Sure."

"Come with me. You might be able to help me with something."

Anna thought they'd leave the store, but instead, he guided her back to the science fiction section. Really? She loved this bookstore and never had a problem in there before, but she wasn't in the mood to feel like crap once more. "Why are we going back there?"

"I want to try something."

"Okay. I want to get to the bottom of this too."

Perhaps he wanted to test whether the illness was all in her mind. She'd hoped that with Rye by her side, she wouldn't experience any ill effects, but she did. When they neared the science fiction section, her stomach nearly turned inside out and her pulse soared.

Rye held on tight. "Easy. Just one more thing."

"What the hell is going on?" she managed to ask.

"I know this seems like a weird request, but can you drop to one knee and place your hand on the floor?"

If he hadn't been the Alpha, she wouldn't have agreed, but his urgent tone suggested she needed to obey. She held out the book. "Hold this."

Trying to act as casual as possible, she dropped to one knee, and her vision turned black for a moment. Had she not reached out to steady herself, she might have done a face plant.

"What do you feel? Is it worse?" he asked.

"Ten times worse," she managed to choke out.

"Good." He helped her up.

"Good?" What was he talking about? If Anna didn't get away from this area, she was going to be sick.

"Let's go."

Thank God. Once she paid for her purchase, he escorted her outside. She spun to face him. "So tell me, what was that all about?" she asked.

He nodded to his black SUV. "I'll drive you back. We need to talk."

Boy did they.

Once she slid into the passenger side seat, Rye faced her. "How much has Dalton told you about the Changelings?"

"He hasn't said anything, but James filled me in, more or less."

"James—as in the man who lives in the stone house?" Rye asked.

She chuckled. "Yes, James, the immortal who's married to Naliana."

"How—?"

She would have thought he'd know. "He was my therapist. It's a long story."

"Therapy? Oh, yes of course; to help from when you were kidnapped by that guy Whitlaw who was after Jillian."

Anna was pleased she didn't have to explain that to him. "Yes."

"I'll try to be brief. Basically, the Changelings get their power from a stone called sardonyx. We've fought a few battles with them over the years to keep it out of their hands. If they ever found a source for this rare gem, there's no telling what would happen to our Clan. I fear they might even be able to wipe us out."

Chills raced up her arms. "They're that powerful?"

"Let's say, they could be if they had enough of this stone. It allows them to steal the Wendayan's powers. They took Kip Landon's brother's powers a few months back."

"That's not good." Though if they wanted to steal her ability to see into the past, she just might let them take it.

"No, it isn't. Since then, we've discovered where some of this stone might be located. The bad part was that the information was obtained from the Changelings."

Her mind soared. "That's scaring me, but what does this have to do with me and the bookstore?"

"This stone might be buried underneath it." He explained how there might have been a mine in the town many years ago, and how once the miners realized that some people wanted to steal it, they buried it around town. "Since then, buildings have been erected over the top of those sites unbeknownst to the developers."

"So now the stone is safe from these Changelings too." Her blood pressure dropped.

He shook his head. "I'm afraid not. They've already burned down one building to find the treasure underneath. Fortunately, my Clan, with the help of others, was able to foil them. Where you were held captive was on the site of the first discovery."

She sucked in a big breath. "I had no idea."

"Hopefully, no one else does either."

Rye still hadn't addressed what she had to do with all of this. "So what does this have to do with me being sick?"

"I believe you hold the key to locating this stone."

Chapter Twelve

JUST AS DALTON and Kalan were about to clock out, Will
Mathers, a rookie street cop entered with Meredith Wilson. Her
hands were locked behind her back, and she looked as if she'd been
given a death sentence.

"What the hell?" Dalton grumbled. Dalton and Kalan both
jumped up and strode over to Will.

"What's going on?" Kalan demanded.

"Mrs. Wilson had a broken taillight, and I pulled her over."

"Hardly a criminal offense," Kalan said.

Will didn't look pleased with Kalan's response. Tough. "I asked
for her license and registration. When she opened her glove
compartment, I spotted a gun."

"I told you it's not mine," Meredith said between gritted teeth.

Will ignored her and straightened his shoulders, as if he needed
to defend his actions. "I asked if she held a concealed weapon permit,
and she told me she didn't. The gun did not belong to her, she said."

Dalton nodded to Merry. "How about taking off the cuffs? I
don't think she'll be a flight risk."

"Thank you, Officer," Merry huffed, her words thick with emotion.

When Will released her, she brought her arms to the front and
rubbed her wrists. Dressed in a navy blue skirt, a peach blouse, and
sensible heels, she looked younger than when he'd first met her,
though he would have thought the opposite given the amount of

stress she must be under.

Kalan nodded to Will. "You have the weapon?"

"Yes."

"How about you log that in and we'll question Mrs. Wilson?"

"Sure." Will took off, clearly not pleased with the reception. He was a good cop, or rather, he would be in a few years.

"It's not my gun, and I have no idea who put it there," Merry pleaded.

While she sounded convincing, Kalan held up his hand. "We'll sort this out. Come with us."

Once they entered her into the system, they escorted her to interrogation room number one. Because Dalton had been the one who'd spoken with Meredith at the bookstore, he took the seat across from her while Kalan stood.

"Can you explain how that gun could have made its way to your glove compartment?" Dalton asked.

"No, but I don't lock my car, so I guess anyone could have stashed it there. My Volkswagen Rabbit is over ten years old, and this is the first time I've had a break in."

"Do you own a gun other than this one?"

She scrunched up her face, acting as if that was a ridiculous question. "I've never even touched a weapon, let alone fired one."

Kalan motioned that they confer outside. "Excuse us for a moment," Dalton said to Meredith. Once in the hallway, he faced his partner. "What do you make of it?"

"She could be telling the truth. If the gun is the murder weapon, and that's a big if, would she really keep it in her car?" Kalan asked.

"Criminals aren't known for their smarts."

"Without evidence, we can't keep her, but if we find out the bullet is a match to the gun that killed Mrs. Wedgewood, we can arrest her."

The process of checking the striations on the bullet casing would take time since their lab tech was working solo this week. "I'll advise her to stay in town, but I doubt she'd run, not with a sick husband at home," Dalton said. "Assuming she didn't lie about that."

"I agree."

No sooner had they released her, than Kalan received a call from his Alpha. They were in the hallway and out of earshot of anyone. As Kalan paced and spoke in a hushed tone, Dalton's thoughts turned to Merry. He should be happy they might be close to wrapping up the case, but something seemed off. A killer wouldn't have pointed a finger at herself and say she had the most to lose—especially when speaking with a cop—and then stash the gun in her car. However, it was always possible she was waiting for the right moment to dispose of the weapon, either by ditching it or planting it on someone else.

Damn. This case was becoming more complicated by the minute. Kalan disconnected, his face drawn. "Rye wants us to meet him at McKinnon and Associates."

Dalton hadn't expected that request. "We needed to speak with Connor anyway about a few things, but why does Rye want us there?" His father might have started the firm, but his brother was now in charge.

"Rye called to discuss what would happen if the Changelings got a hold of the sardonyx. He has a plan and wants our input."

"When you spoke with him just now, I didn't hear you mention the Changelings."

Kalan smiled. "Some of the conversation was spoken out loud, but much was communicated telepathically."

Dalton glanced around. "But you're from different species. How is that possible?" Now more than ever he missed his dad, as there were so many shifter facts he'd never learned about.

"Once we became the Alpha and Beta, we were able to communicate telepathically. It's necessary for the longevity of the Clan. How it works exactly, I don't know, only that it does." He pocketed his phone. "Come on. We can clock out on the way. I'll drive."

As soon as Dalton slipped into Kalan's Jeep, he pulled out his phone.

"Who are you calling?" Kalan asked.

It wasn't police business, but he didn't mind telling him. "Anna. I don't want her to worry when I don't call."

"Don't bother. She's one of the reasons why we're going to Jackson's office."

His tiger woke up, switching into protective mode. "What are you talking about?"

"She's with Rye. Apparently, she has a talent that could be vital to our existence."

ANNA STILL WASN'T convinced she could detect where this sardonyx rock was located, but after the test Rye put her through, she almost couldn't deny it.

"Right this way," Rye said as he escorted her into the building where all the trouble had begun.

She shivered. "This place gives me the creeps."

"I'm sorry. It's where the McKinnon and Associates new office is located. Hopefully, the inside looks different."

When she'd been held captive there, the walls were studs interspersed with pink insulation. Besides being dark that night, she didn't remember much. Pain and fear had a way of erasing details.

The foyer to the new McKinnon and Associates building was classy. A soft butternut leather sofa and two forest green chairs bordered a glass top table that had a few magazines stacked on top. The warm taupe walls, along with the photos of the Great Smokey Mountains, provided a calming environment. An empty receptionist desk sat at one end.

"They haven't hired anyone yet," Rye said, apparently able to read her mind. "Connor is waiting to expand first."

She hadn't asked, but the information was interesting. Just past the reception area was a mostly empty large room, but she couldn't tell what it might be used for. A long wooden table with eight chairs sat across from a kitchen area that included a coffee machine, a refrigerator, and a microwave oven. On the other end were couches and chairs, but nothing to indicate its use. The white walls and lack of wall art implied they were in the process of moving in.

"The meeting is back down this hallway," Rye said, pointing to the left.

He led her down the corridor devoid of any decoration. Perhaps they were trying to keep what they did fairly secret. It wasn't as if they'd have photos of themselves proudly standing over a dead Changeling. She chuckled.

"Something funny?" Rye asked. His brows rose as if he'd like to have some cheer.

"Just my imagination going wild." She'd pictured one of the men from McKinnon and Associates grinning in victory. He'd be naked with blood dripping out of his mouth, and one foot would be on the chest of the dead Changeling.

At the end of the hallway, Rye knocked then entered, holding open the door for her. Whoa. It looked as if she'd stepped into a war room. On one end was a large U-shaped table surrounded by eight chairs. Extra seats were lined up along the wall. On a platform at the front of the room was a table that held a laptop. The entire front wall and halfway back both side walls were covered in white boards, like the ones found in school. A few pieces of paper were stuck to the white boards, and several large colored maps of the area were taped there as well. An image was projected behind Connor McKinnon who was standing at the front, looking serious.

Besides Rye and herself, three men were seated around the table. Kalan's brother, Jackson, Kip Landon, and his mate's brother Sam, who according to Rye had recently joined the firm after serving in the military.

"Welcome, Anna, to our humble office," Connor said. The first time she'd met Connor was at the party to celebrate Teagan Pompley's brother's arrival in town.

Humble indeed. Everything appeared to be state of the art. "Hi."

"Have a seat. We'll begin as soon as Kalan and Dalton arrive."

At the mention of Dalton's name, relief and excitement ran

through her. As if he'd heard Connor's introduction, the room door opened and both Dalton and Kalan stepped in. Dalton made a beeline toward her.

He pulled out the chair next to Anna and clasped her hands. "I just heard you were sick. How are you feeling?" he asked, his concerned words rushed.

"I'm good, but I'm still overwhelmed. I think it might all be a mistake." She had to assume he knew about her newfound *ability*. Other witches were able to start fires or predict the future, but all she could do was locate some stone. If only her talent extended to finding something valuable—like diamonds—she'd be really happy.

Connor tapped the table, and she refocused on the man in front. Her nerves mixed with anticipation. These men had saved her life all those months ago, and now she had the chance to return the favor.

"As you know, things are beginning to erupt in the Changeling world," Connor said. "We've seen what these monsters are willing to do to get their hands on sardonyx, and we can't let them continue. Not only would it put most of the Wendayan population in danger, our very existence might be threatened. Having the human world learn of our kind would have major consequences. The Changelings must be stopped at all costs."

Because none of the men's expressions changed, this wasn't news to them. Clearly, Connor's discourse was directed at her.

He motioned for Jackson to join him on the podium. "Jackson is going to bring up the map we found on John Ernst's computer. He'll superimpose the current buildings in Silver Lake on top of it."

She didn't know who John Ernst was, but apparently he wasn't one of the good guys.

"As you can see," Jackson began, "one of the dots is located in the same position as the Silver Lake Bookstore. We think this is their next target."

She sat up straighter, and Connor returned to stand in front of everyone. "Until today, we were at a loss as to how to retrieve the sardonyx. The Changelings must be in the same quandary or they would have dug it up already. According to Kalan, the folks at Books Galore did not, I repeat, did not put an offer in for Crystal Wedgewood's bookstore."

That made no sense. Why would Crystal lie? "Then who did?" she blurted.

Dalton reached over and squeezed her leg. What was that for? Wasn't she supposed to ask questions? If they wanted her to do something for them, she needed to understand what was at stake.

"We can't be sure, but we're thinking it might have been a Changeling pretending to be from the big store," Connor said.

She jumped ahead to what would happen after the Changelings purchased the building. "And then what? They'd tear down the building in order to rip out the floor?"

"If the Changelings don't know where the stones are located, my guess is that is exactly what they'd have to do," Connor said. "Until today, we had no way of knowing under which floorboard the gems might be hidden either."

She didn't like the way he said *until today*. "You really think the sardonyx is under the science fiction bookcase?"

"Yes," Rye interjected.

Maybe he could sense what she'd experienced because he'd received some pretty powerful magic from his mate.

Kalan pushed back his chair. "I'd like to conduct one more experiment to be sure. Jackson will you bring my knife to me?"

His brother nodded and left the room. Anna was more confused than ever. What did a knife have to do with anything? She thought this was about some stones. A minute later, Jackson returned with a red knife that was made out of the stone she seemed to be affected by. Now it made sense. As he carried it toward her, her throat turned dry, and her eyes began to burn and then tear. She scooted her chair backward then looked around. No one else seemed the least bit affected.

Jackson set it in front of her. "Pick it up."

What game was he playing? She looked over at Dalton. His eyes had narrowed, and his breathing had turned ragged. He was staring at the knife, acting as if he wanted to grab it and throw it across the room. She wanted to do the same, but it was as if someone had cut off her oxygen, and her arms were tingling too much to even snatch the object.

"That's enough," Rye commanded.

In a flash, the knife disappeared and Anna was able to breathe again. "What happened?" she asked in a shaky voice. She planted a hand on her chest to help draw in more air.

"The sardonyx in the knife made you ill," Rye explained. "Proof that you are affected by it. We've never met a Wendayan like you before—or for that matter, any shifter with your talent."

"Lucky me." This time she didn't hold back the sarcasm. Her heart was still racing, and a sharp ache was stabbing her right behind her eyes. "I wonder if I have any other hidden abilities?" She hoped not. Anna was getting rather tired of having sucky talents.

Rye nodded. "We appreciate what you can do."

"So what happens now?" she asked, not liking the direction of this conversation.

"If we can get access to the store, we should be able to dig up the sardonyx before the Changelings can purchase the place," the Alpha said.

"Are you planning to break into the store and hack away at the floor?" she asked, her voice cracking.

The men looked around. Connor spoke up. "Our plan is still incomplete, but we need to work fast. Now that we've zeroed in on its location, thanks to you, we can be in and out in no time."

Assuming they could get in. However, she'd heard Kip was an excellent lock picker. "Then what do you need from me?" she asked.

"Nothing at the moment, but we'd like you to be on hand in case we misidentify the location."

"No," Dalton said.

She swiveled around. "Why not?"

"It makes you sick."

She placed a hand on his. "I appreciate your concern, but I owe these men—as well as you—my life. I want to help."

His jaw tightened, and his fists clenched, probably to keep from shifting. Dalton scanned the room then stopped at Rye. "Fine, but I'm going to be there. I need to make sure nothing happens to Anna."

As sweet as that sentiment was, it was her life. "What could go wrong?"

Rye cleared his throat. "A possible war."

Chapter Thirteen

THE BLACK CURTAINED walls and dim sconce lighting helped center Brother Jacob. While the glowing sardonyx eyes from the metal clad statues didn't provide him with a lot of energy, it gave him the much-needed focus. As the supreme ruler of the Changelings, he had to make his Clan strong again, and that meant finding more of the precious stone.

His Clan had been thriving until those fucking wolves and bears had breached his security and stolen the Wendayan's powers back. The entire compound began acting as if the end was drawing near. Cowards. He'd never let that happen.

A knock sounded on the bunker door, and he clenched his fists as he spun around to face the entrance. This room had been the only place on the compound that had given him any solace, and now someone dared to interrupt him, robbing him of the pleasure of his sanctuary. He'd come in here to think, needing to get away from the constant interruptions and complaints that were slowly wearing him down.

"Enter." Brother Jacob drew up to his full height of six-four and lifted his chin.

John Ernst strutted in. Arrogant bastard. Brother Jacob had not been pleased with his second in command for quite some time, since he was always making *suggestions* on how Brother Jacob should run things. "Speak."

At least Brother John knew to keep his head lowered. "I await your instructions regarding the death of the bookstore owner. Shall I approach her husband and ask if we can purchase the store from him?"

"You are certain the sardonyx is under the building?" He'd been against spending their sparse resources in the first place if the reward wasn't guaranteed, but Brother John had been insistent. While he disliked the man, losing another council member would not look good.

"Reasonably sure."

Brother Jacob slammed his hand on the table. "You need to be sure."

John Ernst raised his gaze, a knowing gleam in his eyes. "It's possible there is a way to be certain, but it will take time."

"We don't have time. What is it you suggest? Are you building some machine to detect the precious stone?" He was being facetious, and hoped Brother John hadn't wasted his time on such a futile endeavor.

"No, sir. Brother Edward witnessed a rather strange occurrence at the bookstore today. He wasn't sure what it meant, but their Alpha was on hand to witness it."

Ernst finally had his attention. "Tell me."

Brother John explained that some woman who the Alpha seemed rather fond of had repeatedly experienced illness around one particular area of the store.

"What do you make of it?" he asked, not sure what to conclude himself.

"While I've never known a human to react strongly to sardonyx, I've heard about one of our witches detecting it. She had the same reaction, but has long since passed away."

Brother Jacob's pulse soared at the implication. "Are you saying you think this woman might be able to find its location—like a human divining rod?"

"It's possible, but I'll need more time to observe her."

"Do so."

For the first time in weeks, Brother Jacob smiled.

DALTON DIDN'T LIKE Anna having any part in an operation that involved Changelings, but the stubborn woman seemed determined to help. With her surrounded by the Clan, as well as himself, she would be safe. While he didn't like that she became ill from the exposure, Dalton understood why Rye needed her.

Connor and Jackson were discussing something on the podium, while Kalan chatted with Kip and Sam.

Several things still bugged him about this whole operation, and he felt it was his duty to comment. "I have a concern."

The group immediately quieted. "What's that, Dalton?" Connor asked.

"We found Meredith Wilson with a gun that could be the murder weapon, so I doubt she'd be receptive to helping us. As for Ed Santaria, we know we can't trust him. Are you planning to enter illegally? I imagine they have an alarm system."

Jackson shook his head. "We're still in the planning stage. We can cut power to the building if we have to, but if we can enter legally it will be for the best. As for asking Ed Santaria, he's definitely out. I asked Ainsley to check him out earlier this afternoon, and she reported he is in fact a Changeling."

Anna placed a hand on his arm, and her mere touch caused his animal to stir. "What do you mean Meredith had a gun?" she whispered.

He thought she'd question him about a Changeling working in a store she visited, not about Merry. "This is an ongoing investigation, and I can't discuss it, but suffice it to say, if the gun proves to have been the murder weapon, she'll be arrested."

Anna sank back in her seat. "I don't believe it. When I touched her arm, I didn't see her holding a gun and killing someone."

"You what?" His voice came out so loud everyone in the room faced him. Damn. Anna might not think her actions could cause problems, but learning something about the wrong person might force him to come after her.

"Anna? Care to explain?" Connor asked.

"I guess it's too late to hide it now." She told them how she'd touched Meredith Wilson's arm and saw what looked like a young Meredith in a hospital bed. "From her profound grief, I'm guessing her baby was stillborn. Does that sound like a killer?"

The pain in her voice tore at him. "People change," Dalton said.

Anna shook her head. "I agree, but if I could touch her once more, I might see something else, though I usually see the worst event first." She stilled then closed her eyes.

"I'll keep that in mind," Connor said, "but we can't have news of your talent leaking out. Witches touching people like that would almost cause as big a stir as humans learning about our kind."

Dalton agreed. News of her abilities needed to remain hidden.

"Dalton," Rye said. "How about taking Anna home? We still have a few more hours of discussion, and we don't want to bore her."

He understood. He wasn't part of the security firm, and Anna certainly didn't need to witness the inner workings of their world. Plus Kalan would fill him in later on anything he needed to know. "Be happy to."

ANNA WASN'T PLEASED they'd dismissed her so quickly, but perhaps they weren't interested in Crystal's murder or whether Meredith was guilty or not. This red stone seemed to concern them more.

Dalton hovered as he escorted her outside, but instead of his nearness bothering her like it might have in the past, she enjoyed it. Add in the warm summer evening that smelled like it was about to rain, and Anna was in a surprisingly good mood, despite what she'd just learned.

"Want to grab a bite to eat?" Dalton asked.

She hadn't thought of food until now. Everything had been too surreal. "Sure."

The evening sun had set, but the sky still glowed with pretty shades of pinks, blues, and yellows, silhouetted against a line of black clouds. They were ominous looking yet strikingly beautiful at the same time.

"What's your pleasure?" he asked.

She'd been about to say indulging in him, but Dalton apparently needed real food. "How about the Silver Lake Café?"

"You got it."

He helped her into his truck. As soon as he closed her door and slid into the front seat, the troubles of the world seemed to disappear. Dalton's presence did that to her. "You seem worried, why?" she asked.

Dalton glanced over at her. "I want to keep you as far from the Changelings as possible, but I'm fully aware of the dire need to keep the sardonyx out of their hands."

That much she'd figured out. "It's not like they'd dare to break in when a ton of you guys are in the bookstore."

"I'm counting on it, but if Connor has to do something illegal, I'd prefer that you not be involved."

"Who's going to arrest me? You?" She half chuckled.

Anna wasn't sure why she found any humor in the situation. Perhaps her joy was because she loved how protective he was of her. It didn't seem his affection was based on her being his fated mate. No, Dalton really cared for her, and that made her happy.

"Hardly, unless I plan to turn myself in as well. The problem is that most of the officers in the sheriff's department are human. Someone might become suspicious if they see light coming from a closed bookstore and call it in."

It wouldn't do his career any good if he were caught. She twisted toward him as he headed down Maple Avenue, past Hope News, and then Nate's Pizzeria on the corner. "Do you think Meredith is guilty?"

His fingers tightened on the wheel. "I'm hoping not, but she said she was upset that Crystal wanted to sell the building, so that means she had a motive."

"I'm upset that my parents gave me up for adoption, but I don't want to kill them."

A small smile lifted his lips. "Is your glass always half full?"

"Not always, but why think negatively? Life is too short."

Dalton reached the restaurant. "I hope you don't mind that we have to park a few blocks away? I'm not sure why it's so crowded tonight."

"Nope, I love to walk."

The blue awning and the cozy outdoor seating made this café one of her favorite places. Dalton held open the restaurant door and motioned her in. "As nice as it would be to sit outside, it looks like it might rain," he said.

"I agree."

Because it was past the dinner hour, they basically had their choice of seats. The cars must have been for the movie theater down the street. He asked the server if they could have a seat near the back, implying he didn't want anyone to overhear their conversation. That worked for her.

She couldn't imagine having to live her life in fear of discovery. Anna mentally halted. What was she talking about? She had lived her life like that—first with the fact she was adopted, and then with the whole concept about her ability to read people's memories. If—no when—she and Dalton mated, she'd have to keep the existence of shifters a secret too.

"This okay?" the waitress asked.

Dalton nodded. Once seated, he leaned back. "Are you scared?" he asked.

"Of what?"

"Of how your life has changed? Or how it might change? Nothing can be done about the past, but the future is up to you."

He sounded like some Himalayan shaman or a fortune cookie. "Are you talking about me helping Connor and Jackson and the rest of the Clan, or are you referring to us?"

A tic around his mouth lifted the side for a second. "Both."

She couldn't be happier that he wanted to talk about their future. "I want to embrace life."

His eyes changed to a pure amber color before he clasped her hand. "I want that for you too."

That was an odd thing to say. "In case I'm not being clear, I want *you* in my life." She didn't wait for him to respond. "What do you want?"

"I just want you."

Her heart melted. "You are such a romantic, you know that?"

His cheeks reddened somewhat. "Don't say that in front of the guys, okay?"

She laughed, loving how easy it was to peel away his layers. Just then the server came by to take their order. Once they made their choices, a loud rat-a-tat sounded on the outside awning. She glanced toward the window. Dalton was right to suggest they eat inside. "Wow. The storm came fast. We made it inside just in time."

"We did."

She smiled. "I do love the rain though."

His brows rose. "I kind of do too. It's rather comforting. I think it dates back to the ancestors on my animal side," he said softly.

She smiled. "Regardless of my heritage, I just love the freedom it brings. Rain is so wild and natural."

"You are good for my soul, you know that?" Dalton's eyes returned to a beautiful shade of brown sprinkled with green. "Perhaps after we eat, you can show me that wild side of yours."

"That was my plan all along." Flirting with Dalton was such a high, giving her hope of a wonderful future.

While they waited for their meal, they briefly discussed the upcoming search for the stone.

"Too bad Meredith is under investigation," Anna said. "If she hadn't been brought in, I bet she'd let you tear up the floor as long as you promised to replace it."

"Why would she allow that? For starters, she's not the owner.

We can't exactly let her know what we're looking for or why we need it. If we did tell her, she might want a cut to keep quiet."

"I don't think she's like that."

Dalton watched her. "You keep defending her. Why?"

That was a good question. "I'm not sure, but there's something I've always liked about her. Even though we have the same taste in reading, it's more than that. She really loves her husband, and I like someone who will stay with a person even though he isn't as vibrant as he once was. I think she said he was considerably older than her." Anna sighed. "Does that sound like a killer to you?"

"Maybe not."

She smiled. "Has anyone told you that you aren't a good liar?"

"Me?"

"I'm sure you've seen a lot in your life," Anna said. "You've dealt with the scum of the earth, and I bet many were sociopaths who could pretend with the best of them."

James was right. Eyes were the window to a person's soul. Right now, Dalton's were swirling with a mixture of greens, browns, and amber. Whether that meant he was excited or pleased that she understood what he went through on a daily basis, she didn't know.

"You're right, which means we have to let the evidence tell us who's guilty."

That implied he didn't want her touching anyone. At least she'd offered.

The meal arrived none too soon. She'd ordered a club sandwich while Dalton went with another hamburger. Apparently, he really liked his meat. The first bite was delicious. Anna must have been hungrier than she'd realized.

Halfway through the meal, his cell rang. When he didn't answer it, Anna had to say something. "It could be important."

He cocked a brow. "I don't want you to think my work is more important than you."

Was he the best or what? "I don't. It could be about those lab results you were waiting for." He'd told her about wanting to know if the bullet that killed Crystal matched the bullets from the gun found in Meredith's possession.

Dalton smiled then extracted his phone. "It's the precinct. Dalton Garner. Yes? It is? Thank you." His shoulders slumped. "Thanks."

"What is it?"

Chapter Fourteen

D ALTON SHOULDN'T TELL Anna what the call was about since it involved police business, but this woman was about to be his mate. "You must be psychic too, because it was the lab. Ballistics came back on the gun in Meredith's car. It's a match."

Anna's cheeks sagged as she glanced away. "I refuse to believe that. Isn't there something you can do to help her?"

"We have to bring her in, but I will do what I can. If someone did plant the weapon on her, it's my job to figure out who did."

Anna's eyes widened. "Yes, that's it. Someone planted the weapon in her car."

He loved how Anna only saw the good of people. "Do you have any suspects?"

"Me? I don't know anything about the case, but what about the husband? The spouses are always the guilty one in every television show."

In real life that was often true too. "He has an alibi."

"Alibi, schmalibi. Anyone can lie and say they weren't wherever the killer was."

"Neither his clothing nor his hands had gunshot residue on them, meaning he didn't fire the gun. Also, the gun in Meredith's car wasn't the gun he'd reported stolen,"

"Okay, but he could have changed shirts to make you think he didn't shoot the gun."

She was a smart one. "Anything's possible, but rest assured Kalan and I will keep digging for the real killer. We'll need more than just a gun in her car to prove without a shadow of a doubt that she killed Crystal Wedgewood."

"Thank you." Anna smiled, and the world seemed to tilt level again.

Dalton couldn't deny it any longer. Anna had wormed her way into his heart. Three months ago they'd met, and in that time, Dalton had come to realize what he'd been missing in his life—a woman to love. He'd never considered himself a lonely man before, but apparently he had been.

Wanting to get her home and make love with her, Dalton finished his burger. Once they paid, they stepped outside. Crap. It was still coming down hard. "I'll get the truck and come back for you," he said.

Anna grabbed his arm. "No, I like the rain."

"I don't want you to get wet and ruin your shoes."

"They'll be fine." Before he could finish the conversation, she dragged him to the sidewalk, opened her arms, and spun around. With her mouth open, she stuck out her tongue.

Dalton smiled. Anna loved life, and because it was contagious, his heart was actually thawing.

Do it, his tiger begged. *Play in the rain like you used to.*

Oh, hell. Why not? About three feet from them, water had pooled on the sidewalk. "Come on," he urged.

Clasping her hand, he rushed them to the puddle. Instead of jumping over it, he landed squarely in the middle, sending a spray of warm water everywhere. Anna giggled, and his tiger roared.

Soaked to the skin, Anna ran down the sidewalk with her arms wide. The few people who'd taken shelter under the overhangs appeared either shocked or delighted. Dalton ran after her. While he wanted to believe he was carefree, he couldn't quite pull it off. His phone that was tucked in his pocket was unprotected.

When she reached his SUV, he stuck his hand in his pocket and pressed the remote, hoping it still functioned. It did.

She slipped in, and he had to stop from being upset that his seat would get wet. Hell, Anna might be right. He was too stodgy for his own good.

With a smile on his face, he jumped in his car and started it up. "Need some heat?" he asked. Anna had wrapped her arms around her body.

"Yes, please."

When she became a tiger, her tolerance for temperature would be much improved. Once they arrived back at her place, the rain had somewhat subsided, but he still parked as close to the door as possible.

She faced him. "That was fun. Thank you for indulging me."

"If you really want to thank me, you can invite me up."

She laughed, and the sound seeped deep into his soul.

Mate, mate. His tiger was practically panting. This time, Dalton didn't bother telling him to shut up since he agreed.

"Come on." Anna rushed up the steps, acting as if she couldn't wait to mate with him—at least he hoped that was what it meant. Right now, his tiger was clawing at his gut, and Dalton had to rub his arms in the hopes of pushing the sprouted hair back where it belonged. He didn't want her to freak if he started to shift.

Anna opened the door, and as soon as they stepped inside, she kicked off her sandals before tearing off her wet shirt. Seeing her damp hair down her back wearing only a pink bra made his nails extend. Dear goddess, but she was a sight.

"Turn around," he said. Anna faced him. "I could look at you for hours."

"No, you couldn't." She nodded to his hands. "Those nails tell me you're excited, not to mention the blue sparks are a dead giveaway."

Damn sparks. She was the only woman who'd ever elicited them. Because Dalton was drenched too, causing water to pool at his feet, he stepped out of his shoes. "Got a towel?"

"Sure." Anna disappeared into the bathroom that sat between

the living room and bedroom.

A cabinet door opened, and she returned holding two towels. She tossed him one then moved within touching range. The woman was tempting him.

"Wouldn't it be easier to just shift into your tiger and then shift back? You'd be naked then."

Maybe that was her ploy for getting them wet. "My clothes would shred." He slipped his phone, keys, and wallet from his pocket and set them on the coffee table.

"You said you have a spare pair of clothes in the car."

Anna unhooked her bra, seductively slid it down one shoulder, and then once she removed it, let it dangle from her finger. His tiger went wild. Using as much supernatural speed as he could, Dalton shucked off his jeans, briefs, and shirt. Naked, he approached her.

Anna held up a hand. "Now you have no excuse not to shift."

He couldn't blame her for wanting to see him in his animal form, especially if she was serious about becoming a tiger herself. It was when Anna stepped out of her pants that he let his animal free. His bones cracked, hair grew, and his vision slightly blurred as the transformation occurred.

"Holy shit." Anna jumped back.

Dalton probably should have warned her that he weighed close to five hundred pounds and was nine feet long. She probably expected something a bit smaller. The slight fear in her eyes caused him to drop his rump to the ground.

Tentatively, she reached out a hand, and Dalton nudged her palm, indicating it was okay for her to pet him. He then remembered her saying that she wanted to before. Clad only in her pink panties, she dropped to her knees. Damn. Her scent was more potent now that he was in his animal form. Without thinking, he licked her hand, and her delicious taste made him want to roar.

"Can you understand me?" she asked.

He really hadn't spent enough time explaining all the facts of shifters to her, but it was probably because he hadn't wanted to scare her away. When she ran her palm over his head, he purred. No one had ever petted him, and Dalton now wished he'd sought it out. The stroking sensation was highly sensual and totally delightful.

He reached up a paw and lightly ran it down her arm, careful not to scratch her with his claws. When she smiled, he was tempted to shift back, as the need to mate with her was growing by the second, but he wanted Anna to have her fill first. It was when she stretched out next to him that he couldn't take it any longer. He scooted out of her reach, spun, and shifted.

"You tempt me too much," Dalton said as he crawled back to her.

Anna propped her head up with her arm, enticing him way past his limits. "Is that so?"

She was a tease. "Did you enjoy the show?" he asked, his heart pounding in his chest.

Anna sat up. "Yes. You have to be the most beautiful animal I've ever seen. I'd love to cuddle up next to you all night."

He chuckled. "For starters, if I didn't break the bed frame with my weight, I would take up the whole bed. Secondly, your touch and smell alone forced me back into my human form. Anna, I need you."

He wanted to tell her that he loved her, but Dalton feared she'd freak, and he couldn't chance losing her.

"I need you too."

She snuggled closer and ran a hand down his chest. What had he been thinking? The hardwood floor was no place for a lady. "How about we find a more comfortable spot?"

Dalton stood and helped her up. Not wanting his wet clothes to damage the wood, he picked them up. "Dryer?"

"Come with me." With their clothes in hand, he followed her toward the bedroom—just where he wanted to end up—watching her luscious ass sway.

She stepped into the bathroom and opened what he thought was a linen closet. Instead, it held a stackable washer-dryer. She dumped her wet clothes in, and he did the same. As soon as she turned on the dryer, he swept her into his arms. Unable to keep away from her any longer, he pressed her against his body and kissed her. Anna stirred something deep and primal inside him like some call of the wild that he had to answer. She tasted sweet like rain and smelled even better—fresh and delicate.

Dalton slid his hands down over her ass and lifted her up. Anna got the message and wrapped her legs around his waist. As he walked into the bedroom with her clinging to him like a second skin, Dalton could feel the heat from her hot sex against his groin. Keeping their lips sealed, he wasted no time as he crawled onto the bed with her securely wrapped around him.

A few seconds later, Anna broke the kiss. "I can't believe this is going to happen again," she said, stroking his arm and then deftly moving her hand to his cock.

He wasn't sure why, but as much as he wanted to respond, it was difficult to form any coherent words with her stroking him. He stared at her lips, willing them to wrap around his cock. Dalton cleared his throat. "It might happen sooner than you want if you don't let up on the speed and pressure."

She looked up at him and grinned. Letting go of her grasp, Anna drew him close. She wrapped her arms around his neck and nibbled on his earlobe. Her warm breath, coupled with her fingers slipping through his hair had his tiger going crazy again. Dalton wanted the mating process to be sensual, exciting, and memorable, but if she didn't stop, he'd have to take her hard.

His tiger was such a cad. "Anna, please."

She looked up at him. "You don't like that?"

"I love it. That's the problem. My tiger is ready to fuck you into next week, but I want to go slow and make love to you the way you deserve, baby." Sitting back in an effort to give his tiger and his libido some space to calm down a bit, he drank in her body. A tattoo on her hip was of a black flower with petals floating upward that turned into beautiful, colorful butterflies. He traced the intricate design. "Does this have a meaning or is it something you just liked?"

"The rose represents all my struggles and dark days growing up, while the butterflies are my flight away from all of it and the hope for happiness and love."

"It's beautiful, just like you."

She gave him a teary eyed smile, and his heart nearly broke. She'd grown up without the love she deserved. Well, that would no longer be a problem, because he would grow old loving her and showing her happiness every day.

Dalton stroked her cheek and looked deep into her eyes, hoping she could see the love he had for her already.

"Why don't you have any tattoos other than the mark on your shoulder?" she asked clearly trying to lighten the mood.

"I'm a cop."

She shook her head. "You can get one on your butt or someplace where it won't show."

He laughed. "You're right. What should I get?"

Her eyes widened as if it would be a present of a lifetime if he did it. "Hmmm. Because I don't think you'd go for the saying, *It's Complicated*, how about an amber colored eye?"

He chuckled. "Why an eye?" He understood the amber part.

"You know. Eyes are the window to the soul, and that way I can look at it and see what you're thinking."

He cracked up. "You're going to tell what I am thinking by looking at an eye on my bare ass? Baby, whenever I'm naked, trust me, you will be able to tell what I am thinking by looking at my cock. You can bet I will be thinking about making love to you, which is exactly what I plan to do now since my tiger has calmed, and I have my control back." Or so he hoped.

Chapter Fifteen

ANNA'S BODY WAS already sizzling with pure bliss, her blue sparks shooting everywhere. Several people had asked in passing about her tattoos, but only Dalton had shown such a keen interest in the reason behind her choices. Then again, the only one anyone could see was the sleeve of roses on her right arm. Besides the one on her hip, she had a tattoo on her lower back. It was of a barbed wire in the shape of a figure eight to show that what goes around comes around.

They were on their sides facing each other, and Dalton was running his hand from her hip up her side, lightly brushing against her breast. The intimate and sensual act practically made her purr in happiness. Wondering if she could elicit an actual purr from his tiger, she stroked his shoulder, before continuing down to enjoy the sinewy muscles of his pecs and abdomen. He claimed he didn't work out, but that was hard to believe.

Anna's hand came over his hip just as Dalton gave a deep throaty guttural sound. While technically not a purr, it was as close as she was probably going to get when he was in human form. With his gaze focused on her face, Dalton climbed on top of her, lowered his head, and with butterfly softness, kissed her. She growled, wanting more. Anna reached up, clasped his head, and drew his bottom lip into her mouth then released him.

"I could kiss you all night," she said.

Dalton's brow rose. "You couldn't last." As if to prove his point, he slid down and plucked her nipple between his teeth.

Bolts of electricity lit her up, not to mention how her blue sparks glowed. He was right. She'd never last, not with the way her body was in such need of him. Anna grabbed his shoulders and hung on tight, and with each flick of his tongue, he took her higher. When he moved to the other side and kneaded the first nipple between his fingers, Anna almost came right there.

"Please, Dalton."

Instead of doing what she'd asked for, he dropped lower and licked her clean. As waves of delight washed over her, she bucked her hips upward and dug her nails into his scalp. His blue orb grew larger and larger and soon matched hers. His groans and moans ratcheted her desires higher. Reaching out to him, she tugged on his shoulders. Dalton must have understood this hint because in a flash, he was once more on top of her with his big cock at her entrance.

"Kiss me," she begged, as she opened her lips to receive him. And receive him she did.

Not only did his tongue delve into her mouth, he slid into her, igniting her to the core. Pulses of incredible lust shimmied up her body, the sparks flying, and her glow expanding even faster. Their tongues twisted, and his scent filled her. Anna wanted to be connected with this man in every way. With each thrust, her desire grew. Dalton's eyes glowed a beautiful amber color, and his dark hair became sprinkled with white.

Her tongue scraped along his teeth, and a tinge of blood floated in her mouth. Dalton broke the kiss. "Oh shit. I'm sorry. I got too excited."

"That's okay. I'm good."

Anna didn't want to break the high she was on, so she pressed her feet into the mattress and met him thrust for thrust. The overwhelming desire to be connected to him stole her breath. Lowering his lips to her neck, she marveled at how their blue orbs overlapped. As he drove into her once more, his sharp teeth sunk into her neck, catapulting her into a new realm of pleasure, while a white light arced between them, forming what looked like a figure eight. Stunned at the beauty of it all, her yearning intensified.

Her climax rushed in and overtook all of her senses. Lights swam in front of her eyes as a cocoon of love surrounded her and held her.

Dalton's chest heaved as he spilled his seed. At that moment, they became one. All sound seemed to disappear as she absorbed Dalton's goodness.

Their blue glows slowly receded, and her body lost all energy. As she collapsed back onto the bed, he kissed her forehead, her nose, and then her lips. "That was life altering," he said.

"Are we mated?" It sure as hell felt like it.

"We are."

"Can I shift now?"

He chuckled then rolled over, taking her with him. "You'll have to wait for the white moon."

"Why?"

He shrugged. "The first time a person shifts, it's always on the white moon. After that, it can be whenever they choose."

That didn't sound so bad. "Will you teach me?"

"Of course. We're a team now."

Anna had never felt so complete. "Team tiger."

Dalton laughed. "I like it, but you can't tell people that."

"Not even Jillian?" Surely, there were no secrets from his sister.

"You can tell Jillian or any other shifter, as long as you're discreet."

Anna hoped she could control her exuberance. This was all so wonderful. "I'll try."

He tapped her butt. "You'll do more than try."

Anna grinned, loving life right now. Dalton pulled her closer and glanced over her shoulder at something on her back. "What are you doing?" she asked.

"Checking out your Wendayan marking."

"My vine?"

"Yes, but now it has the paw of a tiger underneath it."

Excitement raced through her. "Really? It changed? Why?"

"That's what happens when the mating is complete."

This was too good to be true. "Did yours change too?"

He rolled her off then turned to show her his back. "Well?"

She traced the marking. "It's beautiful. I love how the paw print and vine are now one. How did this happen?"

He faced her. "It's magic."

SO FAR, DALTON'S morning had sucked. First thing he had to do was fill out a warrant for Meredith Wilson's arrest. With the ballistic report in hand, Judge Hollars had no issue signing it, though he wasn't happy about being disturbed before he'd had his morning coffee.

Dalton should be satisfied with a job well done, but something was still poking at him. He refused to believe it was Anna's defense of the woman that had increased his doubt. Every criminal insisted they were innocent, so why should Meredith Wilson be any different? The report stated there had been no fingerprints on the gun handle, so it was possible Meredith was telling the truth. On the other hand, it didn't take much to rub them off. Would she have taken the care to wipe away the evidence, and then stash the gun in her own glove compartment? That made little sense. Doubt rarely shadowed him, but this time it was looming big.

Dalton's conscience had no place in what he had to do next—which was to arrest Meredith Wilson. The facts demanded it. Regardless of the circumstances, she had been in possession of the murder weapon. Because there was no need for anyone else to witness her worst day, Dalton wanted to deliver the warrant before she went to work.

He pulled in front of her modest home that needed some up-keep. Her husband must have been the one to cut the lawn since it looked as if it hadn't been mowed in weeks.

Here goes.

When Meredith Wilson opened the door and saw him standing there with a paper in his hand, she clutched her chest, her eyes filled with resignation. "Officer?"

His usual sense of *gotcha* never materialized. He genuinely felt sorry for her, until he remembered she might be a cold-blooded killer. Dalton advised her of her rights.

"But the gun's not mine. I never touched it. Can't the lab tell that?"

"No, ma'am. I'm sorry. You'll have to come with me."

Her shoulders sagged. A voice sounded behind her, and then feet shuffled toward them. An older gentleman appeared in striped pajamas and placed a hand on her back. "Merry? What's going on?"

She faced him. "The gun was the murder weapon. They think I killed Crystal."

His shoulders straightened a bit, and he whipped toward Dalton. "She didn't do it."

Denial was common. "I'm sorry, sir, but this paper says I have the right to take her in." He handed it to him.

Both read the contents. "I'll find a lawyer, sweetheart," the husband said.

Dalton waited until the embrace ended and the tears slowed. Merry clearly loved her husband, but that might be more reason for her to stop the sale of the bookstore from going through.

She said little as he drove her to the station. Once he processed Merry, Dalton headed back to his desk to determine if she had been framed. A good lawyer might be able to go after the reasonable doubt defense, which meant Dalton either had to find the person who framed Meredith Wilson, or prove she did it.

The first step would be to recheck the other suspects—their motives, their alibis, and if they had any past criminal records. He was in the middle of a background check on Tom DeLuca when Kalan arrived.

"You're here early," his partner said.

Not really. Kalan was unusually late. "You got the ballistics report last night?"

"I just saw it."

That explained the lack of a phone call. "I was able to rouse Judge Hollars before he went into work."

"You arrested Mrs. Wilson already?"

"Yes, but I really don't think she did it. Call it my gut instinct." Criminals were more arrogant and smug. Meredith Wilson acted stunned.

Kalan pulled up a chair and leaned close. "What's gotten into you? You're never swayed by your instincts. You go strictly by the facts."

That made him sound so unfeeling. "Anna is a good influence on me."

"Anna?" Kalan stared at him for a moment and then smiled. "Don't tell me you and Anna...you know."

They never used the word *mate* at work. "Yes. It's official." A brief smile stole across his face.

"Congratulations, but you do realize things will become next to impossible real fast."

He didn't like hearing anything negative. "Meaning?"

Kalan glanced around to make sure no one was listening. Discussing anything relating to shifters was chancy. "Your need for Anna will be off the charts for quite a while."

"That's not possible."

Kalan laughed. "That's what I said. Just you wait."

His best chance of focusing then would be early in the morning after they'd made love the night before. No wonder his desire for her was already growing. "Great."

"Now that the case is more or less closed, what are you working on?" Kalan asked nodding to all the papers neatly stacked on his desk.

"Like I said, I'm not sure it is closed. It's possible Meredith Wilson was framed, so I'm doing background checks on all of the other suspects. That's assuming our *mountain* friends aren't behind this."

"They very well might be. Hand me some," Kalan said. "It'll go faster."

"Thanks." Dalton gave him Ed Santaria, in part because Kalan had grown up in Silver Lake and might be more familiar with some of the Changelings. He also gave him Linda Darnell and Carlton Wedgewood. Dalton kept Meredith Wilson's file, wanting to delve into her motivation, as well as Tom DeLuca's. Last would be Julie Dominick, Carlton Wedgewood's secretary.

No sooner had Dalton finished gathering the sparse information he had on Tom than Jillian waltzed in, dressed in a sleek navy blue suit, white blouse, and high heels. With her contrasting blonde hair, he had to admit she looked great. From the way most of the men and women in the room stopped what they were doing and looked at her, they thought she was attractive too. Too bad the young officers didn't seem to notice her engagement ring.

"Dalton," she said in a serious tone that he bet had earned her a lot of respect in the courtroom.

"What can I do for you, sis?"

"I'm here to speak with my client, Meredith Wilson."

His gut tightened. "You're representing Meredith?"

"Yes, is that a problem?"

It shouldn't be. They hadn't discussed anything about the case so far. In fact, he'd barely seen his sister of late because she'd been spending all of her time with her mate. As much as he wanted to share his good news about Anna, now wasn't the time. "Nope."

"Good."

At least Meredith would have a great defense, but he hoped that if Merry were guilty, his sister didn't get her off on some technicality. As soon as Jillian headed off to speak with their lead suspect, Dalton put Tom's paperwork away and ran Merry's name in the criminal database once more but found nothing. To be thorough, he pulled up her marriage certificate for her full name, wanting to check under her maiden name. As soon as he spotted the name Carlyle, he stilled.

That sounded familiar. *Meredith Carlyle Wilson,* he repeated to himself. Merry Carlyle.

Could she be Mary Carlyle, Anna's birth mother? Anna had said she'd traced her mom to Silver Lake. Pulse beating hard, he did a more in-depth search using Zabasearch, which showed the places where a person had lived. Hometown: Vista Lake, Montana. Dalton remembered Anna saying she was from Montana, but he hadn't asked the name of the town.

What if Merry were Anna's birth mother? He couldn't imagine what it would be like to finally find her, only to learn she was a murder suspect. Anna had said when she'd touched Merry's arm, she'd envisioned a younger woman holding a baby, so it seemed possible that Anna was that baby.

Fingers snapped in front of his face. Dalton looked up at Kalan. "Sorry," Dalton said. "I found something and was trying to put the pieces together."

Kalan pulled over his chair. "Tell me."

He explained about Meredith and her possible connection to Anna. "I'm not sure what to do."

"How about asking Meredith if she ever gave up a child? I imagine you don't want to get Anna's hopes up by mentioning it and then find out it isn't true."

That was sound advice, but there was a flaw in his thinking. "Why would she tell me anything? She sure as hell doesn't trust me."

He shrugged. "I suppose you could ask Jillian to find out." Kalan said. "You need to be sure first, but you better hurry. You can't keep this news from Anna. She'll find out at some point."

"That's the problem. If I tell her, she'll want to come in here and demand answers from Meredith."

Kalan shrugged. "It's not like Meredith could harm her."

His partner was right. "I need to think more on it."

"Let me know if I can help." Kalan pushed back his chair and returned to his desk.

For the next half hour, Dalton dug into Meredith's background.

It appeared as if she came from a wealthy family. Not only did her father own several car dealerships, later in his life he'd become active in politics at the State level. If she were Anna's mom at a young age, the parents might have insisted she give up the baby so as not to embarrass them. None of this information, however, was pertinent to the case. In fact, it indicated that Meredith's ability to care for her husband wasn't as dire as it seemed, if her parents were willing and able to help her out.

As frustrating as this job was sometimes, he liked following the leads. The key to this case seemed to be financial. Once he obtained a warrant to search Meredith's bank records, he would ask Daniel Goddard, the man in charge of forensic accounting, to delve into her finances. That would tell him just how desperate she was not to lose her job. It didn't matter that her home implied she was strapped for cash.

Putting off that task a bit longer, he studied Julie Dominick's file. She'd been arrested three years ago for drunk and disorderly conduct, but that didn't mean she was a killer. Wedgewood's company website listed Carlton as CEO and CFO, a Raymond Dougherty as President, and Julie as administrative assistant. According to the site, she had a business degree from the University of Tennessee where Jackson went to school. It might be interesting to see what dirt his friend could dig up on her. Dalton was curious why, with her background though, she wasn't a broker. Was she only interested in landing a rich husband, and thought the best way would be as Carlton's assistant?

Before he could search further, his sister's heels clacked on the tile floor. With a stern look that would scare most jurors, she strode toward him.

"Well? Do you think she's guilty?" he asked.

"You know better than to ask that. It's client privilege."

His sister wasn't here to play. "Fine. Just tell me this. What does your gut tell you?"

"She didn't do it. Why? As she told you, she went straight home after work and didn't leave her home until the next morning. Her husband was asleep, which was why he can't be her alibi. I will admit that she could have lied."

"I agree." He had wondered why she hadn't.

"She told me that before she made supper, she was on Facebook and even PM'd a few friends."

"PM'd?"

Jillian planted a hand on her hip. "Seriously? What rock do live under? PM stands for private message on Facebook. Have you heard of that?"

"Yes, I have." Her words stung nonetheless. They'd been similar to what Anna said about him being a workaholic. "If that's true, it would give her an alibi. Will she let us check out her computer?"

"Absolutely. You'll see that she couldn't be chatting with friends and killing Crystal Wedgewood at the same time."

That might settle it once and for all.

"She also made two phone calls—one to her sister-in-law and one to her brother-in-law—but she wasn't sure of the time. She'd called them because she was concerned about her husband's health. I'm surprised you didn't ask her these questions."

He was too. He must have been preoccupied with a certain delectable woman. "I'll check it out right away. If what she says is true, I'll have the arrest rescinded." He waggled a finger. "But she can't leave town."

Jillian shook her head. "She won't. Now go find the evidence to free her. Then apologize to her."

Dalton hadn't realized how bossy his sister was. "When this is cleared up, maybe the four of us can do dinner and catch up." He was rather pleased with his smooth way of introducing the fact he and Anna were together.

A small smile lifted her lips. "The four of us?"

"You, Brian, me, and Anna."

Her eyes sparkled. "Why didn't you tell me?" She swiped a hand. "Erase that. Why didn't Anna tell me that you two were together?"

VELLA DAY

"Let's say we made it official last night."

A grin split her face. "I am thrilled for you. Anna is a wonderful woman."

"You should be happy for her too." He puffed out his chest. "I'm quite a catch, or so Anna says."

Jillian laughed. "She'll have her hands full, that's for sure."

Dalton slapped a hand to his chest. "I'm offended."

"Uh-huh. Go do your job and prove Merry Wilson is innocent, so we can celebrate."

Dalton saluted and his sister left. The women of the world seemed to be conspiring against him. He pushed back his chair and faced Kalan. "I'm going to do a little more research on Mrs. Wilson." He explained about her being on the computer at the time of the murder.

"She should have told us."

"Most people don't think their computer time can be traced. It was my job to have asked."

"Good point. I'll go see what Mr. Santaria is up to. I bet Jackson and his team would love nothing more than to find some dirt on that man."

Their hatred of the Changelings knew no bounds. "Amen."

Chapter Sixteen

MERRY WILSON SEEMED so thrilled that Dalton was willing to check out her story that she hugged him when he told her his plan. While the action was totally inappropriate, it was something Anna would have done had she been in the same situation.

Dalton had to admit there was a physical similarity between the two women. They both had slightly rounded faces with wide set eyes and pouty lips. Then again, that could be his imagination working, wanting his mate to be happy.

Not only did Meredith sign a waiver for him to check out her computer, she called her husband to explain that Dalton would be over shortly.

Once he arrived at their home, her husband answered on the first knock. The man had changed out of his pajamas, but he still looked like he should be in a hospital. His skin was ashy and his balance suspect as he led Dalton inside. His baggy pants looked a few sizes too big and his shirt was buttoned up wrong. Poor guy. Dalton hoped he'd be able to take care of himself without his wife. However, if what she said was true, she should be home by tomorrow.

"I put Merry's laptop on the dining room table, along with her username and password. She uses the same combination for her Facebook account. I hope you find what you're looking for. I need her." The last sentence took effort, as his breathing was labored. It tore at Dalton's heart.

"Me too." Dalton took a seat at the table while Mr. Wilson

returned to his recliner in front of the television. He lowered the volume, probably so as not to disturb him.

Jillian had said Merry had been on Facebook, so he opened up that page first. When he brought up her account, he had to search to find these private messages, but the icons led him to it. Sure enough, she'd written to two different women—one at 6:04PM and another at 6:10PM making it impossible for her to have killed Crystal. That was good news.

While Merry had given him permission to check her phone records, he didn't think he'd need them. Dalton stood. "Thank you."

"Will you let Merry go free? She isn't capable of hurting any-one."

Dalton couldn't make any promises. "I'll need to take this to the lab so they can confirm what I found."

Her husband wrung his hands together. "Absolutely. Anything to help Merry."

Assuming the techs confirmed that Meredith hadn't somehow manipulated her computer, Dalton would then ask the district attorney to have the charges dismissed. To make it official, he'd have to go back to Judge Hollars and ask for the charges to be dropped, and Dalton wasn't looking forward to that conversation. Most likely he'd get a reaming out from the judge again, telling him he should have checked first.

And he'd be right.

As soon as Dalton returned to the station, he turned over her computer. The lab was backlogged, but the tech said he'd get to it as soon as he could. Having done what he could for now, Dalton spent a little time on his other cases. His plan was to stake out Julie Dominick later this afternoon to see where she headed after work.

He left about a half an hour early in order to stop by the Crystal Winds Spa to pick up something for Anna. Kalan told him the spa carried crystals that might help calm his mate when she was exposed to the sardonyx. While Dalton understood the need for the Clan to find the stone before the Changelings did, it bothered him that Anna had to be the one to suffer as a result.

Because the Blooms of Hope flower shop sat across the street from the Crystal Winds Spa, he parked around the corner on Pine Avenue. Hoping Anna wasn't looking out the shop window, he rushed inside the spa and immediately felt a calming effect. Maybe there was something to this crystal stuff or else the combination of scents was working on him. It smelled like eucalyptus and what he thought might be roses. Whatever it was, he liked it.

As a tiger, he didn't think the pink quartz affected him like it did Kalan and Rye since his genetic makeup was significantly different, but maybe he was wrong about that too.

"Dalton!" Missy said coming out from the back room. "What brings you here?"

No one else was in the store, for which he was glad. Asking about stones wasn't his thing, but for Anna he would suck it up. "I'm looking for a piece of pink quartz for Anna." He looked through the door that led to the back, not sure who else worked there, but a client could be having a massage in one of the back rooms. "I don't know if you heard, but recently Anna came in contact with some sardonyx and had a rather adverse reaction to it. I want something to counteract that."

Missy's eyes widened. "I've never heard of that. I know the Changelings have issues with pink quartz, but never the other way around."

He shrugged. "No one can explain it, not even Anna."

She placed a hand on his arm. "Come into the back. It's where we keep the good stuff." She winked.

After a lengthy lesson from Missy about the various stones and calming oils, Dalton left with a highly polished egg-shaped rock that would fit in Anna's pocket easily. The Eucalyptus Oil, Missy said, was for when she returned home after coming in contact with the sardonyx. Anna could either put some in her bath or just inhale the aroma.

On Missy's advice, he also purchased a vase-like container that held a candle and oil. When heated, the oil would diffuse into the air and bring a sense of peace. He wouldn't judge until he saw it work.

It was shortly after four, which meant it was time to check on Julie Dominick and the grieving widower. Carlton Wedgewood claimed his affair with her was over, but Dalton wanted to see it for himself. It was possible that with his wife dead, he might take back up with Julie. How that pointed the finger at either one of them, he didn't know, but the more information Dalton had about these people, the better. Puzzles were often slow to develop, and he was a firm believer in finding one piece at a time.

Dalton parked across the street from Wedgewood Financial and waited for the two of them to leave for the evening, hoping this wasn't another one of their late nights. While he sat there, he debated calling Anna, but then decided it might wake up his tiger too quickly.

ANNA FINISHED WRAPPING the science fiction book she'd bought for Dalton and set it on her dining room table. It was shortly after five, and she hadn't heard from him all day. This whole mating thing was so new to her; it was throwing her off her game. What did that mean for them? Would they move in together or just date? Jillian and Brian had moved in together after they mated. Then again, Brian had bought a house for them while Jillian was putting her affairs in order in California.

Anna checked the time again. It was two minutes since the last time she'd looked. What happened to her carefree spirit? Damn. Dalton had already changed her.

Needing to talk to someone, she called Jillian since Elana had already closed up shop and returned home. Most likely, her boss would be feeding the baby and wouldn't have time to discuss the life of a shifter right now.

Jillian answered on the first ring. "Hey, girl. I hear congratulations are in order."

Anna stilled, trying to figure out how word had spread so fast. She didn't see Dalton spilling the beans, even to his sister. "Did you talk to your brother?"

She chuckled. "I did. I had to be at the station to represent a client and he told me about your mating. I'm so happy for you."

"Thank you." Now came the awkward part. "I'm not sure what to do now."

"Do? What do you mean? Are you having second thoughts?"

"No! I mean, Dalton hasn't even called or texted all day."

Jillian chuckled. "Oh, sweetie. That's Dalton's way of trying not to think about you when his tiger is going crazy." She explained about the intense need for one another.

Anna walked over to her sofa and dropped down, relieved that she wasn't imagining things. "I was beginning to wonder if something was wrong with me."

"What you're feeling is natural, though it might be more frightening for you since you've never been a shifter."

She wasn't one now. Not really. "So is that why I've been so horny?"

"Yes, and what Dalton is going through is much worse. Not only is he a guy, he already can shift, which makes it worse."

Oh, God. They'd never keep apart after the white moon. "I appreciate the intel—I think."

"Just have fun. Dalton's a great guy, if a little OCD and uptight."

"I know." But she still wanted him. "So now what happens?"

"It's up to you two. Knowing Dalton, he'll want to take things slowly, only because he won't want you to freak. Learning to deal with the new feelings will take time, so don't rush anything. That being said, if you want something, you have to tell him. Trust me, he'll agree."

In the past, Anna was the type to jump head first into a situation and ask questions after the fact. Case in point, she'd packed up what few possessions she had in Montana two years ago and headed to

Tennessee to find her mother, not having any idea where she would live or what she'd do for a living.

Locating her mom hadn't panned out, but she had found a great place to stay and a wonderful job. Never in her wildest dreams would she have thought she'd end up with someone as amazing as Dalton. Even though she was a free spirit, she recognized that some practical things needed to be addressed. "Was shifting hard the first time?"

"Don't ask me," Jillian said. "I learned to shift before I could talk. Wasn't Elana a human before she mated with Kalan?"

Duh. "Yes. Thanks, I'll ask her." Anna had so many more questions, but just thinking about Dalton made her forget them. Her urges were going wild. "Listen, I won't keep you. Thanks for talking to me."

"The four of us need to get together soon."

"Totally." Anna hung up and smiled.

Her stomach grumbled. Perhaps she had time to run to the grocery store and pick up something to make for the two of them for dinner before Dalton called—if he called. With the murder investigation in full swing, he might not have time to see her.

At least she knew the man liked to eat meat. That would make meal prep easy.

As she headed toward the door, her cell vibrated in her hand, and her pulse soared, hoping it was Dalton telling her he wanted to see her. She checked the screen: it wasn't Dalton, but another number she didn't recognize.

"Hello?"

"Anna, it's Jackson. Would you be free for a few minutes to check something out?"

By something, he probably meant the sardonyx. "I guess."

"I really appreciate it. I can pick you up in front of the store in say ten minutes?"

"I'll be ready."

It wouldn't take long to walk through one building. While she wasn't excited about experiencing the ill feelings again, it would help the Clan. If it were as quick as Jackson implied, she'd be back in no time and still be able to see Dalton. For a moment, she debated calling him to say she had an errand to run with Jackson, but Dalton would probably say it wasn't a good idea.

If she was to become a member of the shifter community, she wanted to be useful, and as a Wendayan, she needed to protect other witches from the Changelings.

Once downstairs, she waited for Jackson in front. While she couldn't sense who was a shifter and who wasn't, the hairs on her neck stood up. She had a feeling that someone was watching her, and she didn't like it one bit. But why would someone be watching her?

A black truck pulled up in front, and she clenched her fists. The driver rolled down the passenger side window, and when she spotted Jackson, she let out a breath.

He jumped out and opened her door. "Thanks for doing this," he said. "I know it's not pleasant."

"You're welcome." She hopped in, and he returned to his side. "Where are we going?"

"I'm checking the different locations to see where the Change-lings might target next. A few spots are under places like the church and a school, but I'm thinking they won't bother with something that secure. As for the other sites, I'm not sure if we can convince any owner to let us dig up their floor unless he's a shifter. Even if we can't retrieve the stone, it's good enough to be aware it's there. That way, we can keep an eye on the Changelings to make sure they don't get it."

"That makes sense. If any of the properties are for sale, maybe your team, or rather your Clan could all chip in and buy it to keep the Changelings from getting their hands on it."

Jackson smiled. "You catch on fast."

Two minutes later, they arrived at a convenience store. Good. In a place like that, she could walk around and pretend to look for something to buy. If it had been a doctor's office, they wouldn't let her wander into all of the rooms. Jackson parked then opened her door.

"At least now I understand what the light-headed feeling means, so this time I won't freak out."

"Tell me the moment you're feeling queasy," Jackson said as he led her inside.

Walking with her up and down the aisles, he made small talk about what they needed to buy. As she neared the bathrooms in back, a wave of nausea assaulted her, and she grabbed his arm to steady herself.

"That's enough," he said. "Let's go. Even when the ill feeling passes, pretend you're ill." He grabbed a Ginger ale and once he paid for it, he handed it to her. "Drink this."

"What if a Changeling is watching and saw me take ill?" she whispered.

"Don't worry. There aren't any of those kinds in here."

"Good." Anna couldn't wait to leave. Once outside, fortunately all of her symptoms disappeared, but she drank the Ginger ale anyway. "I still don't understand why that stone affects me so much."

"I don't know either, but wouldn't it be cool if you could repel Changelings because of it?"

She chuckled. "I don't want to even test that theory. They give me the creeps, not that I've ever met one." Or so she hoped.

"I hear ya."

Jackson drove her back to her place. After she said goodbye, she rushed upstairs, anxious to be with Dalton.

BROTHER JACOB PACED his office awaiting John Ernst's report about his *divining rod* woman. Because the partial moon had been red last night, their window of opportunity was closing for infiltrating the wolf and bear Clan's ranks. After his Clan's failure to purchase the bookstore, he was convinced the wolf and bear Clan would try to remove the sardonyx so that Brother Jacob couldn't get his hands on it. Little did Rye McKinnon know that he would fail.

Brother Jacob had ordered several men and women to keep watch over some of the leaders of the Clan to see if they'd ordered any unusual equipment—like a jackhammer—since the only way to excavate the stone would be by digging up the concrete pad. Brother Jacob figured he'd let them do the dirty work first. Once the stone was unearthed, his men would swoop in and steal it. That, however, would require the special talent of Brother Carmen. Because his mother was a black witch, Brother Carmen had the ability to take the form of another person and hold it not just for two days after the red moon, but for three. Knowing Alpha McKinnon, he'd schedule the removal as soon as it was safe. Ha, ha.

A knock sounded on his door. "Come in." Brother John entered with Brother Carmen, their resident witch. "Any news on this Anna woman?" Brother Jacob asked.

"She's at her apartment, sir," Brother John said. At least his second in command wasn't acting like his usual cocky self.

The bookstore didn't close until seven, so the Clan would have to wait until then. Jacob pulled open his desk drawer and retrieved several photographs. "I had Brenda Sims take these photos of some of their more, well-known Clansman." He handed the stack to Brother Carmen. "Memorize their faces. I've listed their names and the names of their mates on the back, should they have any."

"I've already been in contact with Missy Berta, sir," Brother Carmen said. "I can become her for another twelve hours, but it will require a lot of my energy to hold the pose."

"I don't give a damn about your comfort. You have a job to do. I'm sure the place will have several guards stationed outside. You need to rush up to one of them and act very distraught." Brother Jacob outlined the rest of his brilliant plan. He then glanced over at Brother John. "Make sure the cell signal around the Murdoch home is disrupted so there can be no outside contact."

"Yes, sir."

Thank goodness Brother Carmen's scent would be masked when

he took the form of Missy. Not even the great Ryerson McKinnon would be able to tell Brother Carmen was a wolf.

"Then what?" Brother John asked.

"Do what we do best. Kill them all and bring me the stones."

Both John Ernst and Carmen Diaz bowed, turned, and then left.

Brother Jacob smiled, pleased at his perfect plan.

Chapter Seventeen

A S SOON AS Dalton spotted Julie Dominick walking out of
Wedgwood Financial with Carlton, his energy shot up. *Here
goes.* He'd switched out his sheriff's vehicle for his white SUV in the
hopes it would blend in well with the other vehicles on the street, but
his effort didn't seem to have been needed. With the way those two
lovebirds were ogling each other, they wouldn't have noticed
someone screaming bloody murder two feet in front of them.

So much for those two not dating anymore. As they walked
down the street toward the parked cars, Julie leaned closer to Carlton
who smiled then kissed her. Cripes, they acted like eighteen-year olds
rather than two people in their forties.

Wouldn't you do the same if Anna were here?
I wouldn't be able to help myself.

He refocused on the lovebirds. Julie laughed at something Carlton said, and he wrapped his arm around her. After he led her to her
car, he then slipped into his black Mercedes, which was parked in
front of hers. The big question was whether they would head in the
same direction or go to their prospective homes.

Dalton couldn't imagine what it would be like to return home to
a place where his spouse, or mate, had died. His skin crawled at that
sad thought.

A minute later, Carlton headed west and Julie went north. As
much as he wanted to follow her, he needed to be with Anna more.
With each increasing hour, his ability to focus on anything other

than her had deteriorated. On the drive over, the air had been redolent with late summer flowers, reminding him of his mate. Hell, when a woman with a tattoo on her shoulder had walked across the street, his thoughts had shot to Anna's tattoo. Fearing he might shift, he didn't dare think about those butterflies on her sexy hip.

No doubt about it. She was his drug, and he had to have her. Again.

Putting his car in gear, he took off. On the way back to town, he called Anna to make sure she was home. The moment she answered, his bones cracked, which would be hell to explain to any passing motorist if he actually shifted.

"Hey, you," she said, sounding happy.

"Just wondering if you wanted some company?"

"Are you kidding? Of course I do. I was hoping you'd call."

He smiled, but then sobered knowing he'd have to work hard to make sure she didn't think he was only interested in sex. Unfortunately, his tiger didn't seem willing to hold back for much longer. "Be there in five."

Kalan was right. Being mated had ramped up his desires, which Dalton never thought possible, given his strong yearning for her already.

As soon as he turned toward Anna's apartment, the facts of the murder case faded in his memory, and the image of his beautiful mate surfaced. Now he wished he'd purchased a home when he'd arrived in town, so the two of them could discuss moving in together. He would ask now, but both her apartment and his were way too small for the both of them. He preferred to live together in a permanent residence anyway, rather than a rental.

His heart swelled as he pictured the two of them pouring over house designs, trying to decide how big to make the kitchen, and whether to have two, three, or four bedrooms. He hoped Anna wanted a ton of kids. As for decorating and picking out the right shade of countertop, he'd leave that to her, though without a doubt it would be quirky.

He parked behind her brick building, and once she buzzed him in, Dalton took the steps two at a time. Before he even had a chance to knock, she pulled open the door, and the mere sight of her made him growl. The she-devil was barefoot, wearing shorts and a top so thin he could spot her nipples poking out. *Grr.*

Anna grabbed him by the front of his shirt, hauled him inside, and kissed him silly. With their lips in contact, Dalton swung her around, her scent invading every cell in his body.

Anna broke the kiss and laughed. "Whoa. Where did this enthusiasm come from?"

He set her down. "What do you mean? Can't a guy hug his mate?"

She lifted a brow. "Yes, but you're not usually this expressive."

"In the past that was true, but you've inspired me."

Anna plastered her body against his again. "Aw, that's sweet."

As much as he wanted to carry her into bed, he should give her the present first, so she didn't think he was single-mindedly focused on sex. Stepping out of her grasp, he dug the stone from his pocket. Oh, crap. In his hurry to see her, he'd forgotten the candle and oil in the car. He'd have to get it later. Dalton handed her the pink stone. "This is for you. It's to help when you're feeling ill if you happen to be around sardonyx."

"Really? It's so pretty. I didn't know there was something that could combat my bad reaction." She chuckled. "I wish I'd had this a few hours ago."

He stilled. "What do you mean?"

She waved a hand, plopped down on the sofa, and then patted the seat next to her. "Relax. Come. Sit on the sofa, and I'll tell you what happened earlier."

Given how cheerful she seemed, the experience wasn't a bad one. "Did Jackson ask you to scope out a place?"

She smiled. "He did, and I found some sardonyx—or at least I became woozy in one spot, which I guess meant I found the stone. Jackson told me that while the Clan wants to locate the sardonyx, they aren't planning on doing anything about it until the Change-lings make their move."

"That makes sense, but should you need to be around the stone again just touch this quartz and the affect will go away."

She rubbed it on her face and then smiled, her pretty eyes lightening. "I'm feeling calm already."

He wasn't. That little action ramped up his libido. Just as he was about to draw her into a kiss, she jumped up. "I forgot. I bought you a present too!"

His chest squeezed tight. Dalton couldn't remember the last time someone other than a family member had given him anything. When she bent over to pick up his present, his tiger nearly roared. *Down boy. Wait a little longer.*

Anna returned to the sofa and curled one leg underneath her as she handed him what looked like a box.

"You wrapped it?" Now he felt bad he hadn't taken the time to gift-wrap his.

She shrugged. "It makes it more special that way."

Now he really felt like a cad. His other gift was in a Crystal Winds Spa bag, but he couldn't do anything about that right now. Dalton carefully lifted off the tape.

"Just rip it," she said, chuckling.

Aw, what the hell. He tore off the paper and pulled out the book. "*Alien Nomad*," he said, reading the title.

"I hope you haven't read it."

"No." He turned it over and studied the blurb on the back. "This looks great. Thank you."

Anna lifted up on her knees and his tiger went wild. "I know how you could thank me."

He smiled. "Tell me."

She straddled his legs. As her scent seeped deep into him, his body went crazy. When he ran his palms down her bare shoulders, sparks flew off both of them. Anna leaned over and kissed him, causing his cock to press painfully against his zipper. His nails grew.

As he delved into her sweetness, the world seemed to disappear and only goodness existed.

Anna threaded her fingers through his hair then gripped his head, and when she ran her tongue along her lips, his animal clawed his insides.

"Fuck me," she whispered.

He groaned, loving a woman who knew what she wanted. With her on his lap, he slid his hands under her luscious butt, leaned forward, and stood. Her eyes widened as he slid her to her feet. "I want you naked."

"I can do that."

He was about to add *and spread beneath me*, but when she lifted her top off and exposed those perfect tits, his tiger roared, and he lost the ability to speak for a moment. Dalton dropped to one knee, and slipped her shorts down her legs, exposing a thong that made his mouth water. "I didn't stand a chance, did I?"

"No. Because you can be rather reserved at times, I knew I had to take drastic measures. In fact, I haven't been able to think of anything all day but having you. Your bite seemed to have unleashed every latent desire in my body, and I didn't want you to deny me."

He stood and hugged her. "Oh, baby, that will never happen."

Her pretty eyes sparkled with flecks of amber. "That so? Then how about dropping those pants Officer Garner and showing me?"

"You don't have to ask twice." Never in his wildest dream did he expect a woman this amazing to want him. He kicked off his shoes, stepped out of his jeans, and pulled his T-shirt off over his head then dropped it. Anna then helped rid him of his briefs, but in the process she nearly drove him mad with lust. Needing her totally naked, he slipped her panties down her legs. "Step out of them."

Once she did, he lifted her up, and supported her by wrapping an arm under her butt. Walking them a few feet to the nearest wall, he then pressed her back against the door. The kiss that followed spoke of hope, acceptance, and pure passion. Anna planted her feet on his thighs and leaned back, offering him her tits. He couldn't refuse that invitation. Dalton dipped his head, and as he tugged on each pert tip, Anna squealed in delight.

When she wiggled against his cock, his vision narrowed. The image of his tiger running wild with her right beside him came to his mind's eye. Together, they charged forward, and slowly transformed into humans once more.

"Hurry," she begged.

That plea was his signal to unleash his inner animal. With one hand under her butt, he lifted her up. With the other, he aimed his dick right at her entrance. Her blue orb grew as her breathing increased. Needing her now, he drove into her, and heaven descended.

She lowered her head to kiss him, and he greedily drank her in. With her arms around his neck and her legs wrapped around his waist, he plunged into her and savored her sweet lips. No matter how often their tongues entwined, he needed more.

Anna moved her feet to his thighs again and joined in the creation of their wonderful rhythm. Her moans grew, as did her glow. Her heat surrounded him, and he had to draw on all of his control not to come until Anna had been fulfilled. With the way her orb was growing, it would be soon.

She broke the kiss and lowered her mouth to his neck where she sucked on the spot right below his jawline. He nearly lost it as his own blue orb expanded. When Dalton moved his lips to the delicate part where her neck met her shoulder, he couldn't resist her any longer. With swift precision and a strong mating call, he bit her. Their blue glows encompassed each other, and an overwhelming sense of freedom filled him. Dalton held her tightly, hoping to gain a modicum of control, never wanting to let her go.

It was not to be.

Anna lifted up and then dropped back down with such force, his cock exploded just as she screamed her release. Their heart beats matched in intensity, and they remained cocooned until their Wendayan glow began to fade.

Dalton was relishing this moment of holding his mate when his cell rang. He groaned, refusing to release his grip. As he buried his face in her neck again, the damn thing continued to chirp.

"Go ahead and answer it," she urged right before lifting his head and kissing him again.

"I don't want to. I'd rather hold you."

"It might be someone important."

He chuckled. "Okay, okay." The moment he set her down, Anna dashed to the bathroom, and he had to blink at her speed. What the hell? She returned a moment later with a wet washcloth.

The phone was still ringing, and he needed to answer it. Dalton stepped over to his pants and thrust his hand in his pants pocket to retrieve his cell. "Garner."

"It's Jackson. Rye wants us at the bookstore tonight."

He had to be kidding. "Why tonight? We have a lot of things we need to figure out first, like how to bypass the alarm system, and how to make certain no one will notice us." He didn't remember the store having shades.

Jackson chuckled. "Don't worry. It's taken care of. Remember, this is what we do for a living. Besides, we shouldn't have much trouble from the Changelings. Yesterday ended their time of being able to perform their super feats. As for keeping watch outside, Rye asked the Clan to help out."

Dalton's heart squeezed. He'd never had a Clan or even felt like he belonged to any group. If only he'd been born a wolf or a bear, he would have these *Weres* in his corner. Then again, he wasn't sure he could handle being as slow as a bear or as small as a wolf.

"What time?" he asked.

"Seven forty-five. Meet us behind the store by the loading door and tap twice. We'll let you in. And bring Wonder Woman."

Wonder Woman. The name fit though he really didn't want Anna anywhere near the place. "Why? You already know where the sardonyx is."

"We want to be sure. Don't worry. Nothing can happen to her

surrounded by a bunch of Clansmen."

Dalton had to agree that he'd worry more if she remained alone at her home. She'd be safer with him and the rest of the group. "Okay. We'll be there."

Once he disconnected, he faced her. "You heard?"

"Some of it." She walked over to the table and waved the stone. "With this, I'll be fine. Besides, I'd feel safer being with you than staying here alone."

"That's why I agreed." Not having had his fill, Dalton moved closer. "Do you promise to do as we ask?"

Anna pressed against his body and ran her nails over his shoulders and down his arms. "As long as you do what I ask afterward, I'll obey."

He laughed. "Don't I always do what you want?" That was because he wanted the same thing.

"Well, you were willing to let me seduce you."

"True." He nodded to the kitchen. "Did I just see you rush to the bedroom in a flash?"

Her jaw lowered. "Did I?"

Dalton remembered the first time he'd moved from one place to another while his sister had watched, and Jillian had said she'd barely seen him. He, however, didn't think he'd moved that fast. "Yes. I think you have a touch of my speed in you."

She grinned. "You think? Let me try again." She stepped away from him. "Okay, time me." She was at the kitchen before he could count to two. Anna faced him. "Well?"

He stroked his chin, loving her enthusiasm. "How about racing back here and see if you can do better?" She was in his arms before he had the chance to inhale.

"Well?"

"You are fantastic." Dalton couldn't resist tasting her again. Their lips met, and this time, he promised himself he'd take it slow even though his body was still highly aroused. Goddess, how the feel of her long, brown hair in his fingers made the sparks fly. Clutching a handful, he tugged as he dipped and savored her sweet mouth.

Needing more, Dalton broke the kiss and cupped both of her breasts. "I can't ever get enough of them."

She grabbed his cock. "And I can't get enough of this."

Dalton slid her hand away. "Be careful."

He lowered his head and drew one nipple into his mouth, twirling his tongue around and around the tip until the sensitive peak hardened. Anna groaned, and he switched to the other side. Each pull had her pumping her fist on his cock, and her aura glowing brighter by the second.

"Why do I need you again?" she panted.

"Because we're mates," he said between sucks.

She let go of him and pressed her hands to his shoulders. "Then take me again, please."

Dalton stepped back and smiled. "Do you want to ride me this time like you did before?"

Anna wrapped her arms around his neck. "I thought you'd never ask."

Chapter Eighteen

A NNA HAD SPENT the last few years cutting and arranging flowers, never imagining she'd be involved in anything as clandestine as breaking into a bookstore and helping to steal something valuable. While Dalton wasn't pleased she had to be there, the fact Kalan appeared to be okay with the mission seemed to help calm Dalton somewhat.

Right on time, they arrived at the loading dock behind the store. Even though the Clan's Alpha said he would have backup, she felt a pervasive sense of doom hovering around her.

"Are you sure this is safe?" she asked. "I mean what if the cops come?" She'd asked him this before, but she wanted to be certain there wouldn't be any last minute hiccups.

Dalton ran a hand down her arm. "Don't worry. When Kalan called, he told me that Brant Thompson and Drew Compton have our backs. They both work at the sheriff's department and both are shifters. If someone calls in anything about the store, they'll volunteer to investigate."

That made her feel a little better. "Okay, but what if those Changeling creeps show up?"

"We'll fight them and probably end up killing a few." He smiled down at her. "I'll make sure nothing happens to you."

"You better, though I could just hide."

"Or else run. No one can catch you."

Run. That was a plan she could embrace. Dalton knocked twice on the back entrance, and a few seconds later, someone she didn't recognize opened the door.

"Rye and the group are meeting in the back corner," the man said. Once they stepped inside, he then headed out, she guessed to keep watch. Given how many were there, they most likely were the last to arrive.

Dalton placed a hand on her back and led her to where four men had gathered. All of them had been at the McKinnon and Associates' meeting Rye had taken her to. Besides him, Jackson was there along with Connor and Kalan.

As she walked back, Anna couldn't help but glance to the spot where she'd first become ill. Some of the bookcases between the front of the store and the science fiction section had been moved, presumably to prevent anyone from figuring out what they were up to. The bookcases near the science fiction section had also been slid to the side.

As soon as they reached the group, Rye stopped talking and turned to her. "Thanks for coming."

"I want to do whatever I can to help." Being part of such a wonderful group thrilled her. Her whole life, Anna had believed she was alone in this world. Not only hadn't she known shifters existed, she also wasn't aware of Wendayans. Anna had always assumed that the marking on her back had been some form of birthmark.

Rye nodded. "All I need from you is to walk over the spot outlined by the tape. Because we want to find the stone with as little disturbance as possible, we'd like you to tell us if your reaction is strongest where we've marked."

While she wasn't looking forward to it, as soon as she moved away from the designated area, she'd recover. "I can do that."

"Dalton, how about helping her?" Rye asked.

"Sure."

He led her over. Anna inhaled, and when she stepped across the marked area on the floor, a tight band squeezed her chest. Her vision blurred, and if Dalton hadn't steadied her, she might have fallen.

"That's enough," he said keeping his voice low.

Rye came over. "So this is the spot?"

"Most definitely."

"I hate to ask this of you when you reacted so strongly, but the three foot by three foot square is rather large. Is there any way you can place your hand on the surface and tell more precisely where the stones might be located? Any guidance would be helpful."

"I'll try." Anna didn't dare look up at Dalton because his face would be in a scowl.

She clasped his hand and dropped to both knees. Inhaling to keep from getting sick, she methodically ran a palm from left to right starting at the top. To her surprise, some parts of the rectangle actually felt hot. When she completed her search, she looked up at Dalton. "Hand me a book."

"Which one?"

What? "Any book is fine."

He located one on a nearby shelf and gave it to her. She then placed it over the warmest spot. When she lifted her hand, Dalton helped her up. Anna immediately dug her hand in her pocket, and when she clasped the pink quartz, it was as if she'd dived into a cool pool on a really hot summer day. The nausea disappeared, and she was able to move away from the area on her own. "I marked the spot."

Rye smiled. "That's fantastic. We'll get started then."

He motioned to the men, and Jackson carried over a thick piece of plastic about two feet square by three inches high, while Connor walked over with some kind of laser instrument. He held it up to Dalton. "Sweet, right?"

Dalton stepped closer. "That can cut into the cement?"

"Yup. I found this diamond wire cutting instrument that's practically noise free."

That was impressive. "How will you replace the floor when you're done? I didn't see a cement truck outside," Anna said.

Rye smiled and tapped the solid block of plastic. "We'll cut this to fit the space then replace the carpet on top. Where you marked was where the bookcase stood. No one will be the wiser."

Dalton placed a hand on her back. "Let's move to the side and let the men work."

Fine by her. The farther from the sardonyx the better. While she was interested in seeing them work, they didn't need someone standing over them. It was tense enough just thinking someone might catch them—whether it be the sheriff's department, a concerned citizen, or a dreaded Changeling.

Once Anna was seated, Dalton returned to the science fiction section to help. Because only the Emergency lights were on and evening was descending, the store was cast in eerie shadows. She hadn't asked, but she figured Crystal Wedgewood's husband hadn't given them permission to be there. Otherwise, the lights would be blazing.

The saw Connor was using might not be totally silent, but with Rye telling him where to cut, she could barely hear the thing. Anna hoped she hadn't misled them about the location of the stones. She'd feel bad if they had to cut up more than the six-inch by six-inch spot she'd marked.

The drill stopped and then Jackson and Connor huddled over the hole, while the other two watched. As much as she wanted to see them uncover this treasure, Anna remained seated.

"I hit something!" Connor said in a muffled voice.

The tools were discarded, and as best as she could tell by peering between several pairs of legs, they were digging with their hands. Jackson was the first to hold up something that was covered in dirt. She had to assume it was the sardonyx. In silence, the men worked faster. Every few seconds, they'd unearth more stone. How they would know when they found all of the so-called precious treasure, she didn't know.

Rye scooped up the found stones and rushed toward the back, probably to wash them off, and then hopefully put them someplace safe. "Anna would you mind going over to the spot to make sure we didn't miss any?"

"Sure." She went over, but no matter how close she came to the area, she had no reaction. "Nothing's here!"

"Great."

Not wanting to be in the way when they cut the plastic piece, she returned to her seat. A few seconds later, a squeak sounded, and Anna's heart skipped a beat until she realized it was the back door opening. When she spotted Missy looking scared, she jumped up and rushed toward her. "What are you doing here?" Anna asked.

Missy looked around. "It's bad, real bad. Mr. Murdoch had a heart attack." She nodded toward the men in front. "I need to tell Jackson and Kalan."

"Of course, but shouldn't you be with him? Can't you heal him?"

Her heart went out to them. Poor Mr. Murdoch. She'd only met him a handful of times, but he seemed very nice. Missy spoke with the group and then she, Kalan, and Jackson rushed out.

Her eyes widened. "I, ah, did what I could. He's stable now." Missy rushed off.

Now that the gems had been all retrieved, all they had to do was replace the missing cement with the hard plastic, put back the carpet piece they'd cut, and return the bookcase to its original location. This had gone smoother than she had thought.

Dalton came toward her. "Did Missy tell you about Mr. Murdoch?"

"Yes."

"It's such a shame."

"Missy is a good healer. If anyone could help their father, she can."

As Connor finished digging, Rye measured and then cut the plastic to go where the cement had been. Just as he'd pounded it into place, and placed the carpet on top, the back door opened again. Now who was here?

Both of the men who were kneeling jumped up, and Dalton

moved in front of her. "They're here," he said as growls came toward them. "Fuck."

"Who's here? The Changelings?"

"Yes." Dalton remained in front of her as six wolves charged in.

Her heart nearly jumped out of her chest as she grabbed the back of his shirt, ready to run. One dark gray wolf with evil red eyes stalked toward them, while the other five headed toward Rye and Connor. Dalton pressed his hand back to indicate she should not move. That was a command she was willing to obey. If only she could be like Ainsley and disappear, or like Izzy and shoot fire at them.

The wolf howled, and his blood red eyes glowed. The ass acted like he stood a chance against Dalton. Suddenly, fur flew and bones cracked. A second later, Dalton appeared in his tiger form, dwarfing the wolf. The smaller animal growled then stepped back. Dalton, who could move almost as fast as a bullet, lunged at the animal. Bones snapped and a yelp rent the air. When Dalton stepped back, the prone body of the wolf lay on the ground, his formerly red eyes fading to black. A moment later, as the last breath left the wolf's body, he materialized into his human form. Holy shit on a stick. He was naked and very dead.

Dalton roared at her and then took off toward the skirmish. She guessed his angry response meant she should stay put. He wouldn't get any argument from her.

Thanks for leaving me with the dead guy, she mentally chided.

It can't be helped.

Had Dalton just answered her? She must have lost her mind. Seeing a naked dead guy must have caused her brain to malfunction.

Loud, mean growls coming from where Rye, Connor, and Dalton were fighting made her heart pound hard. Anna prayed Dalton could take down most of the Changelings. In comparison to him, the wolves appeared to be slightly larger than big rats.

Five Changelings had surrounded Rye, Connor, and Dalton. Had it not been for Dalton's agility, speed, and size advantage, she would have placed a bet on the Changelings winning.

Teeth gnashed and squeals sounded, as Rye took a light colored wolf by the neck and yanked him around. Two wolves were attacking Connor, while Dalton was holding his own against his two. He rotated toward her, and when she spotted blood dripping down Dalton's flank, she freaked. As much as she wanted to run and get help, she didn't dare leave the building.

Before Anna could decide what she should do, she suddenly twisted and grabbed her side. It was almost as if his pain had entered her body from where a wolf had bit Dalton! Anna staggered backward until she bumped into the wall and jerked from the impact.

From the side door, Sam suddenly rushed in and reached her side just as four additional animals ran in from the hallway with blood dripping from their teeth. Oh, no! When two wolves ran straight at them, her legs weakened. What she wouldn't give to be able to say goodbye to Dalton before she died. The other two charged toward the men.

Sam stepped in front of her like Dalton had and held out his arms. She couldn't let him sacrifice his life for her since he didn't have the ability to shift anymore than she did. Just as she was about to push him aside, the snarling wolves, who were less than three feet from them, both stopped and cocked their heads as if they were trying to determine how to handle both of them.

Then the wolves did the unthinkable—they backed up. The one in the rear actually swayed, and then they both turned tail and jogged back outside.

Sam spun around and grabbed her shoulders. "Are you okay?"

"Yes." *Not at all. I'm quaking from head to toe.*

"That was close," Sam said. "Stay here. I'm going to help the others."

She grabbed his arm. "They'll maul you."

He twisted his head and smiled. "You saw what happened. They won't touch me. Watch."

They hadn't touched either of them this time, but maybe she'd imagined everything from the finding of the stone to the wolves—but she doubted it. Sam sped toward the three men as Dalton helped kill one of the animals attacking Connor. Bodies flew and blood spurted. Glancing at the hallway where the animals had come, she wanted to blockade it to prevent more from arriving, but she didn't dare move. If additional wolves showed up, hopefully Dalton would defend her.

As suddenly as the fray began, the din was replaced with heavy panting and whimpering. How was that possible? Dalton had killed two of the evil wolves, and Rye and Connor had been able to come up with one kill each. The three remaining wolves staggered toward the door. She expected the men to charge after them, but they apparently were going to let them go. What was happening? She had to be in a different dimension. It was the only explanation.

The injured animals disappeared down the hallway. Rye's wolf, who was a beautiful shade of gray and brown, limped toward the same back door and Connor followed him. Now she was even more confused.

Dalton returned to her side and shifted into his human form. As much as she loved seeing him naked, this wasn't the place. Anyone peering in the front window might be able to see him. Dalton gathered her in his arms. "Are you okay?"

"I'm shaken up, but it seems Sam scared the wolves away."

Sam joined them. "If you want to know, I did a little mind meld on them. I was able to get into their heads and convince them that there was no sardonyx here."

"How is that possible?" Sure Wendayans had unique talents, but those kinds of abilities were out of this world. Then again, many of her fellow Wendayans had amazing abilities that no one seemed to be able to explain.

"Beats me. It's just what I do."

"It's impressive." She nodded to the door. "Where did Rye and his brother go?"

"I'm guessing they're making sure those outside don't need additional support," Dalton answered.

Anna's head swam with so many questions. Before she could ask any of them, Sam slipped off his shirt and handed it to Dalton. "You might want to cover up—at least as much as you can. It's not like you can run out to your car in your condition."

"Thanks." Dalton slipped on the oversized shirt. He then toed his shredded clothes. "Damn."

Sam nodded to the bodies. "What should we do with them?"

Before Dalton could answer, Rye and Connor returned fully dressed in their human form, carrying an extra set of clothes.

Rye had a slight smirk on his face as he walked toward Dalton. "The perimeter has been secured." He held out some pants. "Try these on. They might be a bit snug, but they'll cover you."

Dalton pulled on the pair of jeans that barely fit. "My boots might be salvageable," he said, slipping them on. "While they'll function tonight, they're definitely headed for the trash tomorrow."

"I want to thank you for saving our hides," Rye said, holding out his hand to Dalton. "Having someone of your size and strength is a real asset."

While the movement was small, Dalton's shoulders straightened as he shook Rye's hand. He winced then touched his side. Anna did the same thing. They definitely needed to have a talk about these sympathy pains.

"Any time. In all honesty, I haven't been in a fight in a long time. I kind of missed the adrenaline rush."

Rye smiled. "I know what you mean. Why don't you take Anna home? My Clan and I will clean up. We don't need any customers finding blood stains or dead bodies."

Just then Kalan and Jackson charged in, their lips in a thin line and their stride strong. Kalan glanced over at dead men. "I'm glad you killed the bastards."

Rye placed a hand on his Beta's arm. "How's Daniel?"

Kalan shook his head. "Dad's fine. He never was ill. That *person* who looked like Missy was a fucking Changeling."

Why was nothing making sense? She'd spoken with Missy, so why did they say she only looked like her friend? It was Missy. Anna decided to wait until after she and Dalton were alone to ask, though she wasn't sure she'd like the answer.

Rye grabbed Kalan's arm. "That can't be. They can only take a person's form for the first forty-eight hours after the red moon. It's been three days."

Kalan shrugged. "All I know is that Missy never showed up at Dad's. When we arrived there, his cell service had been disrupted so we couldn't call her to check. Once we realized what must have happened and figured we'd been fooled, we came back here. As soon as I had reception, I contacted the real Missy. She said she had been visiting with Izzy all night."

Rye shook his head. "This is really bad."

Chapter Nineteen

BROTHER JACOB HAD no words for the heat and ire racing through his body. How the fuck had his men failed? Again! Sure, they were going against the Alpha and Beta of the Clan, but that was no excuse. His men were well trained.

Brother Jacob paced the small bunker room, waiting for the men responsible for this embarrassing fiasco to arrive. John Ernst told him not only had a few of the men died, there wasn't any sardonyx. Brother Jacob didn't believe it. It smelled of a mutiny. Brother John, at the least, was hiding something from him, he was sure.

Ernst had assured him the stone would be there, but to eliminate his second in command might be the proverbial straw that broke the Council and its members. For now, he'd let the man live.

A knock sounded on the heavy door, and Brother John entered, followed by five men dressed appropriately in their robes. From the scrapes on their faces and the way several were bent over, their wolves hadn't had time to heal their bodies. Too fucking bad.

"Sit," he commanded. Chairs scraped and their gazes remained averted. Thankfully, they acted as if they understood how they'd failed the entire Changeling Clan. "Tell me what happened."

John Ernst looked up. "Brother Carmen did an excellent job portraying Missy Berta. The two Murdoch brothers both believed him, and Carmen was able to lure both brothers back to their home."

"Tell me how without the bears being present, did any of the men die?" Brother Jacob was practically shouting.

"One was a tiger," Brother Richard said.

"A tiger?" Brother Jacob studied them, wondering why they'd come up with such a preposterous lie. "Surely you are mistaken."

Brother John stood. "I've seen the markings on Brother Richard's back. It was a tiger."

"Suppose that's true. It could explain why so many men died, but not how there wasn't any sardonyx."

Brother Richard stood. "When we charged in, it looked like the three of the men had just finished digging. The hole was covered, but there was dirt on the floor. We fought, and then...I don't remember."

Brother Jacob turned around and slammed a hand on the wooden table. "What do you mean you don't remember?"

Brother Richard cleared his throat. "I remember stalking the clansmen, but none of us sensed the stone. The battle was brutal. Then everything went calm."

This time he held his tongue, mostly because he didn't believe a word of it. "Go on."

The man in front of him lowered his gaze. "That's all, sir. They let us live and we left."

Brother Charles stood. "I had something equally strange happen. Two humans were there with them—the girl and a man. Henry and I charged, but the next thing I remember is that we were outside fighting others."

An unpleasant conclusion was forming. Right now, if the bear and wolf Clan had found the stone, it was too late to retrieve it. However, the town had plenty more. To find it, however, would require that girl.

"Bring me this woman. And don't fail this time."

The men grumbled. Tough. If the Changelings were to survive, they needed more sardonyx.

"WOULD YOU MIND staying at my place tonight?" Dalton asked

Anna as he drove them to town. "I don't want you to be alone, and your bed is rather small for the two of us." He plucked the fabric from his leg. "Besides, I need a real change of clothes."

"Of course," Anna said. "I don't want to be alone either, not to mention I have a shitload of questions."

Guilt stabbed him. "I'm sorry. I should have filled you in on what Changelings are like, but I didn't want to overwhelm you."

She looked over at him. "I wasn't talking about them, though I was totally taken aback how that person could look and act so much like Missy, but not be Missy. I mean she knew who was who."

Dalton pulled behind her building. "That really shook up Rye too." As Dalton helped her out, he explained about their red moon and how if they touched a person, they had only two additional days in which to become an image of that person. "Only this Changeling was able to last three days."

"How is that possible?"

"Beats me." He didn't think Rye knew either. "Just like I still don't understand how Sam can alter what people are thinking."

"I know, right?" She explained how one minute two of the wolves were about to attack and the next they were walking away.

His gut soured. "I never should have left your side."

Anna punched in the code to the building, and he followed her upstairs. "You didn't know more wolves would appear. You were busy fighting your own battle. Besides, if they had come any closer, I would have run, darting in between and around all of the bookcases. I might have been able to tire them out. Though to be honest, I was so scared, it didn't occur to me to do that until just now."

The whole thing was too close for comfort. He couldn't wait until the white moon so Anna could shift. Then he'd teach her to defend herself.

The moment they stepped into the apartment, his tiger went wild remembering them making love earlier tonight. Their lovemaking scent still lingered in the air.

"I'll pack a few things," she said.

Dalton didn't follow her into the bedroom. Not only had they made love a few hours ago, she'd been through a lot and needed some alone time to process things. He was willing to bet that Anna had never seen a dead body before. During the fight with the Changelings, he'd glanced over and seen her watching the tussle. Hearing the growls and shrieks of death would forever be imprinted in her head. At least his adrenaline had been pumping so fast that he barely remembered killing those wolves.

A soft whistling sound came from the bedroom. Either Anna was happy to be staying with him or else she was still scared. Not able to keep away any longer, he entered her small bedroom.

"Are you okay?" he telepathed. When he'd heard her voice in his head at the bookstore, he'd been stunned. Sure, he'd been told telepathy between two mates happened, but he never thought he'd be able to do it.

She spun around and smiled. *"I am now."*

Before she asked, he held up his hand. "I don't know how this works, just that it does."

"I'm glad. It's cool. It's like only we can be in the conversation."

She turned back to packing, tossing a pair of jeans, two pairs of shorts, and a couple of tops into a suitcase. From what he could tell, her bras and panties were already in there—not that she would need them. He planned to keep her naked and very busy once they were at his place.

Anna stepped past him and made more noise in the bathroom. She returned with a pouch that he suspected contained her toiletries. "Anything else you want to ask me?" he asked.

"Sam explained what he did. I am curious about what the Changelings are going to do with those men who returned without any of the sardonyx? Won't they want some kind of retaliation?"

His heart pumped faster. "Most likely yes, but the battle for power between them and Rye's Clan has apparently been going on for a long time."

She closed her case. "So all the shifters live on edge, waiting for the Changelings' next attack?"

The way she described it sounded so bleak. "I guess that's one way to look at it, but most of the time they leave us alone."

"Not when it comes to sardonyx."

"That's true." He'd have to have a talk with Jackson about not involving Anna any more. If the Changelings ever found out about her power, they'd try to use it for their own good. He picked up her suitcase. "Ready?"

"You bet." She smiled, and his tiger roared.

ALL LAST NIGHT, Dalton had wanted to tell Anna about Meredith Wilson possibly being her mother, but until Merry was released from jail, he wouldn't. The woman he was fast falling in love with deserved to have a better reunion with her mother than in a cell. Plus, once they had arrived at his place, there wasn't much talking happening, as their mutual need for each other was too strong. They spent the night lost in each other's passion, making love and pushing away the awful thoughts of what they experienced at the bookstore.

As soon as Dalton arrived at work, he received word from the tech department that Merry's computer had not been tampered with, and that the messages had the correct time stamp.

Happy to have her alibi confirmed, he contacted the district attorney and asked that the charges to be dismissed. That conversation went well, but the one to the judge didn't. He called Dalton a few names and told him to be better prepared next time if he ever wanted a warrant again. In the end, the judge gave Dalton Merry's release paper. Why Dalton felt so guilty about the whole ordeal he didn't know. He'd done his job. The facts pointed to her as the killer, which meant he had every right to arrest her.

After he licked his wounds, he called his sister. While she was pleased Dalton had worked quickly to have the charges dropped, Jillian said he should have been more diligent before arresting her. He couldn't argue with her there.

As soon as he hung up from speaking with his sister, Kalan came in. He said nothing as he pulled out his desk chair, sat down, and booted up his computer. His partner must still be steamed about being diverted from the fight. In truth, he, Rye, and Connor—and of course, Sam—had been able to handle who they'd sent.

Dalton went over to his partner's desk and leaned a hip on the corner. "You have to let it go."

Kalan didn't look up. "I can't. I should have suspected they'd pull something like this."

"It'll eat you alive if you let it. No one could have seen this coming."

Kalan let out a breath and finally looked at him. "I know, but it's hard. It didn't help that as Jackson and I drove to my parents' house, I pictured my father dying." His jaw trembled. "Jackson called Mom but couldn't get a hold of her. He spoke with our sister, and Blair nearly had a heart attack herself. I'm not sure she'll ever forgive me or Jackson."

Dalton didn't know what to say. He never was very good dealing with emotions. "The only way to take your mind off of this is to figure out who killed Crystal Wedgewood."

Kalan perked up. "You're right."

Dalton explained that the judge would be sending out Meredith's release papers later this morning. "When he does, I'll drive her home. I want to ask her if she could be Anna's mom."

"How can she be sure?"

"If she gave up a child for adoption, I can suggest both she and Anna take a blood test."

Kalan nodded. "Good idea. So where are you on the investigation?"

He told him about seeing Julie and Carlton kissing. "That doesn't mean much."

"I know, but it adds one more piece to the puzzle. With Meredith in the clear, and no gunshot residue on Carlton's clothes, we need to take a serious look at the other three suspects."

"What should be our plan if the Changelings killed Crystal because she decided to renege on selling the property?"

"We're basically screwed unless the lab missed something in their analysis."

Kalan twirled a pen on his knuckles then pointed it at Dalton. "Could be Carlton killed his wife, then was smart enough to change his clothes. His hands were bloody, making the detection of GSR difficult."

"It's possible he wore gloves at the time of the murder."

"True."

"Anna also suggested that possibility. Without us having access to that other shirt, however, Carlton might have pulled off the perfect murder."

"Damn."

Dalton stood. "I need to wait for the signed paper from the judge and then take Merry home. Do you want to check out either Tom DeLuca or Linda Darnell?"

"I'll take Tom. Even if he's at work, I wouldn't mind making sure we didn't leave any evidence in the store."

Dalton liked that idea. "That works for me."

He returned to his desk and decided to do a little bit more research on Linda Darnell. Jackson said he'd look into Julie Dominick and whether she had any problems at the University of Tennessee where they both went to school.

About an hour later, the delivery he'd been waiting for arrived. After he logged in the release document, Meredith was brought out. The poor woman had bags under eyes, and her shoulders were slumped.

"Mrs. Wilson," he said, wanting to give her the respect she deserved, "I'd like to drive you home."

She nodded. "Thank you. I'd call my husband, but he isn't supposed to drive until the doctor gives him the okay."

"I understand. I'm very sorry this happened."

She reached out and touched his hand. "You had a job to do. I understand."

Dalton was about to argue that if he'd been more thorough, she might not have had to spend even one night in jail, but he decided to accept her comment. "Thank you. I know you want to get home to your husband as quickly as possible, but I'd like to speak with you about something personal. Could I buy you a cup of coffee?"

Chapter Twenty

MEREDITH'S FEATURES PINCHED. "I guess. I really could go for a good cup. The service in your hotel was less than stellar."

He chuckled. The bad coffee was his biggest gripe about working there. "Tell me about it."

Because the Silver Lake Café was several blocks away, he drove. During the short trip, Meredith sat with her back rigid and gazed out the side window. Not that he could blame her, but it was as if she thought he was driving her to her execution instead of setting her free.

When he parked in front of the Café, he rushed to her side to help her out. She stood then faced him. "Is this about Crystal's death? Did you figure out who murdered her? Or do you need me to do a little snooping?"

He couldn't keep back his smile. As sure as he was standing there, Merry Wilson was his mate's mother—determined, strong, and sassy. "It's not about the murder, and no I don't know who is responsible, but you have given me an idea. Come inside."

Once seated, they each ordered a large black coffee. Meredith added a piece of apple pie to her order. Dalton refrained. Now came the hard part. If he mentioned Anna's talent of being able to see into a person's past and the woman before him wasn't a Wendayan, he'd have a lot of explaining to do. However, at some point, he might have to tell her about what Anna was capable of.

The waitress brought over the coffee, and that first sip hit the spot. If he messed things up between Anna and her mother, she'd never forgive him. "Merry, I asked you here because during my investigation I uncovered something." Technically, that was true since he had learned her maiden name matched that of Anna's birth mom. He wouldn't have thought anything of it had Anna not told him about her vision.

She picked up her cup and her hands shook. "What was it?"

"Anna Fairchild was given up at birth in Montana by a woman whose name was Mary Carlyle, only I'm wondering if Anna didn't misunderstand, and it really was Merry Carlyle."

Merry's face paled. "You think that's me?"

He leaned back in his chair and studied her face. "You tell me. Anna is twenty-five, and her birthday is Oct 17th. Does that ring a bell?"

She set her cup down. "Anna is…my daughter?"

For the first time in his career, he couldn't tell if her stunned expression was one of dismay or disbelief. "You tell me."

"How did you find out?" She glanced off to the side. "I told no one."

"You'll have to ask Anna, assuming she's your daughter. A blood test can confirm or deny it."

Merry faced him again, her breath coming out fast. "I did have to give up a daughter on October 17th, twenty-five years ago. Oh, my God. I never thought I'd find her." Tears streamed down her cheeks, and she wiped them away. "You must think I'm terrible, giving her up, but I had my reasons."

"I'm sure you did." Merry probably hadn't been more than a kid herself when Anna was born.

She bit down on her lip. "I'm so confused. I should be jumping up and down, but I guess I'm afraid she'll hate me—assuming it is her."

He reached across the table and placed a hand on hers. "That's where you're wrong. If Anna is your daughter, I can assure you that she is the most forgiving person you'll ever meet. You know her—

albeit as a customer. How do you think she'll react?"

"She's always sweet, unlike some of our customers. Did she ever say if she had a tattoo of a vine on the back of her shoulder?"

He smiled. Her Wendayan stamp. "She has a lot of tattoos, but that marking isn't a tattoo, is it?"

Her cheeks reddened. "No."

Well, well. Dalton couldn't wait to hear this story. A blood test might not be needed after all.

"ANNA?" ELANA CALLED from the front of the store.

Even though Anna was in the middle of cutting the baby's breath for the arrangement she was working on, her boss must need her to retrieve something from the back room. Anna rushed to the door that separated the two rooms and stuck her head out. "What do you need?"

"You have company." When Elana nodded toward Meredith, joy spread through Anna.

She'd been released! *I knew she was innocent.*

"Meredith, so good to see you." Anna wiped her palms on her apron, a bit confused why the manager of a bookstore would take the time to stop by and see her. Sure, she read, but Anna didn't buy that many paperbacks. Oh, crap. She probably wanted to see if she was still suffering any after effects of being in the science fiction section of her store. "How can I help you?"

Meredith looked over Anna's shoulder into the other room. "Is there someplace where we can talk in private?"

That sounded ominous. She hoped someone else hadn't been murdered at the store. Even if they had, why come to her? Anna glanced to Elana who nodded. "Sure, we can chat in the back room."

Her heart suddenly dropped to her stomach. Dalton must have mentioned the vision Anna had seen, and her blood pressure shot up. He had no right.

Meredith appeared uncomfortable more than upset, so perhaps

she wasn't here to chastise her for intruding in her privacy, though it wasn't like Anna could help it that she saw things.

Once in the back room, Anna moved her vase, scissors, cuttings, and flowers she had yet to place into the arrangement off to the side. She then dragged the chair from the desk to an area next to the counter and motioned for Meredith to sit.

She shook her head. "I'm too nervous. I'd rather stand. Actually, I'd rather pace."

Okay, that wasn't good. "What is it? Is it about Crystal?"

"No. I spoke with Officer Garner, and he mentioned that you'd been adopted."

Chills covered her. Her past was something she kept private. "I was."

Meredith grabbed the back of the chair. "Maybe I do need to sit down. I want to tell you something about me."

Anna hopped up on the counter, feeling more secure up there. It was where she sat when she wanted to think. "Go on."

"I'm not sure where to start, so I'll start at the beginning. I was seventeen and a senior in high school. I'd been accepted to Bozeman State University in Montana and was so happy. My life was perfect. I had a bright future, and I was in love. My boyfriend, Tommy Sanders, and I wanted to do something romantic on Valentine's Day, so I suggested we steal away to my parents' cabin in the mountains." A small smile lifted her lips. "If they'd known what I was planning to do, they would have locked me in my room. I told them a bunch of my girlfriends and I wanted to spend the weekend there, and they actually believed me."

While Anna wasn't sexually promiscuous, she never had parents who cared enough to question where she was or what she did. "I take it something happened?"

"Yes. My father, who was a powerful and influential man, loved me in his own way, but he also wanted to control me. I was never allowed to do anything even remotely crazy since it would shed a *bad light* on the family." She waved a hand. "Long story short, Tommy and I had a wonderful and wild fling."

The image returned of her holding a baby with an older couple looking on. She could fill in the blanks. "And you became pregnant?"

Her eyes widened. "Yes, how did—"

"Why else go to a secluded place with a hot guy if not to have some privacy?" Perhaps Dalton hadn't mentioned her vision after all.

"True. Stupid me, I was certain that I couldn't get pregnant, but I did."

Anna placed a hand on her stomach, not sure what she'd been thinking having unprotected sex with Dalton. Now that they were mated, it might turn out to be a good thing. "What happened?"

"My parents were furious. The scandal nearly killed my dad."

"And Tommy? How did he react?" Most young men didn't want the responsibility.

Meredith smiled. "He was so excited about being a father that he asked me to marry him."

"That's sweet. I'm glad you had support."

"Me too." A dark cloud passed over her face, and she looked off to the side. Meredith pressed her lips together, and her chin trembled. "A week after I graduated from high school, we were going to be married. We'd decided to elope since my parents said they were cutting me off. No college, no nothing. I didn't care. I was having a baby and marrying the man I loved. How we were going to support ourselves, I wasn't sure, but he had a good job as a garage mechanic."

This was a lovely story, albeit a sad one, but Anna wasn't sure why Meredith was telling her. They weren't exactly friends. "So are you still married to him?"

"No. Tommy was killed in a car wreck on his way to pick me up for the wedding."

Anna sucked in a breath. She couldn't think of anything more tragic. "I'm so sorry."

Meredith dragged a hand down her face, her eyes watery. "Thank you. I had the baby, but without Tommy, I realized I couldn't work and raise a child, so I had to give it up for adoption."

That must have been the vision she'd seen. Like a huge wave crashing down on her, reality sunk in. "When was the child's birthday?"

"My daughter was born October 17th. She'll be twenty-six this year." Merry looked up at Anna.

"And you think that child might be me?"

She stood. "You are."

A million questions bombarded her. "How do you know?"

Meredith smiled. "Your detective shared a few things about you. The most important piece of information was that you have a Wendayan stamp on the back of your shoulder."

Dalton knew Merry was her mom yet said nothing? Her gut clenched. "Why is my stamp so important?"

"Because Tommy was a Wendayan. Our daughter would have his stamp too. I know that's not one hundred percent proof that you are my daughter, so I brought this." She dug her hand into her purse, extracted a piece of paper, and handed it to her. "It's my daughter's birth certificate. I named her Anna."

"I never knew."

"I didn't either until now. I'm so pleased your new parents kept the name."

Anna gripped the edge of the counter and then pushed off. Excitement, anger, and confusion all bombarded her. Anna was overwhelmed with emotion at possibly finding her mother, but feeling a bit betrayed that Dalton knew Meredith was her mother but said nothing.

Anna straightened her shoulders. "I was told my mother's name was Mary Carlyle."

Meredith fumbled in her purse and withdrew her driver's license. "That's me. Meredith Carlyle Wilson, or Merry for short."

Anna gazed down at the license then back at the woman in front of her. The two of them were about the same height, though Merry was an inch shorter, and they had the same color hair. There was a slight similarity in their facial features, but she wouldn't say they looked alike. "I'm speechless."

Merry swiped a finger under her eyes. "Me too. I never in a million years thought I'd find you."

"You looked?"

"Of course, I looked. Giving you up was the worst day in my life. That and being arrested for something I didn't do." She blew out a breath. "And the day Tommy died."

Anna had to hold onto the counter again, trying to regain her balance. She'd just learned that she already knew her mom. Learning her father was dead was another blow. Totally confused, she looked at Merry Carlyle Wilson, who seemed as overwhelmed as she was. "This is probably awkward, but can I hug you?" Anna asked, sniffling.

Merry, or rather Mom, opened her arms, and suddenly it was as if the whole world was smiling down on her. Anna stepped into her embrace and let her warmth surround her. Not used to being close to people, Anna moved back. "I have so many questions."

"I imagine you do."

"Tell me about my dad."

"He was such a free spirit." Merry ran a hand down over Anna's bare arm. "I imagine you're a lot like him."

Her heart swelled. "I wish I'd met him."

"Me too."

"What were his talents?" She already had enough, but she didn't need any more surprises.

"Tommy was unique. He could touch a person and see something about their past."

Anna's heart rate spiked. "I can too."

Merry moved closer and placed a hand on her shoulder. "Do you see it as a curse? That's what Tommy used to say."

"For the most part." She explained what she'd seen when she'd touched Merry at the store. Anna was rather surprised that the hug didn't bring out more images. Then again, her mind was too busy spinning.

"That was me holding you. The people you saw were my parents. I think they came to make sure you were taken away."

"I'm sorry." She couldn't imagine giving up a child. "Are you a Wendayan?"

"No. I only found out about Tommy's talent when he'd touched my arm and had a strange reaction. He explained what he could about Wendayans."

"I didn't learn about them until I moved here." Now wasn't the time to get into the circumstances under which she learned about them.

"I always hoped you were adopted by a good family"

"Yes, I was but I just never felt really close to them."

Her lips trembled again. "I'm sorry. I've regretted every day of my life that I had to give you up, but I couldn't have taken care of you."

"I understand."

"Thank you." Merry dug her hand into her purse, located a tissue, and blew her nose. "I'm not sure what's supposed to happen next."

How did one step into the person's life and pretend the last twenty-five years had been different? "I don't know either, but we need to learn more about each other. Catch up."

"I already feel like I've found the missing piece to my soul," Merry said.

Anna wanted to share more of her life with her newfound mom. "You'll find out soon enough, but Officer Garner and I are dating." She didn't want to bring up the topic of shifters just yet.

Merry smiled. "I figured. As soon as he spoke your name, his eyes lit up."

The man did have good eyes. "I heard your husband is ill."

"Yes. George is having problems with his heart, and he's only sixty-three. It's very sad."

Anna retrieved her phone from the counter. "Let me have your number."

Merry pulled out her cell. "What's yours? I'll call you and then you'll have mine."

Once they swapped numbers, Merry said she needed to return to the store. "Stay in touch," Anna said.

Merry chuckled. "You don't have to worry about that. I'll never lose touch with you again."

Wow. All these years she'd been looking for her, and to think she'd met her two years ago. Life was just so strange. Anna walked her out and then stood by the window as she watched Merry climb into her Volkswagen. They were alike in more ways than she'd thought.

"What did she want?" Elana asked once Anna turned around.

"You'll never guess."

Chapter Twenty-One

WHEN DALTON RETURNED to the station after dropping Merry off at her house, he wanted to tell Anna what he'd learned, but Merry had asked that she be the one to tell her. While Anna wouldn't be happy with him, he needed to respect Merry's request.

Kalan wasn't at his desk, which meant he was most likely checking out Tom DeLuca. Dalton needed to get on the stick and see what Linda Darnell was up to. Meredith had told him that Linda didn't work today or tomorrow, which meant she might be home. Merry had also scribbled down Tom's and Ed's schedule.

Wanting to be as inconspicuous as possible when he watched Linda, Dalton stepped into the locker rooms at the back of the station and changed into his civilian clothes. Using his own vehicle like he had before, he headed to Linda's house. What he expected to learn from her off-work hours, he didn't know, but often times when a person thought they'd gotten away with a crime, they became careless.

On his way to the stakeout, he called Jackson who answered right away. "Dalton, what's up?"

"Just wondering if you've found any dirt on your fellow alumni?" Dalton asked.

"I'm just finishing up now. Turns out, Miss Dominick was having an affair with her married business professor, a Mr. Ralph Teasdale, but they broke up after his wife died of suspicious causes."

Dalton whistled and his pulse spiked. "Did the police think she was responsible?"

"The case was never solved."

"Interesting. That just shot her up to the front of the class."

"She was questioned but never brought in," Jackson said. "Other than that, her file looks clean."

"I appreciate the info." Dalton would have to revisit her just in case since he didn't believe in coincidences.

"Do you need any other help?" Jackson asked. "Connor is looking for something for Sam to do. He's in training, and the more work we can give him the better. Besides, if he works for free, the client won't complain." Jackson chuckled.

Dalton pulled into a convenience store so he could rethink his plan. "As a matter of fact I do."

At the end of the conversation, they decided that Sam would watch Linda Darnell while Dalton kept tabs on Ed Santaria. Even though Sam had many talents with the beasts, if those talents failed, they'd kill him. Dalton, however, could probably handle several wolves at a time.

Everyone, including Rye and Kalan, was convinced that Ed had been involved with the higher up Changelings in either the sale of the store or somehow in figuring out when their Clan had planned to dig up the sardonyx. It was the only logical explanation for the leak.

"I have one more thing to ask," Dalton said.

"What's that?" Jackson asked.

When Dalton finished explaining his need, he turned around and returned to town. Because Anna wouldn't get off work for another hour, Dalton had time to do a bit more research into Ed's dealing with his fellow wolves. Jackson said he'd dig too.

Before he saw Anna, Dalton had to figure out the best way to handle the dicey situation regarding her newfound mother. Knowing Anna, she'd be in quite an emotional state after realizing her dream. What she wouldn't be pleased about was that he hadn't called her right away and told her about Merry, but he had his reasons. One way to help smooth the way between them was to do something spontaneous. She'd like that.

Then the irony hit him. What was the definition of spontaneity anyway? If something took a bit of planning, did it count as being spur of the moment? Hell, if he knew. The fact he just thought of it and would execute his plan within a day was good enough for him.

After a futile attempt at learning more about Ed Santaria and his connection to the Changeling Council members, Dalton headed to the grocery store. When he arrived home with the goodies in hand, he placed them in the basket he'd had to buy. He figured a cooler didn't say romance like a picnic basket.

Shortly after the Bloom's of Hope closed, he called Anna, but she didn't answer. Shit. His gut soured. His mate connection could sense she was pissed, so he left a voice message, but nothing short of a visit would do. He could have used telepathy, but if she was trying to avoid him, he wanted to give her some room to stew.

Disconnecting, he picked up his surprise and headed to her place. After their last lovemaking session, Anna had given him the code to the back door, but that didn't mean she'd let him in her apartment. However, once she sensed him, her developing animal side wouldn't be able to refuse him—or so he hoped.

With the picnic basket in hand, he strode up the back staircase and knocked. "Anna, please let me in. I can explain."

As she neared the door from the inside, his tiger woke up. She eased it open a few seconds later. "Why didn't you tell me about my mother?" she asked, her lips remaining firm.

He hadn't wanted the conversation to go like this. *"Because she asked me not to tell you. She wanted to be the one,"* he telepathed, needing that connection with her.

"I guess that makes sense," she said. Anna lowered her gaze to what he was carrying. "What's that?"

He lifted up the basket. "I thought we could go on a picnic."

She opened up the door. "Really?"

Excitement rushed through him at the thrill in her voice. That was easy—too easy. The moment her scent reached his tiger, he was tempted to toss the damn thing down the stairs and drag her into bed. Her hair might be in a neat ponytail and her plain white blouse and jeans covered most of her, but his body was thrumming with pleasure at being close to her. "Really."

"Why?" she asked as she slipped the basket from his fingers.

"The truth?" She nodded. "It's a peace offering."

"Oh."

Damn. Her mad state returned. "I need to explain. Two days ago I figured out that Meredith, or rather Merry Wilson, might be your mother after I spotted her maiden name."

Anna planted a hand on her hip. "Why not tell me then?"

"At the time she was in jail, and if she had been guilty of murder, I didn't want you to know what your mom had done. Besides, I wanted to ask her first about whether she could be your mom before I got your hopes up."

Her shoulders relaxed a bit. "When did you know for sure?"

"This morning, but until you get a blood test, I'm not sure how you can be sure."

"I'm sure. Merry had my birth certificate with my name on it."

"That's great." He waited for her to say more, but she stood there gnawing on her lip, probably digesting the information. "So how did the meeting go?" he asked.

As if he'd said some magic word, Anna snapped out of her daze and smiled. "Wonderful. I think I was in shock for most of it though."

"What did she say?"

Anna recounted the conversation about why her mom had to give her up. The death of Tommy seemed to shake Anna.

"How tragic. Did you believe her?"

"Yes, why wouldn't I? My dad was a Wendayan, as am I."

"If you're sure that's all that matters."

"I am, but I will get the blood test just in case I'm wrong."

He hugged her. "I'm very happy for you."

"Me too."

Even the skeptic in him had to admit Merry Carlyle Wilson seemed to be Anna's birth mother. "Since I have a basket full of food, do you want to go on a picnic?"

"I'd love to, but the weather doesn't look so good." She stepped over to the window. "Thunder clouds are everywhere."

Damn. He'd been so focused on Anna that he hadn't notice. "Then how about we eat here?"

Good idea. It's closer to the bed, his tiger said.

You're a pig, she telepathed right back.

Dalton cracked up. He had no idea she could hear his tiger! "I can see I need to work on blocking my thoughts better—or rather my tiger's thoughts."

"No. I like knowing what you're both thinking," she said.

"You don't need my tiger to tell you." He nodded to the floor. "Do you want to put down a blanket or something? We can pretend we're in a grassy field with the tinkling of a small stream whispering in the distance."

"That's perfect." She smiled, and his heart cracked. He loved this woman. He really did.

Together they spread out a blanket she'd located from her linen closet and placed the basket on top. Dalton opened the wine and poured it into the plastic cups he'd brought. "I hope you like fried chicken," he said, taking out the food.

"I do."

At the store, he realized how little he knew about the woman who was becoming everything to him. "What else do you like?"

"Hmm, let me see." Her eyes shone. She picked up a strawberry, bit off the end, and then slowly seduced the poor fruit.

Dalton might have been able to keep in control had she not moaned. "Stop it."

"What? You asked what I liked, so I wanted to show you."

"I meant, what else do you like to eat?"

She picked up the bag of potato chips and broke it open. "I like to lick salty things."

She was so going down. "What else?" he asked, enjoying the game she was playing.

Running her fingers on the basket lid, she made tiny swirls with her forefinger. "I do like to eat, but I like to touch things more."

Wait until after she shifted, then Anna wouldn't be able to say those kinds of things without pouncing on him. "Me too. Maybe you'd like to touch something besides that basket."

"You mean something hard? And throbbing? Or are you talking more about bumpy things?"

Bumpy things? Did she mean his pecs or possibly his abs? It didn't matter.

Dalton set down his glass and stood. When he held out his arms, Anna grabbed his hands and stood up then practically disappeared into the bedroom. He followed her. "Why did you rush in here?"

Please say because you want me to ravish you.

"I do," she responded. When she moved closer to him, his libido went crazy. "All that talk about touching has me too excited. Food held little interest once I thought about what we could be doing."

Wrapping his arms around her waist, he nipped at her lips. "Oh, yeah, what's that?"

Her fingers clutched his cock through his pants. "This."

He laughed. "You got it." Dalton ditched his shoes and stepped out of his pants. The shirt was easy to discard. All through his little strip tease, Anna hadn't moved. Instead, she just stared at him. "Need help with your clothes?" he asked.

"I do."

She ran her hands down her hips, and his tiger went wild. Starved for her, he undid the buttons on her shirt with great efficiency and then peeled her blouse down her shoulders. Once off, he bent down and kissed her neck before traveling lower. "I love your rose tattoos. They are so you."

Dalton wrapped an arm around her waist and pressed his chest against her. Anna's lips parted, and he dove down, devouring her offering. If he weren't careful, his tiger would emerge just when he was ready to impale her. She was everything he wanted in a woman—self reliant, sassy, and best of all—his.

When her hands grabbed his butt, he slid his fingers along her spine, loving how the soft curve led to her delicious ass. "We need to get rid of these pants."

She plopped down on the bed, kicked off her sandals, and then ditched her jeans. The moment he spotted her black panties, his mouth watered, and his blue orb vibrated, creating waves of color around him.

He slid his hands under her legs and moved her to the middle of the bed. Straddling her, he unhooked her bra and tossed it to the side. "Now for the pièce de résistance."

Anna giggled. "You are a romantic. Don't deny it."

"You've made me one." Sliding down between her legs, Dalton tugged on her panties and pulled them off.

He inhaled and growled, his tiger refusing to wait any longer. The first swipe of his tongue had him soaring, and her taste once more became imprinted on his brain. His tiger demanded a quick release, but Dalton wanted to wait. Anna deserved to feel loved.

She pressed her feet into the bed and lifted up. "More."

He answered by flicking her tiny nub with his tongue while he reached up, cupped her breast, and kneaded it. Her glow grew with each twist of her nipple and swirl of his tongue, while her sex perfumed the air.

As Anna tugged on his shoulders, her nails dug into his skin as she panted out small gasps of air. Her eyes were shut. She was close, and he wanted to push her over the edge several times before he took his release. Lifting his head, he slipped a finger into her wet opening, and as soon as he pressed on her trigger point, she yelled and bucked. Sparks flew inside her blue orb, and then she dropped onto the bed, expelling a big sigh.

Easy woman.

She patted his shoulder. "That was awesome," she said.

As much as he wanted to keep licking her, she'd weakened his control. Dalton crawled on top of her, putting his weight on his elbows. "I hope you aren't done?"

She winked. "Never. Just taking a breather."

ANNA SHOULD NEVER have questioned Dalton's integrity. He had two good reasons for not telling her about Meredith being her mother. And to think he understood her well enough to know she'd be upset was beyond wonderful. No doubt about it, she loved Dalton Garner. His bringing over the picnic lunch was even more proof that they belonged together.

She stroked his head as he played with her hair. He lifted the strands to his nose and inhaled. "You smell so good," he whispered.

His tender touch and wonderful words excited her as much as any lick could. "Would you like some reciprocating love?" she asked.

He looked up, his brows pinched. "Does that mean you want to suck on my dick?"

She had to work hard not to laugh. "Yes, I want to make love to your hard tumescent shaft."

He cracked up, just as she'd hoped. His glow ebbed for a moment and then grew again. "Only if you want to, but I'm ready to burst as it is."

She loved his taste and how much power she felt when she pumped her fist and sucked on him hard.

Dalton rolled over and folded his hands behind his head, looking super sexy. Already his chest hair was sprinkled with his tiger's white hairs, and his teeth had sharpened.

Don't get distracted. He won't last long. Even Anna could sense his urgency.

"You got that right," he telepathed back.

Damn, she needed to remember he could hear her thoughts when she was thinking about him.

When she drew him into her mouth, her inner walls cramped

with need. Ever since the first time he bit her, her body had slowly been changing, and she could almost feel her own tiger growing from within. With every day that passed, she yearned to be with him more and more.

On the next stroke and lick of her tongue, a dribble of cum trickled into her mouth. He was so about to explode. As Anna readied to crawl on top of him, he slipped out from under her and growled. Ooh, she'd excited the Alpha in him.

"Get on your elbows and knees," he commanded.

Oh, how she loved when he came from behind. Obeying, she did as he asked. As he leaned over her, he widened her legs and pressed his cock against her opening. Her heart swelled with love for him.

Cupping her breasts and rolling her nipples between his fingers, he plunged in, stretching her way too wide. "Ah, it's too big," she managed to eke out.

"All the better to love you with, my dear," answered Dalton.

When he kissed her neck, she relaxed those inner muscles that had a firm grip on him, and the slight pain subsided. Slowly he withdrew, but continued to nibble on her neck all the while gently pinching and pulling on her sensitive nipples. His tender touch, along with his scent and his larger-than-life presence made her wild with need. Anna pressed her hips back to signal she was ready, and the next thrust sent spikes of lust all over her body. Her hands and arms pulsed blue as he drove into her again and again. The hairs on his chest turned coarser and his palms on her breasts, rougher.

Maybe it was her imagination, but when she ran her tongue along her teeth, they'd sharpened too. Holy hell.

"Anna, I love you," he whispered, his lips pressed against the shell of her ear.

The emotion from today along with his loving words caused tears of joy to well up in her eyes. *"Back at you."* she telepathed, unable to speak.

She did love him, but saying the words was so very hard for her.

Dalton scraped his teeth against her neck as he tunneled into her, and joy spread over every inch of her body.

"Oh, baby." Dalton wrapped his arms around her waist and sunk his teeth into her neck. A moment later, his hot seed filled her, and her orgasm claimed her hard, taking her to new heights.

Grabbing her elbows to keep balanced, a strong vision of the two of them racing in a field filled her head. As they loped together, total bliss came rushing into her. Never had she been so happy. They were mates forever.

Chapter Twenty-Two

FOR THE NEXT few days, Anna remained beyond happy. She'd found her birth mother, and Dalton told her he loved her. Life couldn't get any better than that. To quell the naysayers, she and Merry—Mom—decided to have their blood tested, but Anna wasn't worried. She was confident it would prove she was Merry's daughter.

The only negative right now was that Dalton had to spend a lot of time keeping a close eye on the remaining suspects for Crystal Wedgewood's murder. She understood he had a job to do, but the timing sucked since she didn't like being away from him when their relationship was still in its infancy. While the white moon had yet to appear, she swore her tiger was developing, which meant her intense desire for him was hard to deny.

It was close to four o'clock and because business had slowed so much, Elana decided to leave early. She said she was missing Aiden. Anna was okay with that. It gave her more time to dream about Dalton while she cleaned up.

Close to closing, her cell rang. It was Jillian. "Hey, stranger," Anna said, hopping up onto the back counter.

"I know, right? Work has been crazy, but I thought if I wait until work slows down, I'd never call. I was wondering if you wanted to grab some dinner and a drink tonight. I know Dalton is working crazy late hours."

"He is. I'd love to do dinner," Anna said. "Where and when?"

"You okay with McKinnon's Pub and Pool?"

"Sure."

"How about tonight at 7:00? Or is that too late? I have a ton of work I want to finish before I relax," Jillian said.

"Sounds perfect." Returning to the pub would bring back a happy memory, since it was where she and Dalton had their first date. Because of his busy schedule, they had yet to return and play another game.

As soon as Jillian disconnected, she texted Dalton to say she was going to practice at the shooting range and then go out with his sister. Anna wouldn't be surprised if he had been instrumental in setting up the date since he was always saying how guilty he felt when he had to work late.

After she closed up the shop, Anna rushed upstairs to her apartment to change. While she was meeting Jillian for drinks and some dinner, afterward she planned to stop over and see Dalton, so she wanted to look her best. Yesterday, she'd splurged and bought this cute turquoise bra and panty set that matched the roses on her tattoo, and she couldn't wait to model it for him.

To mask the surprise, she pulled on a pair of jeans and a rather plain, body-fitting pink top. Once ready, she headed to the shooting range, hoping to feel closer to him. It was where he'd first asked her out, yet Anna hadn't been back since that time. Even though no one had threatened her life recently, it wouldn't hurt to hone her skills.

The image of those snarling wolves at the bookstore surfaced, and she decided to revamp her opinion about not having been threatened. Thank goodness Sam had shown up when he did and performed his mind voodoo on those Changelings, or she might have been injured or killed, especially since she'd been too freaked out to run. Even if she had a gun with her, she doubted she would have had the time to draw the pistol and shoot.

Once at the range, she rushed inside, excited to practice since it might be something she and Dalton could do together in the future. Most of the stations were free, so she stepped to the end lane and set her gun on the counter. Once she loaded it, she tried to remember everything Dalton had taught her about the grip and her stance.

Confident she was ready, she shot off a round. However, when she checked her success, it wasn't as good as she'd hoped. For the next half hour, Anna focused more, pretending those snarling wolves were the target instead of a black outline of a man.

When her arms grew tired, she set down her weapon. Only then did she notice that Linda Darnell was practicing in one of the booths. That was cool. It was nice to see another woman at the range honing her skills.

Anna had to meet Jillian in ten minutes, so she stashed her gun and headgear and stepped to the rear to watch Linda shoot for a few seconds. She had nice form, but her accuracy needed work. Not wanting to disturb her concentration, Anna left.

Her Jetta was parked near the street, and as she wove her way through the cars in the lot, some sixth sense shot up. It was the same creepy feeling she had when she and Dalton had approached the bookstore the night the Clan dug up the sardonyx.

Suddenly, a wave of dizziness assaulted her, forcing her to stop for a moment to regain her balance. It was warm outside compared to the shooting range, but not so hot to make her woozy. Had she stepped on a place where sardonyx was located? She'd have to ask Jackson about it later. Needing the calming effect of the pink quartz stone, she shoved a hand into her pocket, only to remember she'd left it at home. Great.

Move. Jillian is waiting. Anna looked around, but didn't see anything that screamed danger. Stepping away from this area that made her ill, her composure returned. As she neared her car, she spotted three men in a black SUV two spots from where she was parked. Something about them set her on edge, so she dug her hand into her purse and clutched the gun.

"Anna, are you okay?" Dalton telepathed.

She nearly jumped out of her skin, but then remembered that she and Dalton could communicate telepathically. *"I'm not sure."* He might have sensed her short-lived illness. *"Three men are just sitting in a car near mine."*

"*Where are you? What are they doing?*" His tone came out almost strangled.

"*I was just leaving the shooting range when I sensed something that made me dizzy. I think it might have been some sardonyx. As I was trying to compose myself, I noticed the black SUV with them watching me, but they aren't doing anything. Oh shit, I take that back. One of them is opening his door."*

"*Casually turn around and act as if you forgot something inside the range,*" Dalton commanded. "*I need time to get there."*

The other two men jumped out of the car and came toward her. "*Ah, I don't think I have time."*

Not waiting for Dalton to give her further instructions, Anna took off and was in the woods behind the building before she bet they'd even reached where she'd been standing. Given her speed, she could evade them better being in the open.

Heart pounding from the exertion and sheer panic, she was rather pleased with herself for evading them. The trees were thick and the underbrush dense, making it hard to move about. Well, this sucks.

Shouts sounded, and she swore one of them called her by name. Her pulse shot sky high. "*Ah…Dalton, what should I do?"*

"*Where are you now?"*

Duh, he might be able to hear her, but he couldn't see her. "*I'm in the woods behind the building, but it's really dense in here. I can't move about very well."*

"*Hide somewhere, but don't make any noise. They'll be able to trace your whereabouts if you do."*

Really? She couldn't take a step without crushing a downed branch. "*Okay."*

"She went this way," one of the men said as they rounded the building. "Let's split up."

Well, that wasn't good. *Think, think.* At least this time she had a gun and could move fast—real fast.

"*Dalton, if I shoot one, will I get into trouble?*" she asked.

"No, baby, but let's not resort to that. I'm on my way now."

She might not have a choice. They were closing in on her. Hiding didn't seem to be an option either. She'd have to make a run for it—assuming she didn't impale herself on a branch.

If they shifted, she didn't think she'd be able to shoot all of them before one of them attacked. From what Elana had said, bullets didn't affect the shifters like they did people or regular animals. Well, crap.

Anna studied the terrain trying to decide which way to go. North seemed to be her best option. She'd make noise but that couldn't be helped. As Anna took off, the whizzing of a gunshot close to her head nearly stopped her heart. Bastards.

"Are you okay?," Dalton asked.

Not emotionally. *"Someone shot at me. Should I try to shoot my way out?"*

"Crap. You're not ready for a showdown."

He might be right.

Because she'd moved so fast, she had a good minute to think things through before they caught up with her again. If she managed to climb a tree in time, she wouldn't be able to really hide. Even in their human form, their sense of smell would be acute.

She wished she knew why they were after her, though knowing the reason wouldn't help her out of this dilemma. It had to be those Changelings. They probably wanted retribution after the failed attempt at retrieving the sardonyx.

Indecision about her next move assaulted her. If she ran too far from the gun range, Dalton might not be able to find her. Her best bet would be to take a wide path to the west and circle back. She might even be able to reach her car before they gave up looking for her.

"I'm at the shooting range now," Dalton telepathed. *"I'll head north."*

She told him her plan, but just as she was about to take off again, three wolves appeared. *"Ah, Dalton, they're here. And they've shifted."*

"*Stay where you are.*"

What? They were gaining ground. "*Why?*"

"*So I can use you to find them and take them down.*"

He better know what he was talking about. "*I'll try.*"

Her heart lodged solidly in her throat, Anna hid behind a tree, all the while keeping the animals in sight. They were coming at her from three different directions. Damn. Dalton would never make it here in time.

With her gun hand pressed up against the tree for better support, she waited for them to reach her. Her plan was to kill the closest one before taking off.

A slight sound behind her had her heart dropping to her stomach. She spun around and aimed the gun at the noise. Two of the most beautiful white tigers approached, and she nearly dropped to her knees.

"*I didn't know you would bring Jillian,*" she telepathed.

The smaller of the two swiped a paw in the air.

"*Stay where you are, and for goddess sake, don't shoot,*" Dalton said.

At his rather lighthearted comment she nearly laughed from the relief.

"*I promise.*"

"*You might not want to look either.*"

At that comment, she didn't respond. As the two tigers emerged into a small clearing, the three wolves stopped and glanced at each other. She expected the cowards to turn tail and run, but instead they remained where they were, their chests puffed out and their heads high. Having seen what Dalton did against the wolves at the bookstore, these wolves didn't stand a chance, especially since there were two tigers. The Changelings had to know this was a suicide mission. On the other hand, they seemed arrogant enough to think they could win.

Dalton's and Jillian's tigers didn't move. Instead, they waited, probably to see what the wolves would do. Then, as if the three wolves could communicate telepathically, they charged Dalton and

Jillian. Anna closed her eyes.

Yelps and growls sounded, forcing her to look. She winced a few times when one of the wolf's claws gouged Dalton's side, but for the most part, the wolves didn't stand a chance. In less than a minute, all three wolves were collapsed onto the ground, blood covering their bodies. None had died however.

The two victorious tigers turned and headed back toward her. *"Why didn't you finish them off?"* she telepathed.

"It would only bring more. Besides, I want them to return to their leaders and tell them not to mess with you ever again or death would be guaranteed."

He did have a point. *"What should I do now? The wolves will recover, and I don't want to head back and then have them find me."*

"Follow us," Dalton telepathed.

Both of them shot forward so fast, she lost them for a second. Anna rushed after them, and by the time she reached them, both had shifted and were pulling on their clothes.

She placed a hand on Jillian's arm. "Thank you. I guess this wasn't what you meant when you said you wanted to get together and catch up."

"No, but I'm glad I came."

Dalton embraced Anna. "You sure you're okay?"

"I am now, though admittedly I was scared shitless."

He smiled. "I could tell."

Dalton kissed her forehead and stepped back. "I asked Jillian to come because I didn't want a fight. I was hoping they'd take one look at us and run."

"They were stupid not to."

"Agreed," he and Jillian said in unison.

"So, anyone up for dinner?" Anna asked. "I'm starving."

"Absolutely," Dalton said.

Blood was seeping through his pants. "You're bleeding."

Dalton waved an arm. "I know. I'll have to stop at home first." He turned to his sister. "You want to join us?"

"Don't you two want to be alone?"

"I always want to be alone with Anna, but since she's hungry, I need a reason not to ravish her. Why don't you ask Brian to join us?"

"I will. Hopefully, I can pull him away from the dresser he's making."

"Meet us at the pub in say twenty minutes."

Jillian smiled then shot off. Dalton turned to her. "Ready?"

"You bet."

Chapter Twenty-Three

"YOU WANT TO throw in the towel on this murder?" Kalan asked Dalton.

Dalton moved his computer to the side of his desk, so his partner's face wouldn't be blocked. "Not yet, but I'm close. You know how Smythe hates it when we have a case go cold."

They never gave up on a murder case, unless they were positive a Changeling was involved. While they had arrested a few of the slimy bastards in the past, it was difficult to prove their guilt. Wolves didn't leave human fingerprints.

Dalton's cell rang, and he checked the caller ID. "It's Merry Wilson," he told his partner. Dalton answered. "Hey, Merry."

"You said I should keep my eyes and ears open for anything strange going on."

He sat up straighter. "I did. What did you see or hear?"

"I was putting away some books on one of the shelves, when Tom must have had the same idea because he was on the other side. A few seconds later, Linda joined him. I couldn't see them, but Linda asked Tom out for this weekend."

That wasn't all that newsworthy. She'd previously told him that she and Tom were an item despite comments to the contrary. "What did he say?"

"First, I heard Linda grunt in pain, as if Tom had grabbed her. He told her to leave him alone or he'd get a restraining order against her."

Dalton's pulse spiked as he scribbled some notes. "Do you mind if I put you on speaker? Kalan Murdoch is sitting next to me."

"No, I don't mind."

"What did Linda do?" Dalton asked.

"She whimpered a bit then asked why he would do something like that after all she'd done for him."

Dalton wondered what that meant. "And what did Tom say?"

"I couldn't hear the rest. Either he was whispering or he'd walked off."

That conversation gave him another reason to continue the surveillance. "Thank you, Merry. That was helpful. Stay safe."

"I will."

Once he discontinued, he looked over at Kalan. "What do you think?"

"Isn't Sam watching Linda?"

"He hasn't been for the last three days. She didn't do anything out of the ordinary, so Connor pulled him, saying he had something else for his new recruit to do."

Kalan tapped the desk and stood. "I guess you have your work cut out for you."

"What about you? Don't you think you should watch Tom?"

"He's the victim here. I'm going to spend my time on the husband. I still think either he, or Julie Dominick is good for it."

"Suit yourself."

Because both Tom and Linda would be at work for two more hours, he wanted to take advantage of his free time by checking in on Anna. Tonight would be another long evening, and he wasn't sure he could keep away from his mate until then.

The Blooms of Hope shop was only a few blocks away, so Dalton decided to take advantage of the warm summer day and walk over. Once he arrived, he looked in the window, not wanting to disturb Anna should she be with a customer. Only Elana was visible. Hopefully, Anna was in the back and not out on some errand. Dalton pushed open the front door, and the intense scent of flowers enveloped him. Even with the rich scent in the air, he could still make out Anna's delicate signature, and he swallowed a smile.

Elana looked up and grinned. "She's in the back."

"Thanks."

As he stepped through the opening to the back, he debated closing the door, but then figured if they had any privacy, he'd want to make love with her. This visit was about discussing a big step for him, not getting his rocks off—though that would be nice too.

Anna set down her scissors and practically skipped over to him. She threw her arms around his neck, and his tiger roared. "Hello stranger. What brings you here?" she asked.

"Can't a man just stop by to see his *mate*?" He whispered the last word even though Elana was one. The customer with her was not.

"He sure can." Anna stood on her tiptoes, and when she kissed him, his bones cracked and hair sprouted on his face. Damn.

Dalton enjoyed a few more seconds of wondrous kissing before stepping back. "We can't get started 'cause I won't be able to stop if we do."

"Spoilsport." Anna hopped up on a clean corner of the table and looked cute up there.

"I've been thinking about getting a tattoo," he announced, positive she'd be happy with his new revelation. Anna would believe she'd influenced him—and she'd be right. Before meeting her, Dalton never would have considered getting one.

"For real?" Sparks shot off her arms.

"Yes."

"What will you get? A serpent or maybe a sheriff's badge?"

He hadn't considered anything like that. "I want it to represent you, so I'm going to get a turquoise rose tattooed right here." He pointed to the area right below his shoulder.

She jumped down off the table. "That means so much to me. In fact, I've been contemplating getting something too."

"What would that be?"

"Hold on." She stepped behind the counter to the desk where

her purse sat on top and fished out a photograph. "Merry, or I guess I should say Mom, gave me this picture of my father. I thought I'd have his face tattooed on my arm between my roses."

"Will it fit?"

"I might only have room for a partial face, but I'll know it's him. I'm also going to add one more thing, but I'll show it to you when I get it. When do you want to go?"

He laughed. She was spontaneous. "Can they do a tattoo in two hours? It's all the time I have."

"I bet it can be done, but the problem is that there isn't a tattoo artist in Silver Lake. We'd have to go to Andersonville."

He cupped her shoulders then drew her to his chest. "Can I take a rain check? I have to work late tonight."

She leaned back, looked up at him, and stuck out her tongue. "Sure, but you owe me one."

"Trust me, when I get you alone, I'll give you all the orgasms you want."

She punched him in the chest, but he barely felt it. Goddess but he was one lucky man.

After he gave Anna a thorough kissing, he walked back to the station. Because it might be a long evening, he stopped at the Silver Lake Café for a burger to-go along with a large coffee. If Kalan was going to check on Carlton Wedgewood and Julie Dominick, Dalton should be able to touch base with Tom DeLuca and Linda Darnell. Neither would be off work for a while, so it would give him the chance to find a good vantage point in which to study them.

Dalton had already looked up the make, model, and year of the cars they drove, so he would be able to tell if they were home. Merry said they both got off work at five, while she and Ed stayed until seven.

Dalton had already figured out the best spot for watching Linda, but he hadn't even seen Tom's place, so that needed to be his first stop. Turns out Tom lived about five miles from the town center in a Craftsman style home. Without a garage, he'd be easy to spot if he'd returned home from work early. Dalton's plan was to watch Tom for a bit then head over to Linda's place.

He wouldn't be surprised if she decided to go out with some girls for the evening to blow off some steam after her less than pleasant interaction with Tom. Jillian had told him that women liked to talk about their men problems when they were together.

Dalton enjoyed his burger in peace but rationed his coffee, anticipating a long night. A few minutes before five, Tom pulled into his drive, catching Dalton off guard since the man's shift wasn't up for another few minutes. Perhaps tomorrow he'd call Merry and ask her what happened.

Tom jumped out of his car and raced into his house. Something must be important for him to rush inside like that. Dalton leaned back, ready for a long and boring evening—or would it be? Dalton had the camera ready to snap a photo of Tom should he leave.

Come to think of it, it was always possible that Tom's rebuff had upset Linda so much that she'd show up to talk with him. That was wishful thinking because Dalton always enjoyed a little action.

Dalton thought back to Ed Santaria's comment about Tom desiring Crystal. Clearly, it didn't mattered to him that she was married. If he'd been the killer type though, Tom would have offed Crystal's husband and not the woman he loved. Then again, he might have been of the mindset that if he couldn't have Crystal, no one should be able to have her. Shit. This was more complicated than a soap opera—not that he'd ever watched one.

About a half hour into his watch, another car turned down the road that matched the description of Linda's vehicle. This stakeout suddenly turned more intriguing. She pulled into Tom's drive, got out, and slammed the car door. Like Tom, she appeared to be in a hurry, striding up the steps and ringing the bell repeatedly. Not even waiting a few seconds for Tom to answer, she pounded on the door then shouted his name. This wasn't looking good for dear old Tom.

The door opened, but Dalton couldn't see who answered, though no one else but Tom seemed to be inside. She must have convinced this person to invite her in, because seconds later she stepped inside. Dalton took a few photos of her car parked in the street, but because of the angle of where Dalton was parked, her license plate number wasn't in view. If he needed proof that Linda had been at Tom's house, he had to get a shot that included the plate.

Being in his civilian clothes, Dalton felt at ease walking down the street. As long as he didn't move too close to the house and kept his face averted, he doubted they'd even notice him. He eased out of his SUV and casually walked down the street. When he reached her car from across the street, he zoomed in and snapped a few pictures.

Just as he turned back around, shouts sounded from inside the house and Dalton's animal clawed at him, begging for release. The last thing anyone needed was for someone to see a white tiger to be running loose in a suburban neighborhood. Had it not been for his shifter abilities, he doubted he'd have heard their voices. Too bad he couldn't understand what was being said.

Stay hidden, he commanded his tiger. Ever since those last two fights, his tiger had been antsy to run free. The white moon would occur in a few days, and Dalton had promised him his freedom then.

What sounded like a gunshot suddenly rang out, jerking him out of his musings. The front door to Tom's house slammed opened and Linda rushed out, heading straight for her car.

"Hey, Linda!" Dalton called, trying to pretend he just happened to be in the area.

She froze. Her eyes widened and then her body stiffened. Sticking her hand in her purse, she withdrew a weapon. Well shit. "Don't come any closer," she warned.

Well, that wasn't going to happen. Dalton was a little pissed that his spare piece was snug in his glove compartment, but he could handle her without it. Shifting, however, wasn't an option for many reasons. Primarily, he didn't think he needed to. According to Anna, she'd watched Linda practice at the range, and while she had good form, Linda's aim wasn't all that precise. Secondly, he didn't want to be the one to break the news to the world about his kind.

Dalton watched her body language as he eased closer. His mind spun with possibilities. Had Linda just shot Tom? Dalton wasn't one to jump to conclusions, as it was equally possible, Tom had shot at her but missed.

The best way to find out was to ask her. "Did Tom just threaten you?" he asked holding up his hands.

"Threaten me? No." She glanced over her shoulder then returned her gaze to him.

"Interesting. I thought I heard a gunshot. Did you shoot Tom?"

She lifted her weapon and aimed it at him. Dalton could disarm her before she blinked, but he wasn't willing to chance anyone might be watching. "Linda, you don't want to do this. Put down the gun." With his hands still raised, he moved closer, noting the increase in her respiration. Her arms shook and her gaze turned wild. *Please don't do anything else stupid, like shoot a cop.*

"I can't do that. You don't understand. Don't come any closer." She waved the gun at him. Like that would help?

Dalton stopped. "Try me. I'm a good listener."

He glanced at the picture window, hoping Tom was watching and not dead.

"Is that so? You want to listen to my tale of woe?"

"I do." Dalton wasn't sure if keeping her talking was a good idea. He hadn't called for backup and he needed to check on Tom, but if by telling her story she'd let down her guard, he'd listen.

"All right I'll tell you what that SOB did to me. He promised me we'd live in a cabin in the woods, so I moved to Silver Lake to be with him. I even gave up a good career as an office manager. Working at a bookstore as a flunky sure as hell was not my dream job, but I took it—for him. And what did Tom do? He dumped me for Crystal. A fucking married woman!"

It didn't matter if she had a valid reason for being angry. Shooting someone was never the answer. "Not all relationships work out." *What am I doing?* He'd been trained to agree with her. "But to lure you here and then dismiss you is terrible."

She looked back at the house. "You got that right."

"It didn't matter to him that Crystal was married?" Dalton asked, sounding outraged. That question wasn't an act.

"I know, right? I told him it was wrong, but did he listen? No."

The puzzle pieces were falling into place. "You were right to leave him." Not that she said she had; quite the opposite. From what Merry had told him, it appeared as if Linda wanted to get back with Tom, only he didn't want to be with her.

"Damn straight. Even after that bitch died, did Tom come back? No." Tears were streaming down her cheek, and Dalton doubted Linda could see straight enough to shoot him.

Slowly, the front door opened an inch, but Dalton kept his focus on Linda. "Did you kill Crystal? I mean if you did, you had every right. She stole your man." That was a crock of shit, but in Linda's frame of mind, it was what she wanted to hear.

"Damn straight. She wasn't even sorry she was a cheater and stole Tom from me."

The front door opened another foot and Tom appeared on his knees with one hand on his stomach. He was bleeding profusely. "You bitch," he growled.

Linda spun around, lifted her weapon, and got off a shot. Before Dalton could talk either of them down, Tom raised a gun and fired, hitting Linda squarely in the chest. Her weapon clattered to the ground, and then she dropped to her knees. Tom groaned, let go of his gun, and slumped against the door. From the way his eyes were closed and his arms dangled by his side, he'd passed out.

With the threats neutralized, Dalton called 911 for two ambulances. He rushed to Tom to assess his damage. As he passed Linda, he kicked her gun into the grass. "Don't even think about touching it."

She didn't respond. In fact, from the way her eyes were rolling back in her head and how she was swaying, she had no intention or ability to move. "Help me," she whispered, blood dripping from her mouth.

"Tom first."

Once at the man's side, Dalton lifted his shirt off his back, bent down and rolled Tom over. He then pressed his shirt against the wound to stem the blood flow. Tom opened his eyes. "She shot me."

"I can see that," Dalton said. "Did she say why?"

His face turned even whiter. That wasn't good. "She was jealous of me and Crystal. Bitch killed her too."

"Save your energy. The ambulance is on its way."

Tom grunted and passed out again. Damn. Needing to check on Linda, Dalton rolled Tom onto his side, hoping that position would help keep pressure on the wound.

Dalton then rushed to Linda whose face was on the cement with her eyes open. He placed two fingers on her carotid artery and felt for a pulse but detected nothing.

Sirens sounded in the background, and relief rushed through him. He could only hope Tom made it. He might be immoral, but at least he wasn't a killer.

Chapter Twenty-Four

A NNA WAS NERVOUS. The white moon shone brightly in the clear, dark sky, which meant tonight would be the night she would become a tiger, and she couldn't wait. Dalton claimed it was rather easy to shift, but she wasn't as convinced. Elana had told her how her brother, Brian, had tried a ton of times and had failed. Apparently, Anna had seen him shift for the first time when he'd rushed in to save Jillian. From what she'd learned, it was only because his mate had been injured that his protective instincts had allowed him to enact the change the first time.

"Don't worry," Dalton said. "You'll do fine." He picked up his car keys and led her outside.

"Elana said it was fun and easy, but her brother really struggled."

Dalton cupped her shoulders, and his delicious scent helped calm her. "You're a free spirit. You have no mental barricades. Besides, you believe in shifters while Brian didn't think he was one, so he blocked out his abilities."

"I was lucky. I was able to watch you and Jillian in your tiger forms."

"Ready?"

"I guess." The first shift had to be on a white moon, so it wasn't as if she could ask to try tomorrow.

"I have the perfect place," Dalton said with more excitement than he'd shown since he'd found out Linda Darnell had killed Crystal out of jealousy.

Anna hopped in his SUV and rolled down the windows. She loved this time of year. The days were warm but the nights cool. "Do you think we'll be alone? I don't want to run into any other animals."

He smiled. "Even if you did, where we're going, they will be friendly shifters."

She'd take his word for it. When he headed toward Elana's house, she became confused. "Why are we going here? I thought this area was only for the Clan members."

He grinned. "That's true, but I am a Clan member now."

Even though he was driving, she grabbed his arm. "What do you mean? I thought you shied away from any group."

"That was before I outed myself as a tiger—or rather before I had to shift to keep those wolves from killing you and the others. I always believed that the wolves and bears wouldn't accept me for being different, but I was wrong. Rye personally invited me to join them. He said that a shifter was a shifter. It never mattered to them what kind of animal I was."

She couldn't be happier. "That's fantastic."

"I think so too. Wait until I show you where we're going. It's beautiful."

He drove in about a mile, and then turned down an unpaved, bumpy road. "The owner doesn't mind you trespassing?" she asked.

"Nope." When he reached the end of the road, he stopped and jumped out. Dalton came over to her side and opened her door. "Before we undress, I want to show you something."

"It's dark."

"But you can see, right?"

She hadn't even thought about it before, but yes, her vision was sharp and clear. "I can. The white moon helps."

Dalton grabbed her hand and led her across the small field that smelled sweet. The cicadas were trilling in the trees and a hawk was flying overhead. The wind whispered throughout the surrounding trees. He led her past a few boulders and down a small slope.

"Can you smell it?" he asked.

"Smell what?"

Dalton wrapped an arm around her. "The water."

They traversed down a long, sloping hillside, careful not to trip over any downed branches. At the bottom, they came to another small clearing where a four-foot wide, fast moving stream ran through it. "It's beautiful."

Dalton faced her and took hold of her hands. "This is my surprise. I just bought the land. I want to build a house on it for us."

Anna was speechless. "You bought this land?"

"Yes, do you like it?"

"Like it? I love it." Her heart beat fast. Saying the word love just now reminded her that she'd never told Dalton how much she loved him. Saying it in the heat of passion had never seemed right. "But not as much as I love you."

Before he had the chance to respond, she drew his face to hers and pressed her lips to his. He groaned and returned the kiss, gently at first and then with more intensity. Both of their orbs glowed, and suddenly, she was overwhelmed with such desire that she felt as if she might shift. Her scalp itched and her body began to burn up, but she didn't care. All she could think about was having him. Grabbing his butt, she squeezed each hard cheek then dragged her hands up his back, loving all the bumps and ridges.

Running her tongue over her teeth, she jerked when one of her teeth cut her. Blood tinged her mouth. Unsure of how that had happened, Anna stepped back.

"I feel your pain. What happened?" he asked.

"My teeth just sharpened, like yours."

He gathered her in his arms and pressed his lips to her ear. "Shh. It's all right. It's just your tiger fighting for release. Relax, and go with the flow."

What did go with the flow really mean? Aw, hell. It didn't matter. Her hands itched with a need to feel his skin. Anna leaned back. "Touch me everywhere. Please."

"I think you should get naked first to enhance the pleasure."

He was right. When they eventually shifted, she'd have to be naked anyway. Because it was warm, she hadn't worn much, which made undressing easier. After toeing off her sandals, she kicked them to the side. Her T-shirt took little effort to remove as did her shorts. She'd not worn a bra, so all that was left were her panties.

When she'd finished stepping out of them, Dalton hadn't moved. "Why are you still dressed?"

"I was too caught up watching you."

He was being silly. She moved closer and slid her hands under his T-shirt and palmed his pecs. While she loved every part of his body, his chest had to be one of her favorite areas. He flexed and she grinned. "Do it again."

Dalton moved his right pec and then his left. He then clamped his palms over her breasts. "See if you can do it."

It took a few tries, but finally she was able to move one and then the other. He pinched his fingers together and slowly slid them off her breasts until he was only holding onto her nipples. All it took was for him to press on them lightly and twist her sensitive nubs for her glow to fully bloom.

That seemed to be the key to unlock her hormones, because suddenly her body was flooded with lust, joy, and glorious passion. "Take off your pants," she said trying to sound as forceful as possible, though the command sounded closer to a plea.

He cocked a brow as if his mate shouldn't make demands.

"Please?" she added.

"You bet." In a flash, he was naked and pressed up against her.

The divine sensation of his skin on hers set her off again. Her nails grew, and her bones cracked, followed by an ache rippling through her. When he leaned over and drew a nipple into his mouth and slid two fingers into her wet hole, her world turned black. She staggered back and suddenly found herself on the ground without remembering having fallen.

How was it possible that her knees weren't touching the dry

leaves, yet she was staring at Dalton's shins?

"What happened?" she telepathed, not trusting her ability to speak.

"You shifted, that's what happened." The joy in his voice was unmistaken.

I did? As much as she wanted to run around, she wanted to make love with him more. *"How do I shift back?"*

"Don't be scared. Do you want me to join you?"

"Not yet. I need you too much."

Dalton chuckled. "I hear you. Picture yourself as a human again," he said out loud.

Anna concentrated, imagining staring into a mirror, seeing herself dressed in blue jeans shorts and purple tank top. Once more her vision blurred than faded to black for a moment as she spun around and lost her balance once more. She landed on her rear with a hard thump. "Oh."

The sound of her own voice took her by surprise, but when she managed to open her eyes, her legs and arms were all human.

Dalton dropped down next to her. "I realize the shift only lasted a few seconds, but how did it feel?"

"I'm not sure. It was different."

"I think you were so turned on that you shifted." He ran a knuckle down her face. "I do love you, Anna Fairchild. You are too adorable for words."

"While I do love hearing you tell me that, I would appreciate a little bit more showing." With that, she dragged him down to the ground with her.

A second later, she was on top of him, and Dalton grinned. "Then ride me for all I'm worth."

"My pleasure."

"WHAT DO YOU think?" Anna asked as she held up the tattoo artist's drawing of the sword next to a partial image of her father's face.

"It looks amazing, but why a sword?" Dalton asked.

"To me, one side of the double-edged sword represents strength, something I needed growing up—like when I was given up by Merry, when my first set of foster parents didn't treat me well, and then all the times I thought I was a freak and would never fit in."

He liked her take. "And the other side?"

"That represents where I am now. It's the good side." She smiled, and his body heated. "The goodness happened when I met you and fell in love."

Her words made his heart soar. "It may not seem like it, but you and I are very much alike. After my dad died, I tumbled into darkness too. Nothing made much sense to me either." While one of the tattoo artists was a shifter, the other was not, so he had to be careful with what he said.

Anna clasped his hand. "I keep forgetting. I'm sorry."

"Yeah, me too. The one and only benefit of his dying so early, was that it made me the man I am today."

She leaned over and kissed his cheek. "And that's the man I love." She nodded to the pattern he was holding. "Which rose did you pick?"

"The one like yours. I asked him to do it in the same turquoise color."

"That's sweet. Let's do this." She returned to her chair.

His artist was Renfro, a shifter, but the woman, Sabrina, working on Anna was not. While Dalton was interested in what Renfro was doing on his arm, he couldn't take his eyes off Anna. Having the tattoo even of a partial face of her father meant a lot to her. She'd never met him, but he'd given her his Wendayan gifts. At least now, she wouldn't have to think she was different.

Now that her powers had combined with his, she'd become a force to be reckoned with. In the last few weeks, he too had discovered that he could touch someone and see into their past. While his skills weren't as developed as Anna's, that talent had proved very useful just last week when speaking with a suspect—

who, by the way, had been guilty as sin.

The two artists worked quickly and precisely, but in the time he and Anna had been in the shop, no one else had come in. He worried how they could remain in business. "Did you know Silver Lake doesn't have a tattoo parlor?"

Renfro's brows rose. "That so?" He glanced over at his partner. "Sabrina and I don't have a lot of business right now. Maybe we should consider opening a new shop down there. I appreciate the tip."

"No problem." Another shifter would always be welcome, but he kept that comment to himself.

Once their tattoos were complete, they thanked their artists and left.

"So what do you want to do now?" Anna asked eying his new addition. "I really like it by the way."

"I do too. How about we go for a run over at our property, and then go out to dinner?" Even though Anna had moved in with him, they didn't have a set routine for cooking. Too often, he'd work late and the meal she'd cooked would grow cold.

"Sounds like a plan, but what do you say we eat first and then go for a run? I'm in the mood for a little hide and seek, and it's better when it's dark."

Too often when they played that game, he lost. Anna was amazingly good at slowing her breath and remaining still. If the clouds covered the sky, finding her was extra difficult despite her light coloring. "I'm game, but I'm winning this time."

She laughed. "You wish." Halfway back to Silver Lake, her cell rang. "It's Merry," she said. "Hey. What's up? I'll ask." She turned to him. "Merry invited us to dinner. You up for it?"

"Always."

She returned to her conversation and requested the time. "See you soon."

Dalton loved how Anna's eyes lit up when she was around her mother. The requested blood tests had come back, showing they were indeed mother and daughter. If he didn't know the story behind their meeting, he'd think they'd known each other their whole lives. Thankfully, Merry's husband seemed to be on the mend. His doctor had changed his medication, and it was working.

"Did you tell Merry you were getting the tattoo?" he asked.

"Yes, but not that it was of Tommy."

"I hope George isn't upset when he sees it, assuming he can tell who it is."

She shook her head. "He's cool with it. He understands that it happened long before Merry met him."

When they arrived at Anna's mom's house, they piled out. As soon as they stepped inside, her mom hugged them both then escorted them into the living room. "I'm so glad you two could come." She turned toward him. "I know how busy you are, Dalton."

"Now that Crystal's case is closed, I have more time on my hands." Silver Lake didn't have that many murders.

"Come and sit down both of you. Dinner's in the oven. What can I get you two to drink?" Merry asked.

"A beer if you have one," Dalton said.

"Water for me," Anna replied.

He glanced over at his mate. In the few months they'd been together, she'd rarely ordered water. *"You feeling okay?"* he telepathed, not wanting to worry Merry.

She smiled, looking like herself. *"Water is good for the body, especially after getting a tattoo."*

Dalton didn't want to drink alone. "Merry, can you make mine a water too?"

"Sure." Anna's mom brought in a tray filled with four glasses of water.

George came downstairs. "Is that Anna and Dalton I hear."

Dalton stood. "Yes, sir." He shook his hand.

When Merry passed out the drinks, Anna clasped her glass with both hands. "I have an announcement to make."

His tiger sat up. He would have noticed if she'd been ill. "What is it?" he asked.

Anna grinned. "I'm pregnant."

Thankfully, he hadn't been holding his glass or he might have dropped it. "For real?" They hadn't decided whether to mention shifters in front of Merry and George, so he telepathed his next thought. *"I knew something was different."*

She nodded. *"Different? How so?"* she telepathed.

"Your scent had changed, but I thought you might have been working with different flowers than usual." She grinned then set her glass on the coffee table as Dalton jumped up. He drew his mate into his arms and held her close. "When did you find out?" he asked out loud.

"Yesterday, but I wanted to surprise you."

"You did."

A whimper sounded from Merry. She swiped a finger under her eye. "I never thought I'd be a grandmother."

"I hope that's a good thing."

"It's wonderful. I can see many hours babysitting," Merry said with a load of cheer in her voice.

Anna smiled. "I'm counting on it."

During dinner, they talked about the house plans and when their home would be completed.

Merry cut off another slice of meatloaf. "I almost forgot to tell you that Tom came back to work today. He says he's one hundred percent, but he looked a little peaked to me."

Dalton was glad he'd survived the gunshot wound, though Tom wasn't one of his favorite people. No cheater ever could be. "That's great news."

Once they finished eating, Anna and he insisted they clean up. When they finished, they hugged Merry and George goodbye. Dalton normally would have stayed longer, but he really needed this run. No telling how long Anna would want to go on runs while pregnant. He wasn't even sure who to ask about whether it was safe to shift in her condition, though Elana might be able to shed some light.

Once Anna was settled in the car, he reached over and clasped her hand. "Other than the day we mated, I think this will go down as the best day of my life."

She unbuckled her seatbelt and scooted closer. "That so? You want to make it even more memorable?"

"If you don't mind waiting a bit to run off the meal we just ate, I'd be happy to."

"Then what are you waiting for, cowboy?"

Dalton laughed. Being with Anna was the best present he could ask for.

The End

Don't forget to sign up for my newsletter to receive three free books, as well as up-to-date information on my stories. If you prefer to only receive notices regarding my releases, follow me on BookBub.
http://smarturl.it/o4cz93?IQid=MLite
bookbub.com/authors/vella-day

I hope you enjoyed Anna and Dalton's story. Up next is PROTECTING HIS WOLF. It's Sam and Lexi's story (she's a newcomer). Here is a sneak peak of the first chapter.

Chapter One

L EXI LARAMIE GROUND her teeth together. "Are you crazy? You
have no right to sell me. It's barbaric!"

Her dad lifted his hand and slapped her so hard across the face
that she stumbled backward, slamming against the sharp edge of the
trailer's kitchen counter. Pain shot up her spine, but she refused to
show how much his actions had hurt her, both physically and
mentally.

Lexi was so damned tempted to kill the bastard right here, right
now, but she wanted him to suffer with the poor decisions he'd made
in his life. Let the gambler he owned money to come after him and
dole out his own brand of justice.

"Release me," her wolf begged. *"I can take him."*

He's not worth it.

Her dad was a wolf too, and while he had been strong in his
youth, in his current drunk condition, he was a mere shell of a man.
His once thick brown hair, now in need of a haircut, was peppered
with gray. The once broad shoulders were beginning to round from
lack of exercise. She too had been devastated by her mom's death,
but did she go out and get drunk and gamble every night? Hell no.
She mourned her mom while keeping a job.

He raised his hand once more, but she wouldn't let him strike
her again. She swiped the blood trickling down her cheek, ready to
defend herself. Could she kill him? Probably. Her Wendayan mother
had imbued her with great strength and agility. Deciding to use that

talent instead of her ability to shift, Lexi executed a roundhouse kick to his midsection. As expected, the old man tumbled on his ass and landed with a grunt. Lexi stood over him. "Don't. Ever. Hit. Me. Again. You understand?" She refrained from saying what she might do if he did.

His eyes darkened with fury as he half rolled over. "You will pay."

"Me?" Lexi stepped back, planted one foot in front of the other, and lifted her fists. "How much money do you owe this time?"

Her father lifted up onto his elbows. "Ten thousand dollars. Because he knows I don't have that kind of cash, Justin Kapok said we'd be even as soon as I hand you over to him."

Her stomach churned with a strong ache. Kapok was a known gangster in their wolf Clan. One time at a bar, he'd tried to convince her to hook up with him, and she'd said no. Apparently, that had been the wrong thing to say to such an influential man. That night he made it clear that his goal was to find a powerful mate to help him climb the Clan ladder. Asshat. He bragged that his woman would be popping out pups one right after the other to increase the Clan's population. She wasn't against having a lot of kids—just not with him. For Justin, the concept of love seemed totally foreign to him.

"What possessed you to play poker with someone of that man's caliber?" she asked, aching in so many places, especially in her heart.

"He asked me to play." Fear for his life suddenly replaced the angry lines around his eyes and mouth.

She loomed over him again. "I'm twenty-four years old. Last time I looked, human trafficking was illegal."

The dim light from the one lamp in the trailer's living room flickered, casting a sickening yellow pall over the room. Spittle dripped down her father's chin, but he didn't bother wiping it away. He rose to his feet and teetered, and then tapped her chest hard. "You're my daughter. I raised you; spent money on you. I can do whatever I want with you."

He was delusional. "You need help. Serious help."

Quicker than she thought possible, Bill Laramie grabbed her arm and shook her. Lexi had had enough of being manhandled. Stealing herself against the upcoming pain, she slugged him hard, and he folded like a weak collapsible chair. Damn, her hand hurt.

His head hit the stained carpet and his eyes rolled back in his head. He was out for the count. Good. Lara should feel guilty that she'd had to resort to violence against her father, but if she hadn't defended herself, no telling what he might have done next. Probably tie her up and then call Justin to come get her, and she couldn't let that happen.

"You shouldn't have hit me," she said to the unconscious man. In her mind and heart, the pitiful person on the floor no longer was her father. The man she remembered had been clean and funny. When he wasn't out working one of his two jobs, he'd played with her and her brother when they were growing up. What a shame that man had left this earth long ago.

"I'm leaving, Dad. Don't try to follow me. You'll never find me." It didn't matter he couldn't hear her; she needed to say it.

Blood had congealed on her cheek caused by the blow, but right now, she wasn't worried. Her wolf would heal her soon. With a heavy heart, Lexi spun on her heels and ducked into her temporary room at the far end of the trailer. She'd been stupid to agree to move back into his filthy hole in the wall last month, but her father had been so convincing. He told her that with her help, he could clean up his act. What a crock. The man hadn't even tried.

Lexi quickly packed her one bag. Less than five minutes later, she was out of there, not daring to look over her shoulder. Once outside, the cold Vermont air bit into her skin, but at least it convinced her she was still alive. It was close to midnight, and even though she had excellent shifter vision, she needed the moon's light to guide her. Her vision was blurred from the sheen of tears.

Unfortunately, as soon as Lexi slid into her 2001 Toyota Camry and twisted the key to start the engine, she flooded it. "Come on, come on."

After waiting a minute, Old Betty fired up and she took off. Lexi hadn't reached the edge of Windwood, Vermont before it occurred to her that while her dad wasn't savvy enough to find her if she charged down south, Justin Kapok was. Damn. Credit cards would leave a trail of her travel. That meant she'd need cash.

Slowing down, she fished her phone from her purse, and dialed her brother's number. He answered on the second ring. "What's up, sis. Shouldn't you be in bed?"

"Funny." She didn't need to remind Ronan that her temporary teaching job had ended in December, and she hadn't found another position yet. "Look, I'm sorry to bug you, but I really need your help."

SAM POMPLEY HELD up his beer mug and tapped it against Connor McKinnon's shot glass. "To a job well done," Connor said. "Any time we take down a you-know-who, it's a good day."

"Amen." Sam tossed back his drink. Shouts from the back room echoed through McKinnon's Pool and Pub. Someone must have won a game.

Their case involved a Changeling who had tried to swindle one of the storeowners in town. The owner happened to be a fellow clansman of theirs. The owner had immediately contacted McKinnon and Associates for help. After tailing the culprit for a few days, they'd caught the bastard with the stolen merchandise and returned it to the store. The best part was that they'd been able to bring the thief in and he'd been arrested—not the usual end for a Changeling.

"For me, the game changer had been when you were able to get close enough to the man to do a mind meld on him." Connor set his empty glass on the bar top.

Sam leaned back and smiled. "I can still see the guy's face after he realized he'd led us right to the stolen pavers," he said before draining his glass.

Connor chuckled. "I bet the bastard will be pondering for years to come how that happened."

"That's why I love what I do."

They both laughed. Connor waved to his brother Finn, who was tending bar. "As much as I'd love to stay out all night and talk about our company's highlights, I have to be up early. From the sounds of the winds out there, a winter storm is rolling in, and I don't want to get caught in it like I did last winter."

"I thought you enjoyed romping in the snow." Connor was a werewolf.

"I do, but it's not smart to attract attention in the middle of town."

Sam wasn't a shifter, but he understood the need to be circumspect. "We see wild animals crossing the street from time to time. I don't think it would attract too much attention if you hoofed it."

"You'd be wrong. People think bears are cute, but wolves? They're touted as a menace to society because they eat the farmers' chickens. It's not like I haven't been mistaken for a real wolf and been shot at."

"That would suck."

Finn waltzed over, and Connor slapped a twenty on the bar. "You leaving so soon?" Finn asked.

"Work calls or rather my bed calls. This should cover both our drinks. Keep the change, little brother."

Finn grinned. "Thanks."

"You didn't have to do that," Sam said.

Connor clasped a hand on Sam's shoulder. "You deserved it after helping catch that thief."

Sam slid off his stool. Both of them had parked in the alley in back because all the close spaces had been taken up in front. Bad weather always brought people inside. As they stepped out back, a strong blast of wind air snaked up Sam's jacket, forcing him to button up. A scraping sound in the direction of the dumpster caught his attention. "What's that?" he asked.

"I sense a shifter." Connor stopped, looked around, and then headed in the direction of the noise.

The wind whipped around the alley, lifting the snow covering the ground and shooting swirls into the air. Unfortunately, the fresh air wasn't enough to mask the stench of the trash. Sam caught up with Connor just as he lifted the lid of the big trash bin.

"What the hell?" Connor said.

Sam peaked in. A small wolf was inside, her face smudged with some kind of food goo. Her eyes widened, and then a low throaty growl escaped. While Sam wasn't a shifter, he knew that werewolves or any kind of shifters didn't dumpster dive. "What are you doing in there?" he asked, knowing full well he wouldn't receive a response.

Connor nudged him. "She's obviously hungry."

That much Sam had figured out. During his many tours in Afghanistan, he'd seen hunger, and it tore at his heart every time. He addressed the pretty wolf with the gold and brown snout. "If you shift, I'll buy you dinner."

The wolf shivered and then bared her teeth in a highly aggressive manner. Not to be deterred, Sam edge closer, and the poor creature backed up despite having little room to maneuver. While he was no shifter expert, from her body language, the poor thing was scared.

"If she shifts, she'll be naked, and I doubt she'll like that," Connor said.

Sam hadn't been thinking. He whipped off his jacket and placed it on the rim of the dumpster, trying to ignore the brutal cold seeping into his skin. "Put this on and then come out."

He nodded to Connor that they give her some privacy, and they jogged back to their respective cars. As Sam unlocked and then slipped into his four-door truck, the jacket disappeared. He started the engine and turned the heat to high, watching and waiting. A minute later, a petite woman crawled out wearing his camouflaged wool Pea Coat. The fabric covered her butt, but not much else, causing something inside him to spark. What the heck was that about? Okay, those legs of hers were attractive.

She darted down the alley to an old Toyota Camry, and he

winced at what it would be like running barefoot. While it was lightly covered in snow, rocks protruded randomly, making the way painful. Their dumpster girl, however, acted as if she was moving across a soft carpet. She jumped in the back of her car, hopefully to change.

A few minutes later, a knock sounded on his window. The woman was holding out his jacket. Instead of lowering his window, he pushed open the door, and she jumped back.

"Thank you," she said before turning away.

Sam snatched his coat, slipped his arms in the sleeves and jerked it up and over his shoulders. "Wait. My offer still stands to buy you dinner."

She shook her head. "I'm not fit company."

Connor's door eased open and he got out, but he remained by his car. "Where are you staying?" Sam asked in as non-threatening a tone as possible, hoping she didn't say her car.

She wrapped her arms around her shoulders and rubbed her arms. Thankfully, she wore a down jacket and a wool cap. "I'm just passing through."

"That didn't answer my question. You have to sleep somewhere." If she owned a car, why was she looking for food in a dumpster? Her speech sounded educated, so she probably wasn't a thief. "Do you need any money?" Sam pulled out his wallet and extracted the only two bills in there. "Here's forty bucks. Go buy yourself some food."

"I can't. Thank you though."

Before he could stop her, she ran off and hopped into her car. Normally, he would have shrugged, content that he'd tried to help, but there was something about this delicate creature that spoke to him. He refused to address how his sexual interest in her had flared. It must have been that second beer he'd had.

"What's she doing?" Connor asked as he stepped next to him.

"Leaving, I guess. I tried to give her money, but she wouldn't take it." Her engine sputtered. The car chugged a few feet and then died. She slapped her hand on the dash then lowered her forehead to the wheel.

"I'm going to see if she needs help," Sam said.

Connor reached out to stop him. "Let her come to you. It's less intimidating for her that way."

His friend had a point. "I'll give her a few minutes, and then I'm stepping in." While he hadn't been a mechanic in the service, he knew his way around a car engine.

They returned to their warm cars and waited. Sure enough, five minutes later, their little dumpster girl stepped out from her car, the wind buffeting her so much she had to battle against it.

As much as Sam wanted to shield her from the weather, he believed what Connor said; their little wolf needed to approach them. This time when she knocked on Sam's window, he rolled it down. "Change your mind?"

"Kind of. My car seems to have run out of gas."

He didn't need to ask why she didn't buy some more. "The offer for the money still stands."

She pressed her lips together. "How about that meal instead? It's hard to think on an empty stomach."

"Dine in or drive through?"

The cute shifter smiled briefly. "Either works for me, as long as it's warm."

"I have a plan. Get in the back of my car, and I'll speak with my boss."

"Your boss?"

"The other man." He nodded to Connor's car. "I work for McKinnon and Associates. We're a security agency." Her eyes glowed, implying she might be running away and could use someone to look after her—or else that had been wishful thinking on his part. He stepped out and held open his truck's back door. "Hop in. I'll get your luggage."

Wolf lady sucked on her bottom lip as if she couldn't decide whether to trust him. "Why are you doing this?"

That question took him by surprise. "Because I'm a nice guy?" Her eyes narrowed. "I just returned home after several tours in Afghanistan. Helping others is ingrained in me."

Her shoulders seemed to relax. "What about your friend?"

She was cautious, and he liked that. "Connor McKinnon runs McKinnon and Associates. He's a good guy. Trust me."

The wind howled and more flurries fell. "Okay." She slipped into the back seat but kept her gaze on him. Someone must have done a number on her. By the cut on her cheek, she'd had a rough time lately.

Sam hoped he was doing the right thing in giving her shelter, praying the Changelings hadn't sent someone as lovely and vulnerable as this woman to infiltrate their camp.

PACK WARS (Paranormal)
Training Their Mate (book 1)
Claiming Their Mate (book 2)
Rescuing Their Virgin Mate (book 3)
Box Set (books 1-3)
Loving Their Vixen Mate (book 4)
Fighting For Their Mate (book 5)
Enticing Their Mate (book 6)

MONTANA PROMISES (Full length contemporary)
Promises of Mercy (book 1)
Foundations For Three (book 2)
Montana Fire (book 3)
Hart To Hart (book 4)
Burning Seduction (book 5)
Montana Promises Box Set (books 1-3)

ROCK HARD, MONTANA (contemporary novellas)
Montana Desire (book 1)
Awakening Passions (book 2)

HIDDEN HILLS SHIFTERS (Paranormal)
An Unexpected Diversion (book 1) – FREE
Bare Instincts (book 2)
Shifting Destinies (book 3)
Embracing Fate (book 4)
Promises Unbroken (book 5)

SOUTHERN SHIFTERS KINDLE WORLDS
Bear 'N Dirty

WERES & WITCHES OF SILVER LAKE
A Magical Shift (book 1)
Catching Her Bear (book 2)
A Surge of Magic (book 3)
The Bear's Forbidden Wolf (book 4)
Her Reluctant Bear (book 5)
Freeing His Tiger (book 6)

Author Bio

Want 3 FREE books? Sign up for my newsletter.

COPY AND PASTE INTO YOUR BROWSER:
http://smarturl.it/o4cz93?IQid=MLite

Check out my latest interview on You Tube:
youtube.com/watch?v=sQo5pyyVMDI

Not only do I love to read, write, and dream, I'm an extrovert. I enjoy being around people and am always trying to understand what makes them tick. Not only must my books have a happily ever after, I need characters I can relate to. My men are wonderful, dynamic, smart, strong, and the best lovers in the world (of course).

I believe I am the luckiest woman. I do what I love and I have a wonderful, supportive husband, who happens to be hot!

Fun facts about me

(1) I'm a math nerd who loves spreadsheets. Give me numbers and I'll find a pattern.
(2) I just moved to Costa Rica and live on the beach!
(3) I also like to exercise. Yes, I know I'm odd.

I love hearing from readers either on FB or via email (hint, hint).

Social Media Sites

Website:
www.velladay.com

FB:
www.facebook.com/vella.day.90

Twitter:
@velladay4

Gmail:
velladayauthor@gmail.com